⊸THE⊸
ONTARIO PROJECT

THE ONTARIO PROJECT

HENDRIK HOITINGA

Printed in the United States of America
ISBN 978-1-967279-14-2 (hc)
ISBN 978-1-967279-15-9 (sc)
ISBN 978-1-967279-16-6 (e)

2025.11.03

This book is printed on acid-free paper.

Blue Ink Media Solutions
1111B S Governors Ave
STE 7582 Dover,
DE 19904

www.blueinkmediasolutions.com

Table of Contents

BOOK 2
OUT OF THE BLUE

DEDICATION

In memory of my grandfather

Pake Hendrik

Cloth cap and wooden clogs

Great guy

Thanks to my supportive wife Gilly, for her love and guidance.

Thank you to my friend Margaret Alison for her prayerful support and inspiration.

Authors favourite passage of Scripture.

'Trust in the Lord with all your heart and lean not on your own understanding. In all your ways acknowledge him and he will make your paths straight' Proverbs- 3:5-6

Thanks to Alex Sanders and the Blue Ink Media Solutions Team.

BOOK I
INTO THIN AIR

Prologue; Present day
Monday 1st March 2021
Moncton - New Brunswick-Canada

Thousands of people, worldwide, had died. Thousands more still in hospitals everywhere. Army barracks, school buildings, sporting venues and other larger buildings had been transformed into makeshift hospitals. Bedding, ventilators and other equipment had been brought in.

But vaccinations had now been tested and approved. Again, various spaces had been utilised to set up vaccination centres, current nurses, retired nurses, and volunteers had been droughted in to inoculate people.

One such building was the 'Cock-a-hoop Basketball Club' set in an industrial estate to the north of the city. Letters had been posted, dates, times and place mentioned as to where they could get the first of their two doses. The elderly and vulnerable first. The double doors at the front of the building were both open, in the foyer was the registration table, also boxes of facemasks, in case they didn't already have one, then they would be seated in the main hall of the venue, on the basketball court. Various cubicles were set up and people would be called and directed to receive their jab, the first of two with another vaccination to be given within three months. It was going well, in other parts of the world similar setups were in progress. Once having received their shot, they would be guided to another area where they would sit a while, in case of any immediate reactions, before leaving via a rear fire-door exit.

Masks were worn, distances apart would be kept, guidelines and floor markings everywhere. Handwash pumps were at the entrance and exit. Erik Erasmussen, at eighty-three, already had his jab. He was the director and manager of the basketball club and despite his age, very sprightly. Wearing a pair of corduroy trousers, a checked woodcutter shirt and his feet in white and blue sneakers, he looked rather trendy. Tall, lanky in build, wearing silver rimmed glasses, he had an infectious smile and very white hair, though not much left of it. He was at the entrance, wearing a red coloured face mask, helping to welcome the people and guide them to where they needed to go. A man arrived. Erik greeted him warmly. 'Hey Joe, how are you keeping?'

'Not bad Erik,' Joe, around the same age as Erik, answered, 'Maureen has caught this dreaded virus, resting at home'.

'Sorry to hear that, wish her well' Erik said, personally knowing his daughter Maureen who was the city's current mayor, then as Joe had washed his hands and a volunteer, also fully masked, had taken his details, Erik guided him to where he could sit and wait, 'hear anything from that Dutchman?' he asked, pointing him to a row of seats.

'That was a rum thing' Joe answered, sitting down, and looking up at Erik, 'the abduction of that woman, actually Maureen knows more and apparently, he, Sam, is getting married'.

'I suppose to that lovely American woman he rescued?' Erik asked, thinking back to when he met her when she had been in this very building, along with Sam.

'No, actually to that other one, the one from Boston' Joe replied, sitting down.

'When you're done, come into the office, I'll brew some coffee' Erik said, keen to know more about the art assessor who had been instrumental in the rescue of the American woman and who had later gone missing.

'Sounds great, just what I need' Joe answered, and a nurse appeared and called his name.

Businesses were slowly reopening, handwash pumps and signs on floors and posters on windows everywhere. Wash your hands, keep your distance, wear a mask, drink fluids. One such business, was the 'Shapeshifters' health club, situated a little outside of the town on the northern side, not far from where the basketball club was situated.

A woman entered, wearing a floral decorated face mask, and walked up to the reception desk where a tall redheaded young woman awaited her, also wearing a mask, but one which had the club's logo on it, she smiled and said, 'Hello Mrs Rozzini, good to see you back'.

'Hi, I heard you were open again, is it all as normal?'

'No, I'm afraid not Mrs. Rozzini, very limited space and, I'm afraid by booking only, Sorry'.

'That's okay, I understand, I will ring for a booking, but, well, you know about what happened with my husband…'

'Yes, I'm sorry…' the redhead answered.

'Well, I know, it's been a while already, but, well, I feel I need to write to this woman, Alison Hudson, you know, apologise, I wonder, I know she left, but do you have her new address at all?'

'I'm sorry Mrs. Rozzini, I can't give you that, you should contact Detective Sergeant Saunders, at the north side police station, speak with her'.

'Of course, should have thought of that myself, thank you, I will ring for an appointment time later.'

And with that she turned and left.

Waiting until she had left the premises, the receptionist then made a phone call.

'Detective Sergeant Saunders please' she said, watching the departing woman get into her vehicle.

'Hi, it's Rita Falkirk, from Shapeshifters….'

In her office Karen Saunders recalled the tall redhead and said, 'Yes, Miss Falkirk, how can I help?'

'Mrs. Rozzini walked in here just now, she was asking for Ally's, I mean Alison's address, said she wanted to write her a letter, an apology, I felt it didn't sound right, didn't feel right, I remember all that had happened to Ally, so, I said that I couldn't reveal that information, which of course I can't, but suggested she call you'.

'That's interesting, this would be Mrs. Debra Rozzini, I take it, Nico's widow?'

'Yes'

'Thank you, Miss Falkirk, I appreciate your concern, I share that concern also, thank you for calling me'.

'Not at all, Ally was a friend, she gave me her car you know.'

'That red Triumph?' detective Saunders asked, recalling the vehicle, 'You know how to drive it?'

With laughter in her voice, Rita answered, 'Yes, I do now, my dad taught me.'

'Okay, well thanks again Miss Falkirk, bye' Karen said, smiling and then frowning as she wondered why Debra Rozzini would want to know the whereabouts of Alison Hudson.

Detective Sergeant Karen Saunders, of the Royal Canadian mounted Police, stood her slim five-foot six-inch frame up, went over to a metal filing cabinet, opened the second drawer down, rifled through and pulled out a folder. Returning to her desk she glanced up at the clock, looked at the various files on her desk, then shook her head and opened the file she had retrieved. Other cases would just have to wait a bit, she thought to herself, tucking a loose strand of her short cut brown hair behind her ear, a gut feeling was gnawing at her. She wasn't at all happy that Debra Rozzini was looking to know where Alison Hudson was. The large folder contained several smaller sub-folders, and she began flicking through them, refreshing her mind.

Her thoughts took her back to that day, a rainy day she recalled, when the foreigner had come to the station, when he had been shown to her office, where he had then told of being a witness to a kidnapping. She shook her head slightly, smiled to herself and remembered that occasion, as if it was yesterday, yet it happened around two years ago.

It had been this Alison Hudson, who had been forcefully taken, then left for dead on the edge of a ravine. Reading the file, she began to wonder about a few things, something was niggling at her, something puzzled her, and these questions needed to be addressed, the answers might just give a clue as to why, and why now, that Nico Rozzini's wife, now a widow, was keen to find her. Closing the file, making some notes on a pad, she returned to the file to the cabinet, sat down and made up her mind, she would call Sam.

THE PAST; Period 1

The year 1762 – Nova Scotia

Christoffer Rosenborg stood on the port side deck and watched cargo being loaded. He looked beyond the harbour and viewed the landscape. He had not long been here, less than two months. His thoughts took him back to earlier in the year, when, on a misty Sunday morning he had been hammering some crates together, in an area that was called the Haringvliet, in Rotterdam. He had served for over thirteen years with the VOC, the Dutch East India Company. Sailing many times to the far east, negotiating cargo loads, instructing the loading of the ship, documenting the various journeys, the contacts made, the type of cargo available, what would sell best where and when. Thirteen years. But the time had come for him to change direction, to change his lifestyle, to change the work he was involved with. He spoke several languages, enjoyed journaling the voyages and observing the many cultures that he encountered. He wanted to do just this, study and journal his observations. He had, over the years, gathered a variety of goods, was financially secure and wanted a new challenge. Though still only thirty-five years of age, he was an astute operator, knew how things worked, knew whom to contact, where to go. He wanted to observe the skirmishes that he had heard about in Nova Scotia, the French, the British, the natives. He knew that the French would like more in depth reports and it was to a Parisian Newspaper he made an approach and a plan. He would send regular reports that could be featured in their daily paper, in return he just needed someone at the other end, in this case being Boston to where he first intended to go, to help him through customs. He had goods to sell and only a few days prior to sailing from Rotterdam, he had also purchased three masterfully painted seascapes that he knew would sell very well. His new French contact informed him that they would ensure that someone was there to help him through customs, they had just the man, they said. This, through various sources, Christoffer already knew, he had picked up information on this Irish man in Boston who could prove very helpful at the port. Hence the call made to the French newspaperman, whom he knew had that contact, and he was pleased with the result and pleased with himself.

Late that Sunday morning he, along with his crates and luggage, boarded a vessel to Rouen in France, from there he would sail, via Cadiz in Spain, across the Atlantic to Boston. There he would sell his goods and arrange a passage to Halifax.

The voyage to Boston had been uneventful and he duly arrived one afternoon. The Irishman, who had a habit of speaking very quickly and only required very limited time in which to breathe, was ready at the port, along with a horse and cart and furthermore had an address for him to stay whilst in the city.

He had sold well, furs, jewellery, silks, some pots and pans, and of course the seascapes, three of them, which he sold to a very jovial but business-like man called Charlie Parker. Christoffer smiled remembering the large man, puffing a cigar. Recalling the day he had called on him, where he had, with dramatic flourish, shown the wonderful seascapes. The Bostonian had been impressed and bought all three. Since his arrival in Nova Scotia, he had written several reports to the newspaper in France, but it wasn't all as exciting that he thought it might be. In fact, the intensity of these skirmishes had been truly exaggerated. Time to move on. He was on the deck of an English ship, a two-masted schooner that had sailed from Liverpool. Always keeping his nose and ear attuned, he had picked up that this ship was going to head up the St. Lawrence River to Montreal. Not having been to this part of the word before, he studied some rudimentary maps he had come across and decided that this was an opportunity to explore this part of the North American continent.

Once in Montreal he would them navigate by a smaller vessel through some rough and turbulent rapid to reach a town called Kingston. From there he would seek to traverse Lake Ontario and make for Oswego, a port on the northeastern side of the lake and then travel across land back to Boston. Quite the journey but one he was looking forward to, he would journal the travel and even wondered whether he might sell these reports as articles for a magazine or paper. He watched the loading of cargo for a little longer, studying the men at work, studying the man who oversaw the loading, a job he himself knew well, a role he was an expert in. It all seemed to be going well. He took another look around and then decided to head for his cabin, which he had, after some bartering, secured.

Christoffer was born in Denmark, in the year 1727. He came from an influential family, but as the youngest child, he knew any inheritance would not likely come his way. He was often, when just a lad, found by the docks and had decided then and there, when only around fourteen, that he wanted to travel over the seas. When he was seventeen, he left his homeland, sailed on a Dutch vessel to Amsterdam and travelled to Leiden where he enrolled at the university there in 1744. Three years later he was qualified in many of the requirements needed for sailing and was quickly employed by the VOC. He had no regrets, learned a lot, sailed through calm seas and heavy storms and met different cultures and learned about silks, spices and tea. But it was time for a change, time to move on, see more of the world. He spoke Danish, Dutch, French, English and Spanish. Though already a shrewd and learned man, there was more to see, more to learn. Entering his cabin, small but perfectly acceptable, he settled on his bunk which just fitted his nearly six-foot frame and wondered what adventures might lie ahead.

Other than enjoying the beauty of the St. Lawrence River and the often-rugged landscape surrounding it, which he recorded daily, there were no significant events on this first part of the journey. The city of Montreal was a fascinating place and Christoffer enjoyed a few days there before travelling on towards Kingston. Two days after that he boarded a large twin masted sailing ship with a cargo of fur for Oswego. Built in Buffalo, New York, it was less than four years old and was named the 'Antoinette'. Christoffer was impressed with the sleek vessel and its twin masts, the centre one rose high into the sky. The captain was proud to point out that it was close to forty feet in height. The crossing was smooth and Christoffer was pleasantly surprised that contact had already been made for him to join a group of travellers heading for Boston. The nearly three-hundred-mile journey would take ten days and though the journey was arduous and tiring, it was also rewarding with a magnificent landscape. Travelling first to Syracuse, then following a valley between the Appalachian and Adirondack Mountains, they reached Albany and after that came across a town called Rotterdam, named after the city in the Netherlands. Christoffer had never heard of this town which wasn't even listed on an old map he had secured and easily opened a conversation with several inhabitants in a saloon one evening and with ability to speak the Dutch language, much to their delight, had interesting conversations which he, the following day after shaking off a headache from too much drinking, wrote down in his journal.

Then the wagon train, consisting of three wagons, a total of thirteen horses and a group company of fifteen men and women traversed over to Springfield and then on to the city of Boston. However, it was with sadness that upon reaching Boston, Christoffer was informed that the sailing ship, the Antoinette, which had brought him from Kingston to Oswego, had encountered a sudden storm and had sunk, all men and cargo lost. Not very far north of Oswego in an area known as the Rochester Basin. Walking along the dock that day, after hearing this news, he shook his head and remembered how he had thought the cargo looked too much for that fine sleek ship, and angry that whoever had been responsible for the loading, had not picked that up.

It was well into the year 1763 when Christoffer arrived at the incredible trading post in the port of Philadelphia, having spent eight days in Boston where he made a point of contacting Charlie Parker, to whom he had sold the three seascape paintings and when he boarded a ship to head south, he smiled as he waved to the big man, who stood by the window in the large house on the harbourfront where he had only hours before also stood, enjoying a drink with the jovial man. He had also, during those eight days, written up a full account of his trek across from Oswego to Boston, which he sold to a local newspaper. Time again, to move on. Goodbye Boston.

THE PRESENT; Boston

Monday 1st March

Samuel Joshua Price was walking down School Street, turned left into Washington Street, and headed for Quincy Market near Faneuil Hall. Six foot one, slim in built and with short blonde hair, that, he had noticed, was starting to turn grey in places. He had turned forty-nine a month ago and as he was walking many things were trying to prioritise in his mind. The telephone call earlier from Detective Sergeant Karen Saunders was disturbing. He told Chrissie he just needed to go for a walk, to think things through. A breath of fresh air, though having to wear a face mask did hamper that somewhat. Six years ago. Six years ago, his world had turned upside down, his wife, Sonja, had died, peacefully after a short illness. Sam recalled that day, he recalled that day often. It had set him on a journey, a random train trip to Paris, it was a day, in a sense a bit like today, a day where he needed to think things through, needed to make sense of it all, needed to try and understand and come to grips with what had happened and what would be next for him.

Walking along he barely noticed the other pedestrians, barely noticed the traffic and was only vaguely aware that it was a sunny and clear and rather warm day. He turned right into Court Street, remembered to check for traffic, and crossed over to the other side. He and Sonja had not been able to have children, but had been very happy with each other, with life. The journey to Paris and the quite by chance stepping into the Paris Fine Arts Auction house, proved to be the beginning of a new direction. Sam purposefully concentrated on remembering that day even though other thoughts were trying to mingle and vie for attention in his mind. He smiled as he crossed another street, recalling the angry French woman. Sophie. Now a trusted and very good friend. Reluctantly, after a few more moments, he let go of those memories and returned to the phone call earlier. Debra Rozzini was looking for Alison Hudson. Why?

He entered Quincy Market. The aroma of food immediately hit his nostrils. The facemask he was wearing not preventing the smell of herbs and spices to penetrate. He dutifully washed his hands and began walking down the centre isle taking in the various stalls on either side and the thoughts that had been on his mind were momentarily interrupted as he contemplated as to what to eat. Though the situation was still far from normal, far from how it had been before the pandemic, there was hope now. And slowly businesses began to reopen, people began to venture out. Would it all ever be the same as before, Sam doubted it. This worldwide pandemic had caused a seismic change in the way of life. It was not very busy and walking a little further, he made his choice, ordered, and sat down. His up-coming wedding took over in his mind. Chrissie. His change of direction after that trip to Paris had brought him to Boston, had taken him to an old house from where he had just left, had brought him into contact with her. Chrissie. They had tentatively fixed a date in August, hoping that by that time the many restrictions that were still in place, would be alleviated. They had both agreed on a small intimate ceremony, just a few friends. Sam nodded his thanks as his food and drink arrived, took his mask off, and again his thoughts returned to the phone call. Unexpected, worrying.

Chrissie had noticed the concerned look on his face as he ended the call.

'Detective Sergeant Saunders?' she had asked, 'what's happened Sam?'

He smiled briefly, walked over to her, hugged her. Thought about how he felt about her, the woman he was in love with, the woman he was to marry, the woman who, despite at one point thinking he would never fall in love again, had captured his heart. 'Not sure, apparently Mrs Debra Rozzini, Nico's widow, has been asking about the whereabouts of Ally.'

'Does she know? Did Karen ring her too?' Chrissie asked, knowing the detective as she had met her when Sam had gone missing, nearly two years ago.

'No, she felt it best to ring me first, see what I thought, apparently Debra went to the fitness club where she was a member, the one where Ally worked, the receptionist there was suspicious and called the detective, called Karen, the reason given, was she wanted to write a letter of apology.'

'You met Mrs. Rozzini, she was grateful at the time, gave you that painting, maybe it is what it is, she just wants to write an apology on behalf of her late husband?' Chrissie asked, looking up into his face.

'Maybe, but the receptionist, who was a friend of Ally's, felt it was suspicious, detective Saunders thinks it's suspicious, and, well, to be truthful Chrissie, so do I, I mean, why? And, why now?'

'Shall I call her? Call Ally?' Chrissie, pulling away from Sam and looking into his eyes, asked.

Sam, releasing his hands from her waist, leant forward, kissed her lightly on her lips, then said, 'Thank you, yes, please do that, I am going for a walk, need to think.'

In the market hall Sam ate and thought back, running it all through his mind and trying to think as to why he felt troubled.

It had been quite a chain of events, from the moment he had witnessed the abduction, standing in the large doorway of the goods hanger at the railway station in Moncton that day. The rain pouring down. A chain of events that included a rescue and a search, a chain of events that ended in arrests and sadly too, a death. The death of Nico Rozzini. He himself had visited his widow, Debra, and their two children.

She had been understanding, had been calm and composed. Perhaps for the benefit of the children. She had given him the painting, the third seascape, the very painting that had, in a sense, been the precursor leading to this chain of events. So, Sam was thinking, as he ate, why had she come out now, why had she asked the whereabouts of Alison now?

His thoughts briefly focused on the woman, whose swift abduction he had witnessed, tall, blonde, very attractive. Their connection had been emotional, their search together for the daughter that had been taken from her over ten years earlier, had brought them close. Did he have feelings for her at one time? Yes, he did, and, he knew, she had feelings for him. But, Sam, reliving that time in his mind, accepted that it was not to be her. Often, at that time, recalling the words his late wife had spoken to him, before closing her eyes that morning, ever so clearly, ever so softly, 'Go and find someone to love'.

Sam took a sip of his coffee and sensed the tears in his eyes as he recollected. No, it wasn't going to be Alison, for it was more important for her to be reunited with her daughter Terry. But he had, he knew now in his heart, found someone to love. Chrissie. His search for a painted miniature had let him to her door, they had, subsequently, worked together in the search for what had happened to her grandfather who had, not long after the second world war, travelled to Italy and had after that not been heard from again, vanished, into thin air. He smiled at the memory and at the fact that he had not fallen in love with her then. But, as he ate and sipped his coffee, he sure was in love with her now.

Finishing eating and drinking the last of his coffee, Sam again returned to the question that sprang foremost in his mind, why now? Why was Debra Rozzini looking for Ally now? Recalling the day he had visited her, how she had looked shaken, how she had been apologetic, how she had spoken softly and kindly, how she had insisted that the seascape, that was at that time being professionally cleaned, would be his to keep. For Sam this certainly seemed out of character. Had he been wrong? Putting his face mask back on, he stood up and headed for home, still thinking back to that day in the town of Harris.

The year 1866 – The town of Harris

Sara Rebekah Parker walked up the stairs, her heart was heavy. She turned left, past the small reception desk, down the corridor and entered the first door on her left. Entering, she closed the door after her and stood still for a moment. It was a large office. Ahead of her were three windows overlooking the town. To her right was a seating area, three chairs surrounding a low table. How often had she sat there, she wondered, smiling, thinking of all the reports she had read, how she had watched him at work. She turned to look to her right, the beautiful oak desk which had a leather inserted top. Two chairs were set in front and a large leather chair behind it, in which he had so often sat, reading and writing. In the spacious office there was also an oak sideboard with a variety of bottles and glasses set on top and there were two standard lamps. Looking again at the desk, Sara closed her eyes briefly. Henry's desk. Though before him it had been her father, Charlie's desk.

Her eyes moved upwards and looked at the large painting that hung on the wall behind the desk. It was a beautifully painted seascape. Turbulent seas, men struggling to control a sailing ship. She had often admired it. Now, looking at it, she could so much more now, identify with those sailors, struggling in the storm, being tossed about by the heavy seas. It was how she felt. Henry had died, but not just that, Rebekah had died, within days of each other. Her father and mother had travelled over from Boston for the funeral. They had stayed three days and journeyed back. Rebekah had been her grandmother and had married Henry on a day when her father had also married Ruth. Here in this town, here where, when she was eighteen had moved to from Boston. Henry Hopkins had taken her under his wings, had worked and taught her all about every aspect of the workings of the silver mine. He was incredibly well admired, a giant figure in the small town, though he only stood five foot and six inches, as was she. But he commanded huge respect.

The mine had stopped work for the day so that all could attend the double funeral. The following morning, she had arrived, had moved up to the third step of the staircase and had asked the personnel to be in the foyer. She spoke to them, encouraged them, thanked them. She had a gift for speaking, much like her mother Ruth, who, when she and her father returned to Boston over twenty years ago, had been so instrumental in getting the failing business back on track.

Sara walked over to the desk, threw a glance out one of the windows and then sat herself into the big leather chair. She had, over the past couple of weeks, when Henry had become poor in health, already re-arranged some of the files and reports. She opened the bottom drawer on the right-hand side and took out three black covered journals. Henry had given these to her some months back, perhaps already having an inkling that the time was right. She promised him she would read them, a journal of Henry's adventures, from the time he left Cornwall in England, through to the many years he spent in South America and up to his time here, in the town of Harris. But not today, she said to herself, and put the journals back in the drawer.

It was time for work. The mine didn't run itself. She got up from the desk and decided to head down the mines, again to give encouragement to the miners and to show that life goes on. As she opened to the door to what was now her office, she threw another glance back at the seascape that hung on the wall, before entering the corridor, closing the door behind her.

THE PRESENT
Monday 1ˢᵗ of March-Friesland-The Netherlands

Whilst Sam was tucking into his food in Boston late morning, thinking about his visit with Debra Rozzini and recalling how it had been his visit to the mining company to view the seascape painting that had started the events, it was late afternoon as Froukje Boersma sat, deep in thought, by the window on the train from Leeuwarden to Amersfoort. She had spent a long weekend with her older brother and family, something she hadn't been able to do for quite some time. It was great seeing them, seeing her young thirteen-year-old nephew, Alexander, in particular.

She was deep in thought about something she had discovered. It had taken her imagination in all sorts of directions. Froukje had, very much like Sam, needed a time to just get away, think through about her position, her future and going up north to visit her brother was an ideal opportunity to do so. Her colleague, Martijn, with whom she had worked now for several years, the two of them heading up the burglary investigation team, based in Amersfoort and covering a wide geographical area in the centre of the Netherlands, was going to move. He had been offered a new role in the Rotterdam police force, mainly due to recent events and his connection with the chief of police. This, and his romance with the Parisian auction house woman, Sophie, who had also been offered a new position with a prestigious museum in the city, meant they could be closer together.

Whilst of course very happy for Martijn, she had to think through her own options. She was offered the now senior role in the burglary section, a new pay deal and the responsibility of recruiting an assistant. Deciding that it would be good to just get away and think this through, she had rung her brother and invited herself over for the weekend. Something which, due to the covid pandemic, she hadn't been able to do for some time.

Leeuwarden, her hometown, her place of birth nearly 34 years ago. Her long blonde hair in a ponytail, wearing faded jeans and a t-shirt under a red leather jacket, feet into soft sneakers, a brightly coloured facemask covered the required area of her face and carrying a small holdall and her handbag, she had arrived on the Friday evening. Had then had spent most of Saturday morning with her nephew, shopping and treating him to lunch, getting on well with the tall thirteen-year-old, finding out his likes, his interests, and the bond they had was great.

On the Sunday she had visited a market, and it was there, in looking for something to gift her brother and sister-in law and her nephew, that she came across a stall with various antiques displayed on a table. The stall, she noticed, had a sign on the front of the awning that had the address and name of the antique store that had a shop in the city. It was called 'Terugblik' which, meaning 'hindsight', she found rather apt, and it was not a store she was familiar with. She then noticed a box, a cardboard box, sat on the ground and spotted the framed photograph. The glass was cracked in one corner. The image was familiar, she had seen it in books. It was a scene from the second world war, the liberation of the Frisian capital when the Canadians entered.

She picked up the frame, turned it over and read the inscription, 15th April 1945, Royal Canadian Dragoons liberate Leeuwarden. The photograph showed people waving and cheering, armoured vehicles entering the city. Again, turning it over, she noticed that someone had written a description of the vehicle in the photo, apparently a Dodge WC 4wd Utility truck, ¼ ton, two-seater, split windscreen. Obviously, someone with knowledge on military vehicles. This was ideal because Froukje had picked up her nephew's interest in the history of the second world war, and particularly the vehicles used. This photo would be an ideal gift, she would buy a replacement frame for it.

As the train smoothly sped through the Frisian countryside, with its many canals' rivers and lakes, heading south, Froukje thought back to when she made the unusual discovery. She had returned from the market, had then gone to the guestroom and gift-wrapped a few things. It was when taking the photo from the broken frame, that she discovered that there was a letter, taped to the inside of the frame backing. The old cello-tape gave up and the letter slid onto the bed. Although extremely curious, she made herself put the letter aside, carefully dealing with the broken glass, she put the photograph into its new frame, then wrapped this neatly. It was almost lunchtime. Gifts in hand she left the room, threw a glance at the letter she had found that lay so invitingly on the bed and briefly considered sharing her find. She decided not to and went downstairs. Alexander was thrilled with the old photograph, kissed, and embraced his auntie, then rushed upstairs to his room, re-appearing moments later with a book, turning to the right pages he showed her a page showing the details and pictures of the very same vehicle. Later in the afternoon, Froukje went to her room to pack, put her long blond hair back into a ponytail, shoved the letter in her handbag and looked forward to opening and reading it once on her way.

The train had smoothly cut through the flat Frisian landscape with speeds in excess of one hundred kilometres an hour and was approaching Heerenveen when Froukje started to read the letter for a second time. It was dated the 29th of March 1945 and began with 'Dearest Nicholas'

As the train picked up speed rapidly, now heading for the city of Zwolle, it began to rain, the many droplets running down the glass window…

THE PAST
Period 3

The year 1938 – Rochester – New York State-USA

It was dark and it was raining, coming up to half an hour past midnight. The Ford drop-side truck, drove slowly over the gravel road and stopped when a man stepped in front of the vehicle with his hand raised. The windscreen wipers were working hard to clear the heavy rain and the driver applied the brakes and awaited further instructions. A face appeared at the driver's door, and he was told by signals to remain in the truck and turn the engine off. Two men then unbolted the right-hand drop-side and lowered it. There was a line of overhead lamps that swung slightly through the force of the rain. A light was placed about every ten feet and before the driver lost all visibility through the windscreen, he noticed the row of lights led to a building some sixty feet or so further down.

The two men, wearing heavy rain-jackets, with hoods, wearing strong gloves and heavy boots, worked in unison, not saying a word, manhandling the various crates onto a flat-bed trolley that stood on steel rails. The boxes were of different sizes and shapes and a total of fourteen were placed on the trolley. One of the men then released a brake-lever, gave a push and the trolley moved smoothly on the gleaming rails, descending slightly towards the building.

The second man knocked on the driver's window, gave signals to start the engine, then to continue to the turning circle to then head back from where he had come. The driver understood, nodded, and started the vehicle. With the windscreen wipers once again in action, he saw, as he slowly drove forward, the trolley rolling towards the large building. In the rain, the corrugated iron shone in the lights, and he noticed, just as he began turning the truck, that the rails went straight to a roller door, which was only half – way open, and then into it. He completed the turn, was grateful that the heater was once more warming him up and drove back towards the town of Rochester. A few minutes later he drove by the side of the last leg of the Genesee River as it flowed into the lake. He then turned off the make-shift gravel road, onto a firm concrete road and headed towards the East. Meanwhile two men had appeared outside the steel roller door and waited. Moments later an empty trolley came into view which they took hold off and between them pushed and pulled it up the slight gradient to where the first men were waiting, where yet another lorry came trundling along the road towards them. The rain showing no signs of easing up.

Less than a hundred yards away, situated between the large hangar type building and where the two men were getting ready to unload another truck, stood an old barn, a dilapidated barn. It stood on higher ground and from the loft, through a small opening, the lake could be seen. Through a wide slid in the boarding, a young lad was watching the proceedings. Though the barn was far from watertight, there were enough places where it was dry and, protected from the wind, relatively warm. The young boy, fourteen years of age, watched in fascination as the truck was being unloaded, as the boxes and crates were being placed on the trolley. This was the second night he had snuck away from the farmhouse, over half a mile away, to come and see the goings on. He could not get close in the day – time as there were security personnel everywhere. He had first been intrigued when seeing the trucks go past the road adjacent the farmhouse, had first noticed the building of the large hangar, painted a dark shade of green and had found out, mainly through notices that had been placed around the property, that this was a United States Naval facility where new equipment was being manufactured.

Hence the security, the fencing, the guards. Being the only boy with three younger sisters, he was often by himself, often went exploring and had decided to go out at night, when they all thought he was fast asleep, to investigate. Four nights ago, had been his first outing. Quietly slipping from the house, even taking some food and drink with him in his school satchel. That was the night, very cold, but dry, that he decided to check out the old barn, no longer in use, and realised it's vantage point and chose it as his look-out post.

The second night, having been glad that it was a school holiday week and had been able to catch up on sleep during the day, was a stormy night, again it was dry, but the wind howled around and through the barn. It was as he was about to head back home, having no idea as to the exact time but guessing it would be around two o'clock in the morning, when he saw that a gust of wind had picked up a small box, blown it of the flat-bed trolley and it had opened and several folders and papers were gathered by the wind and dispersed in all directions. Two men were frantically snatching and gathering the papers for quite a few minutes. The young lad was totally engrossed and amused as he watched their scurrying around.

Having seemingly recovered it all, the situation calmed down, the papers and folders were stuffed back in the box and the trolley was pushed towards the large building where it rolled under the half open roller door. Feeling quite tired now, and longing for his bed, the lad left the barn and was steadily walking back toward the farmhouse when the wind, still strong and gusting, blew a sheet of paper against his chest where it clung. He plucked it, stuffed it into his satchel and continued to walk home. It wasn't until the following morning, waking with the light streaming into his room, hearing his sisters giggling and laughing downstairs, that he remembered the paper, grabbed the satchel, took out the sheet of crumpled paper, opened it, flattened it out on his bed and read it. Young Wayne Koppell smiled, and his imagination was even further fired up, for the heading on the paper, which was most likely just a label that had been attached to a box or crate, said, in black capital letter, US NAVAL SERVICE, then there were some numbers and below that in smaller but still in capital letters, ONTARIO PROJECT. Wayne carefully folded the paper, put it back into his school satchel and set about to dress and have breakfast.

He was excited and hungry and, though often told not to, he partially slid down the banister and headed for the kitchen.

THE PRESENT;
Milan –Italy

Monday 1ˢᵗ March

As Froukje Boersma was gliding through the Frisian countryside on the intercity train, Milly Parker answered the doorbell in her apartment in the Italian city. Just remembering in time to put her face mask on, she opened the door. A courier stood a little way back from the door, also wearing a mask and spoke to her in Italian, she need not sign anything, and walked away. There, on the doorstep, was a parcel. Well, a box really, and when she bent down to pick it up, she was surprised how weighty it was. She closed the door with her foot and carried the box over to the small table adjacent the kitchen.

Checking the consignment note, she saw it had been posted in San Francisco and there was a letter attached. Ignoring the temptation to open the box first, Millie sat herself down on a stool by the breakfast bar, reached for a knife and slit open the letter.

Dear Miss Parker,

When your father passed in 2010, all his goods and finances were bequeathed to you, which you received in due course. We have since however, discovered that your father had placed a few items in a storeroom in the health facility where he spent the final years of his life. These goods, consisting of a photo album, a bundle of letters, several books, a few journals and a wristwatch, have been boxed up and now finally sent as it has taken us a while to locate your new address, and so please accept our apologies for the lateness in getting these to you.

Sincerely yours

Edwin Buchanan

Bay-Side Solicitors

Her curiosity no longer to be contained, she took the knife and went over to the table to open the cardboard box. She thought about her father, recalled a time when her mother had died, at the time believing it to be through injuries sustained when a tornado hit the archaeological dig she was working at. She was heartbroken, but even more so as she saw her father's health decline after the loss of his wife. Millie pulled out the photo album, which was on the top, then, tied together with a ribbon and with a letter tucked underneath the faded red ribbon, were three journals. She placed these on the table, slipped the letter free and opened it. Milie immediately felt shaken and sat herself down on one of the dining chairs. She recognised her mother's handwriting.

A little later, having emptied the box and disposed of the carboard, she sat again on the stool in the kitchen, a glass of orange juice nearby, and looked at a folder that contained a report. She discovered from the notes her mother had written that the journals had arrived by post, from Halifax, sent by Zeta, her grandfather's sister, on the very day that her mother was born, and also the day her great grandfather, Carlos, had died. These journals were written by Henry Hopkins, who was in charge of the silver mine in Harris, the same one her father, Joshua, would one day be running. They journalled Henry's life and her mother had written down, that, having read them when she was around fourteen or fifteen, that it was this man's adventures that had helped her make the decision to study geology. Also, in the folder that now lay on the counter next to the orange juice, contained a report handwritten by her grandfather, Zoltina, and a special and secret mission that he flew in the war, which he had titled, the Ontario Project. It was this report that Millie decided to read first, it sounded most intriguing, and it began by stating it was the 10th of December, 1941…

THE PAST; Period 4

The year 1941 – San Francisco – Wednesday 10ᵗʰ December

A little after seven pm on a cold evening. The car, a black saloon, stopped outside the house, the driver kept the engine running and a man in the front passenger seat opened the door, got out and opened the rear door as the man appeared in the doorway, closed the front door, and walked down the path. He gave a brief nod to the man holding the door open and got into the car.

Zoltina Huanca the 3ʳᵈ placed his leather holdall next to him and sat back, then leant forward and spoke to the driver. 'Quick detour, the hospital.' Then sat back.

The man in the passenger seat closed his door, nodded an approval to the driver and the car pulled away.

There was no further conversation. The mood was sombre, in the car, in the city, in the nation. Three day earlier, just before eight am, the Japanese had attacked Pearl Harbour in Honolulu. A massive attack, an organised attack, a surprise attack.

Over three hundred aircraft had been involved, setting off from six aircraft carriers that had surrounded the Hawaiian Islands. An estimated two and half thousand men killed, a further twelve hundred wounded, ships sunk and destroyed.

The mood was indeed sombre and Zoltina, known to his family and friends as just Zee, wondered why he had been urgently summoned. He was a pilot. A scout pilot having covered many hours over the Pacific keeping an eye out for the enemy. He had been on leave, having last flown over a week ago. Had he missed something?

The telephone call had been short, 'Pack an overnight bag, a car will pick you up in half an hour.' then after a very brief pause, 'No need to wear your uniform'.

He looked out the window. The roads were quiet. They were coming up to the hospital. Zoltina sighed as he recalled what had happened here. Just over a year ago, his father had died, he had been deployed at the time and later, after having comforted his mother and sisters, he had taken himself to the hospital, to see his father for a last time. Afterwards he took himself to a small waiting room and just sat there. Lost. The plans they had made, the project that was in progress, all had changed. The day his father died, was also the day his niece was born, Emily. A day of joy and a day of sorrow. It had been that night, as he had just sat there, in that waiting room, when a nurse had seen him, had come alongside him, had sat with him, had held his hand, and had cradled his head when he had cried.

Millie. Some time had passed before he had an opportunity to see her, to thank her. He had been unable to utter a word. He smiled at the recollection as she had said to him that the next time he came, he should ask her out. The car pulled into the circular driveway to the hospital entrance and Zoltina got out. He didn't say a word, carried his six-foot frame through the entrance and entered the reception area. She was there, waiting, knowing he was coming. Millie.

He, again, briefly thought back to that time, when, the next time he had seen her, he had found his voice and had been bold in telling her that after his next deployment he would come and ask her to be his wife. Now, as he walked across the foyer, he smiled as he saw her, she walked up to meet him, and they embraced. She was on the night shift and in the hospital, as everywhere else, the mood was sombre. They had planned to get married in the new year, however, with this recent turn of events they felt they should perhaps wait a little longer.

'Where are you going?' she asked, whispering in his ear as she felt comforted by his strong arms around her.

He pulled back to look at her, kissed her lips and said, 'Don't know, an overnight mission somewhere, guess I'll find out soon, must go, but had to see you first, of course' Then smiled at her, looking into her deep blue eyes, and realising again how much he loved her.

Millie studied his deep brown eyes, held his clean shaven and tanned face, kissed him, and said,' Off you go, I have patients to see'.

He nodded, turned, and left.

Back in the car his thoughts returned to the question foremost in his mind, what was this about, why had he been called?

Fifteen minutes later the car stopped by a building on the dockyard and the man in the front passenger seat got out and opened the door for him.

Zoltina nodded his thanks and followed the man's directions to a nearby door. It opened as he approached it, was ushered in by a man wearing dark blue coveralls and followed him through two corridors before being led into a room.

Twenty-two minutes later he emerged, the man in the blue coveralls was waiting and led him through several other corridors and then through a large warehouse and through a small door onto the jetty. There it stood, or rather floated. The Curtiss Seagull single prop biplane. It was almost identical to the one he regularly flew, with the exception, he had been told, of a larger fuel tank.

'Flight plans and documents are on board sir,' the man said, 'she's ready to go'.

Zoltina nodded, then jumped onto the near floater and opened the door, throwing his overnight bag inside, then climbed into the cockpit. Checking all the instruments, he saw that all seemed in order, started the prop engine, and slowly pulled away from the dock area. It was a little after eight-thirty, the sky was clear.

No radio communication, unless in an emergency, climb to no higher than fourteen thousand feet and fly only during the night hours. Checking all the instruments by the light in the cockpit, Zoltina then checked the surrounding area and gunned the engine, picking up speed rapidly, slightly bouncing on the water, then lifted the craft, banked to the right and climbed to the required height.

A mission, a secret mission, a classified, top-secret mission. Once he had set the correct bearing, he thought about the conversation he had, or more actually, the orders he had listened to. Relieved in a way that he had not been blamed for not having picked up any movement by the Japanese in his scout missions, but listened as he was told he was the best for this mission, that it would involve night flying, landing on water and would take several stages, the first to the Port of Tacoma in Oregon, where he would be met, where he would collect an assignment of military equipment and be refuelled.

Once at cruising height he was able to comfortable read through the directions and double check the heading and destinations.

As he flew through the night, his thoughts jumped from one thing to another, from this assignment he was given, top-secret, classified, military equipment, to his lovely Millie, to his friends and fellow mariners and soldiers who had perished in Pearl Harbour. He thought about his father, about his heritage, about the company his father had set up and that he was to continue and manage, would have already been doing so, had it not been for the impending war. Deciding he would need a drink of strong coffee, he felt for the flask in his holdall and unscrewed the lid. The plane flew on beautifully, the engine purring quite softly and evenly. The sky was clear, there was hardly any wind as he crossed the night skies towards Portland.

It was a little after midnight when he saw the lights of the city and started his descent towards the water of Port Tacoma. His destination was a large chemical plant on the east side docks. Lights would guide him he was told as he watched the altimeter drop. Slighting banking to port he lined up the craft and then saw several beacon lights. Slowing the plane, he adjusted the speed and got ready to land upon the water, glistening in the night sky. The landing was smooth, and he noticed someone with two torches guiding him towards the large building.

He glided the plane alongside the dock and cut the engine. A small tanker wagon was approaching. Fuel. He opened the door and was beckoned out. A tall man wearing thin glasses held out his hand, shook it vigorously and said, 'Welcome sir, please, come inside and rest a while, we will see to the refuelling and the loading of the cargo'.

'Thank you' he replied and followed the man inside the vast building, noticing the various chemical tanks and several banks of dials and monitors as he was led to a well-lit and tidy cafeteria. He was told to help himself and was given directions to the toilets, then left to it. Twenty minutes later he was collected, escorted back to his plane and the same man stood on the dockside, shook his hand, and wished him a safe flight on this second part of his journey. Zoltina thanked him, boarded his plane, threw a cursory look at the equipment that had been stowed and climbed into the cockpit.

The sky remained clear, the wind remained almost non-existent and restarting the engine it wasn't long before he moved away from the dock, lined up the craft and pulled the throttle. Next destination, Fort Peck in Montana. Knowing the distance, Zoltina figured that he would only just have enough fuel in the enlarged fuel tank to reach it and hoped that he wouldn't face a strong headwind. He was soon at the asked for cruising height and was pleased with the performance of the engine as he crossed the night skies heading east.

Making sure he regularly checked his instrument, Zoltina wondered briefly what might be contained in the various crates that had been placed on board the small plane, and moreover, he had noticed four metal canisters and pondered on what they might contain. Classified. He was when he returned, not able to reveal this mission to anyone, had signed documents. Deciding to think on other matters he flew on through the night sky, thinking that he should arrive at his next destination just before daybreak. There he would stay, there he would sleep, there he would remain until he would fly out when darkness fell.

The fuel gauge was slipping down towards empty when he started his descent towards the waters of the mighty Missouri, the longest river in the United States. He noticed in the already brightening light, a wide a smooth area, just to the west of Fort Peck, the beacons already lit, and smoothly touched down, then turning slightly towards where someone was guiding him in. There was no dock, no large building, just a small wooden jetty and he expertly manoeuvred his plane beside it.

Cutting the engine, he got out and was again cordially greeted, this time by a young man who welcomed him, told him the plane would be well guarded and would he follow him to a nearby house where he would be able to spend the day, of course to perhaps, in the first place, sleep.

Zoltina agreed that sleep would be first on the agenda, took in the surroundings as day was breaking and was impressed by the vastness and scenery of this part of the country.

A rather plumb woman with rosy cheeks and sparkling blue eyes, her dark hair tied in a ponytail, greeted him warmly. As the sun was fully over the horizon and the new day was beginning, Zoltina lay down on the bed and promptly fell asleep.

Just over halfway into the third leg of his journey, the weather changed, and the wind increased. He had slept well, had eaten well and had been able to have a restful day, leaving the small house just after seven in the evening. It was cold but dry then as he had boarded the plane, checked the instruments, noticed his full fuel tank, and had again briefly looked over the contents of the cargo. It wasn't long before he again took off into the night sky, this time, another long haul, to Duluth, Minnesota, and to an oil refinery there. The earlier part of this flight had all gone very well, crossing the clear night skies, but, then the cloud cover thickened, and the wind increased, he could feel the engine straining a little harder, saw the speed drop slightly. Then the rain came.

Zoltina was an experienced pilot, already many hours under his belt and one of the top pilots who could fly the Curtiss Seagull. Concentrating on the instrument panel, he flew on, thinking that with this weather, he might struggle to make the distance.

But the rain passed, the wind eased, and it was a little after one o'clock in the morning when he saw the lights of the city of Duluth and checking his maps, steered the plane around towards the industrial harbour area and easily spotted the oil refinery. Circling around, Zoltina descended and came in from the west, landing smoothly and once again noticed someone had two torches lit and waving him in.

Refuelled and after some light refreshments and a pit stop, he was once again airborne, this time a shorter leg, to the southeast, to Green Bay, Wisconsin, where he would overnight with the last leg the following night.

There were a few more folks around when he landed on the waters of Green Bay. Again, being guided in and escorted to where he would spend the night. Having at the very beginning checked over all the maps and routes, he knew that for his final leg, he would have to ensure he stayed out of Canadian airspace as he crossed over Lake Michigan as well as going no higher than ten thousand feet on this leg. Then to the south around Cleveland and Buffalo to land on Lake Ontario near Rochester.

And so it was, on the third day of his mission, at just before four o'clock in the morning, he landed the craft smoothly on the waters of Lake Ontario. Steering the biplane towards a waterside hangar, Zoltina was unaware that on the shore, not two hundred yards away, he was being observed by two youngsters, as he was focused on the man with the two torches who was guiding him towards the jetty by the large hanger.

Keeping low, a young lad crawled closer to the hangar, which was not far from the old, dilapidated barn, where for several years now, Wayne still occasionally went to in the middle of the night, to observe and note the goings on at the Naval station. He had recently, three months ago, started dating a girl from school. She had originated in the lowlands, arriving on American soil when just four years old. She was very keen on photography and had received, on her sixteenth birthday recently, a camera from her father and mother, one that had been purchased in Rotterdam just six months prior to it being bombed by the Germans in the month of May 1940. A gift from her father who had visited the city as part of his role in the Navy.

Wayne and his girlfriend Mies, who was now known as Missy, had met, and crept up to the old barn, often they would spend time together, chatting, frolicking and at times just watching the goings on at the Naval Base. On occasions Missie brought her camera. This Friday morning was such an occasion, and on a clear night, despite the cold temperature, they had walked down to the shore as she wanted to take some pictures of the lake by the night sky, and then heard the plane.

'Keep down' Wayne had said, whispering loudly, 'hand me your camera, please' asking nicely for he knew she was protective of the Zeiss Ikon Centex camera that had been given her.

Wayne took photos as the plane smoothly landed on the water, then crawled closer to the hangar where he had spotted a man waving torches. Missy crawled after him and soon they were side by side. 'Let me take some shots" she said, and he handed her the camera, knowing she knew far better how to use it.

The sixteen-year-old took several shots, zooming the lens for close ups and captured the pilot, the man with the torches, two more men as they came from the hangar and of the crates and cylinders that were unloaded.

Then it began to rain, looking at each other they nodded and retreated, eventually returning to the old barn. Dawn was beginning to break when the pair left, Wayne returning to the house close by where he lived and Missy a little further along to her house, promising to develop the film very soon.

Zoltina was escorted into the large hanger and directed to a side entrance where a chauffeur was ready to drive him to a nearby house where he would spend the rest of the night and following day and would be picked up in the evening for his return flight, taking the same route but in reverse. On the way, though a little tired now, he thought about this mission he was on, having again noticed, as he exited his plane, the various boxes and cylinders, this time noticing a label that was on one of those boxes. Written boldly on a label on the side of one of the crates, the words, 'Ontario Project', and wondered what that might be about.

Not much later he was taken to a nearby house where he could sleep and rest until nighttime when he could commence his return journey. As he got into bed, Zoltina pondered about a time when he might learn exactly how he was involved in the war effort, or perhaps this mission might forever be kept a secret. Shoving those thoughts aside, he thought of his wife Millie and looked forward to going home.

THE PRESENT; Myrtle Creek – Oregon

Monday 1ˢᵗ March

Claire Symonds, on her way home, had briefly stopped by the war memorial, recalling the time she had stood there, some ten months ago, thinking about her grandfather and uncle, and thinking about a boy she once knew. Luke. Where was he now?

She walked on and reached the house, walking up the path and remembering the time that Thomas had walked up to the house that day. She had seen the car stop, she had seen him get out, she had defiantly walked out onto the porch and challenged him, all five foot four inches of her, asked him who he was and that he had better turn around.

So long ago? She wondered, no, it just seemed a like ages. She unlocked the front door and entered. It was time to carry on her search, her investigation. One she had started nearly a year ago. Thomas and Cynthia were not here, they had received a call for help from the Spanish woman, Letitia Teremos, and had flown out earlier. Claire headed upstairs, pressed the number pad to unlock the door and entered the room. The search engine room as Thomas had dubbed it. She was going to have another crack at solving the disappearance of a woman. Holly. It had been her vanishing that had started Robert Pentegrass into researching missing people, something he then did for nearly twenty years until his death last year. The death that had brought Thomas Klaassen over from Sweden for he had been gifted the house in Robert's will. A close friend in high school days, Thomas had been astounded to find out what Robert had been up to over the years. He learned that Claire had been one of around thirty – five people that Robert in his research had located and saved, this with the help of the Portland police and a woman, Cynthia, who had been there when Claire had been rescued. Learning of this, Thomas had decided to follow up on what Robert had begun, starting with a case, that had been mentioned in Robert's will, though it was interrupted by an urgent call which then sent Thomas flying over to

Spain and subsequently was embroiled in case with the help of Cynthia where he met the Spanish woman, Letitia Teremos. It was her who had called, who had rung Thomas. She needed their help and they had not hesitated in making arrangements to go there.

Claire punched in the code for the computer and brought the screen to life. It had been the disappearance of Holly, Robert's girlfriend back then, that had started him on this journey to find others, subsequently earning him the nickname, dubbed by the Portland Police, of 'The Searcher'.

Holly had simply vanished. Claire had, having discovered that it had been the disappearance of Holly that had set in motion Roberts searching, found a file, and realising that he had not been successful, decided to follow up this search.

'For you Robert' she had audibly whispered. Beginning the investigation shortly after Thomas and Tia had returned from Spain last year.

It hadn't been long before she made a startling discovery. A connection with a case that Thomas had been part of and had explained to her, for she had found out, that Holly's grandfather was Wayne Koppell, and following his line in order to hopefully work back and find out more about Holly, she discovered, that he had also gone missing, that he was the captain of a ship called the 'Taciturn' an exploration vessel, and it had simply vanished into thin air when on an expedition on Lake Ontario, back in 1963.

As this intrigued her, she then gasped when she read the names of those who were on this vessel when it went missing. For she knew two of these names. Calling to Thomas to come and see, she showed him the screen. Roger Sutherland and Natalie Umbrego. Two people who had been involved in the case that Thomas had referred to as the mystery of the three monks.

But the trail had not led to anywhere, no further information was to be found. With Thomas and Cynthia now off to Spain to help Letitia who had problems with a neighbouring family that were known drug growers, she was determined to again try and find out what had happened to Holly, who had vanished on New Year's Eve, or actually, New Year's Day in the year 2001.

She had, not too long ago, found out a little more, for she had found out that Holly, who had been watching the firework display at midnight, had been seen leaving with two women.

The screen came to life, showing the idyllic beach and palm tree scene that Robert had set up. She would never change it. It would be a constant reminder, of the lovely man, who suffered with a type of Asperger syndrome, who had located and organised her rescue. 'So,' Claire said to herself,' the new year's party at the Rozzini household, who were there, and who were these two women, who had been seen with Holly? Getting up from the desk chair, she walked over to the window and looked up at the blue sky, briefly thinking about Thomas and Cynthia, then returned to the desk and began to type on the keyboard.

Cynthia Barnes looked out the window down to the Atlantic Ocean far below. The sky was clear, not a cloud to be seen anywhere. Her thoughts went back to only two days earlier, it was early in the evening, and she was standing on the East Bank Esplanade in Portland. Beside her were her parents, both having now recovered from the covid infection. Thomas had offered to come, but Tia, as she was known to her friends and family, insisted she just be with her parents at this time. The three of them stood silently and looked over the water of the Willamette River towards the bridge. The Morrison Bridge. Thirty years ago. It had been thirty years ago that her younger brother had left the house after dinner, had cycled his bike to the bridge, and had then leaned the bicycle against the railing, stepped onto the saddle and then jumped over the railing. into the water some twenty metres below.

The coroner's report suggested that the impact would have most likely caused an immediate blackout, death had been quick.

Tia, dark brown hair, tied in a ponytail and standing five foot eight inches tall had her arm around her mother's waist and leant her head on the top her mother's head. Her father, well over six foot, from whom she obviously got her height, had his arm around her shoulder from the other side and the three of them stood linked for some moments. Thirty years. Suicide because he had been bullied at school. Tears rolled down the cheeks of her mother, tears rolled down her cheeks too, her fault, she was to blame. Though she had been forgiven by her parents, she still carried the guilt with her. Her phone rang. Tia sniffed, extricated herself from her parents and reached into her pocket for the phone, saw that it was from Thomas.

'Sorry to ring, needed to get in touch rather quickly' he began.

'It's okay, what's happened?' Tia answered, sniffing once more, and trying to get to her handkerchief from the handbag that was slung across her shoulder.

'Letitia called, quite worried, she needs us, well, particularly you, with your knowledge of the law, we need to fly out there.'

'Okay, I'll call you back shortly' put her phone away, blew her nose and explained to her parents that she had to go. Ever since her brother had taken his life, she had changed her ways, had vowed to never again be the person she had been before and to do whatever she could to help others. This aim became even more clear and focused when she met Robert Pentegrass and for over ten years had worked together with him in the hunt and search for missing people. Her parents understood, they hugged, and Cynthia left them on the esplanade and headed for their home, calling Thomas back and planning their flights.

He sat next to her on board the flight to Bilbao. Thomas. She looked across to him as he was reading some report, that he had printed out shortly before leaving Myrtle Creek. He had then driven to Portland, met her and boarded a flight to Atlanta, from there, earlier today, they had boarded the connection to Spain. Tia smiled to herself as she thought about the time she had been on this same flight, but then sitting several rows behind him.

In a place called Truro, Nova Scotia, situated about halfway between Halifax and Moncton, Karina West escaped from the Nova Institute for Women.

And in Myrtle Creek, Claire was looking into the disappearance of Holly Koppell, Thomas and Cynthia were on their way to see how they could help Letitia Teremos in Spain and in Amersfoort Martijn Vogel put the phone down after having listened to a lengthy conversation from Froukje and what she had discovered in Leeuwarden.

THE PAST; Period 5

The year 1945 Leeuwarden – Netherlands – April

Nicholas Robbins stirred to wakefulness. Keeping his eyes closed he first realised that his head was thumping inside. Concentrating on pushing the banging sound into the recesses of his mind, he then became aware of three things, first there was the sound of the birds that filtered through, second was, though his eyes were still closed, he could sense that it was light and the third was the movement, of a body that was beside him.

He tried to remember, tried to recall. Thankfully the thumping was subsiding, and he tentatively opened his eyes. It was indeed quite light, and a sideways glance caught sight of the bedside table alarm clock revealing it to be just past nine o'clock.

He took in a deep breath and memories of the previous evening began to create various images in his mind. Sitting up slowly, he glanced to where she lay, the blond woman, though, at merely eighteen, a teenager really. He slipped from beneath the sheets and recalled more clearly now, that though he had ended up in bed with her, their encounter had been kissing and caressing only. He had been sensible, even though the alcohol he had consumed throughout the evening had affected his speech and movement. The thumping in his head reminded him not to drink so much ever again. Standing by the window in just his boxer shorts, he peered around the curtain. It was sunny. For a moment he had to recollect what day it was and sifted through the memory banks of his mind. It had been Sunday, just a little before noon when they had trundled into the city, to a massive greeting and cheers of the people who joyfully greeted their liberators. Looking out the window Nicholas noticed it was quiet outside. It was Wednesday now, he remembered, for two events came to mind. The first, on the morning of Tuesday, shortly after a debriefing and listening to a plan of action to drive the Germans, that were still in some force to the west of the city, near a town called Franeker, back, for late on the Sunday and into Monday, backup had

40

arrived in the form of the Nova Scotia Highlanders and a third squadron of his Dragoons to consolidate their progress, was a letter his commander gave him.

A letter from his mother. Turning away from the window he looked at her. Though she had briefly stirred, she was once again sound asleep. This was the second event. She was the second event. He moved closer to the bed, looked at her and then made up his mind, gathered his clothes and boots and left the room. After a brief wash in the small bathroom, he quietly headed downstairs. He became aware of someone being in the kitchen, heard voices, likely the girl's parents. No way he wanted to introduce himself at that moment, not sure as to what reception he might get. He needed to get back to his unit that had been put up in a local school not far from where he was. Ever so quietly, he left the house.

Nicholas wondered how many others had been to parties as the invitations had been overwhelming and plenty. Many young women flirting their attention with smiles and laughter. A city liberated, joy and thankfulness abound. Taking only one wrong turn, Nicholas found the school and made a point of striding upright and with determination. He was hungry. He knew they were moving out in the afternoon. But he knew the war was over. Knew he would soon be able to head home. He saluted the man by the school gate and entered the building. After reading the letter from his mother he had been given the previous afternoon, he wasn't sure he wanted to go home at all. For the situation back there wasn't as he had hoped, wasn't at all as he felt it should be.

He had been angered by the contents. He was resolute in going to town, seeking a party, seeking a girl, seeking some female company, seeking a way to forget what his mother had revealed to him. It hadn't taken long, the people in the city were overflowing with kindness, many girls had been milling around his unit and it wasn't long before he spotted a girl that drew his attention. She was slim and tall, she was blond, and he could see that she had a lovely figure and the loveliest blue eyes. He smiled at her. She smiled back.

After a busy morning, after a debriefing and after reading through instructions for their next move, RSM, regimental sergeant major, Nicholas Robbins got his team together and it wasn't until late in the afternoon that he realised he had lost the letter. Unbeknownst to him, whilst quickly gathering his clothes, the letter had slipped from his tunic inside pocket and had dropped and slithered under the bed.

Three days later, having successfully pushed the Germans towards the east away from the town of Franeker, Nicholas and a small part of his team made their ways back down south, heading for the port city of Rotterdam.

Monday 1ˢᵗ of March

Sophie Louise Pontiac disembarked from the tram, crossed the road, and walked into the top end of the Peppelweg, a street in the suburb of Schiebroek. Getting the key from her handbag, the slim brunette inserted it into the door to the foyer entrance, then, often thinking about her fitness, took the stairs to the top floor. Whilst across the ocean and right across to the West side of the States Claire was deeply concentrating and looking at her screen and a clock on the wall showed it to be just after nine in the morning, Sophie entered the apartment where the hall clock showed it to be just after six in the evening.

She had been at the museum, an induction day, getting a feel for the new job she had been successful in obtaining. Curator of the museum of art. A new challenge, a new responsibility. It had been an informative, but rather tiring day and as she took of her coat and entered the lounge, she was reminded of the time she had been here before, in fact several times. Heading through to the kitchen she rummaged around to get some dinner on the go, opened a bottle of white wine, poured herself a glass and went back to the lounge. The first time she had been here, she had been wounded, had been cut, with a knife. Sam had come to her rescue, had driven to Amsterdam, had collected her, brought her here, taken care of her wound. It had been here where she first met Martijn, a man she was now in a relationship with and recalled the time she had been here, with him, when on a second occasion she had come over from Paris to help the Dutch policeman with the search for Sam when he had gone missing. She had then, she thought back, sipping her wine, been here again, with Martijn, when they had returned from Cologne, when they had been investigating a story regarding the painting of a monk.

This apartment was Sam's, but it was now going to be theirs, to use, her and Martijn who would be moving in after his colleague Froukje had returned from her holiday. Getting up from the sofa, Sophie returned to the kitchen and saw to her dinner. A little later she walked around the apartment. Sam had told them they could repaint, refurnish, whatever they wanted to do. Her own possessions would arrive in two days' time having just rented a van to bring over a few bits and pieces, mainly her wardrobe and her computer equipment, along with numerous files which would be of help in her new job. Finishing her meal and walking towards the kitchen she heard her phone ring.

In Amersfoort, Martijn checked the time on the clock on the wall and figured that Sophie must be at home now, their new home to be, Sam's apartment, and he was not only looking to ask her how her induction went, but also to share some news he had earlier received from Froukje, and he recalled the conversation…

'Martijn, hi, it's me, on my way back, on the train, just approaching Zwolle, I have discovered something rather interesting'.

'You do sound excited, did your visit with your brother and family go well?' Martijn asked.

'Yes thanks, very well, it was good to see them all, now, I found an old photograph in the market, a scene from the second world war, and knowing that my nephew was interested in army transport, bought this, it had a broken frame, so, I replaced it, but then, and this is the exciting bit, a letter fell out from behind the photo.'

'Now that does sounds interesting, a treasure map maybe?' Martijn asked, smiling and sensing Froukje's excitement.

'Ha ha, no, it's a letter, actually it's a 'Dear John' letter, though not from the girlfriend, but from this man's mother, writing about what she had learned, anyway, that's not the exciting bit, though I can imagine that the chap might well have been upset, no, it's his name, he was a RSM, a Regimental Sergeant Major, Canadian, and his name was Nicholas Robbins. So, you must be thinking, and?'

The train then pulled into the station at Zwolle. Martijn frowned and thought, but the name didn't ring a bell, 'Yes, and? You have more to tell, so, come on now!'

Froukje smiled, watched several people entering the Intercity train that started in Leeuwarden and would end in Rotterdam. 'I did some searching, had my tablet with me, decided to do some sleuthing, punched in his name and that's when I found the exciting bit'.

'Okay, go on'.

'When you and Sophie, and I know Sam was also involved, were following the trail of the three monks that you told me in detail about' Froukje said, again smiling as she remembered the account that he, with some flourish, told her.

'Are you teasing me? Martijn asked, smiling as well and recalling when he had told her all that had occurred, then said, 'As I recall, you demanded the whole story!'

'Okay, okay, but, hey, listen, there was a part where you said about an Englishman, an artist, and this French woman, the one who had the painting, the one, who you said had been chased, well, I recall you saying that they both vanished, disappeared, in some expedition or other, in Canada, on a ship that vanished?'

'Yes, the ship was called…' Martijn began.

'The Taciturn!' Froukje finished, then,' yes, well, he, this man, this Nicholas, he was the leader of this expedition!'

'Never, wow, that's very interesting, so, his name was Nicholas. Tell me again his last name.'

Robbins, Nicholas Robbins'…….

Martijn heard the phone ringing and then Sophie's voice, 'Hello mon cherie'.

'Hey, how was you day?' Martijn asked, speaking in English as his French was very poor and he at times, struggled to follow the conversation when Sophie spoke rapidly. She smiled at hearing his voice and told him all about it. It was when he had listened for a while, that he then had the opportunity to relate a phone conversation that he had with Froukje, a lengthy conversation, all about a man named Nicholas Robbin.

Meanwhile, many thousands of miles to the west, across the Atlantic and all the way across to the West coast, to San Francisco, Alison Hudson, her phone in her hand, pondered over the lengthy conversation she had just had with her good friend Chrissie. She had never met Debra, the wife of the late Nico Rozzini. She paced up and down her lounge, now and then stopping, many things seemingly randomly appearing in the forefront of her mind. Why was this Debra, suddenly, so interested in writing an apology? It wasn't as if any of what had happened, was her fault, from what she had remembered and from what Chrissie had just told her, she had been quite friendly, quite understanding, and obviously still quite in shock when Sam had visited her, not long after the death of her husband. Sam had said she had been rather quiet, had been sorry at that time, of all that had happened, had told Sam she had not been aware of anything that had occurred ten years earlier, not been aware of the abduction of the child, of young Terri, when she was just seven. Pacing the room, Alison remembered how the woman had even given the painting to Sam, which now hung in Tammy's apartment in New York. A woman she had yet to meet but had heard a lot about, especially from her daughter who had met up with her only recently, very much involved in the mystery of the three monks. But why would this woman Debra, want to apologize to her, why now. Detective Saunders was suspicious of this fact, her friend at the health club, Rita, to whom she had given the Triumph Stag car, had been suspicious, Sam and Chrissie had found this also rather strange. Alison stopped, turned, and headed for the kitchen, a coffee was needed, and then, she would call Terri, who had, only very recently, being allowed to return to work as the restrictions were slowly being lifted. The museum had re-opened, though with many new rules and guidelines and limiting the numbers that could come in, one had to now book a timeslot to monitor those restrictions.

Whilst making a fresh brew of coffee, she thought about Simon. It was coming up a year ago now, that she had first encountered him. Had met at the police station in Albuquerque, had commandeered him and his motorcycle to take her to the bus terminal. Smiling she recollected the ride through the city, clinging on to him. So much had happened since then, Terri being held at gun point, the stolen painting, Terri flying over to Paris, meeting up with Tammy from New York and Sophie in Paris. The brew was ready, tucking a strand of her long blonde hair behind her ear, she poured herself a mug then began to get her thoughts into some sort of order and concentrated on what to do next, what to say to Terri and whether or not to ring Simon, recalling the time he had made the trip to see her here in San Francisco.

THE PAST; Period 6

The year 1956 – San Francisco

A time to be born and a time to die. Millie Huanca was thinking, recalling a piece of scripture from the book of Ecclesiastes. A time to be born and a time to die. Across from her in the beautifully ornate study of their house, sitting in one of the two comfortable leather chairs that were placed either side of a low oakwood table, sat young Emily. Millie sat back in the large highbacked desk chair and watched her for a moment as she was fully immersed in the book that she was reading by the light of the standard lamp beside her. The study was quite dark, only one window that looked out over the street, there was dark wood panelling around the lower part of three walls and three tall bookcases, made of oak, were situated against each of those walls, containing numerous books. Her late father-in-law, Carlos, loved to read. She herself loved to read and young Emily, fourteen years of age, loved to read. A time to be born and a time to die, Millie thought again, for it had been on that day, a little over fourteen years ago, when Emily was born and, less than an hour after having seen his third grandchild, Carlos had on the way home, sat down by a streetside café, and had simply passed away.

Much had happened over the past years. Remembering another few verses from that same piece of Scripture, Millie whispered, 'A time of war and a time of peace'. The war had ended over ten years ago, it was peace time. But there hadn't been peace everywhere. She again looked across the desk to young Emily. Such a lovely young girl, but as she was quite a few years younger than her two sisters, it seemed there had been strife. Furthermore, her father, Micheal, had strayed, had been unfaithful and had subsequently up and left. Emily's mother, her husband's sister, Zefora, had taken to drink. The situation in the home had severely broken down and, on an occasion, when Emily's sisters, Katrina and Zoe, had caused the breakage of a vase in the lounge and had then told their mother that it had been Emily who had broken it, her mother had lost her temper and had struck her several times.

That day, young Emily had, in the early evening, packed a few things, some clothes and schoolbooks, had left the house and had gone over to see her uncle 'Z' and aunty Millie, where she had cried and told the story. The following morning Zoltina had gone over to confront his sister and his nieces who immediately broke down and cried, confessing their lies. They had the previous day been quite shocked at their mother's retaliation. That had been less than a month ago now. Emily had never returned home to live, instead, accompanied by Millie, had collected her personal belongings and Millie and Zoltina had processed an application to formally adopt her. Millie smiled as she glanced at the young girl again. She and Zoltina had been unable to have children, but Emily was their daughter now. A time for peace, she thought, then as she opened a drawer to look for another pen, as the one she had been writing with had run out of ink, she spotted a small folder, it had a rubber band wrapped around it.

Strange, she thought, she hadn't seen that before and her husband, not a reader, hardly ever set foot in this study, yet it was his handwriting on the cover, which simply read, 'The Ontario Project'.

Zoltina was walking home, for a brief stop, a quick bite to eat and a change of clothes, before he would set out again to the wharf as he would captain the boat, the third boat in their fleet, their company, that his father Carlos had set up, 'Huanca Bay Transport' the third and largest vessel, named after himself, Zoltina 3rd, for the daily evening cruise and dinner across the bay. He walked along Hyde Street, then turned right just as one of San Francisco's famous streetcars trundled past, having come from Fisherman's Wharf, and heading into the city centre, to Union Street.

Meanwhile Millie undid the rubber band and opened the notebook, written, quite neatly she noticed, by her husband, and began to read.

THE PRESENT; Moncton

Still Monday 1ˢᵗ of March

It was late in the evening. Detective Sergeant Karen Saunders was feeling tired, she had been doing a lot of reading, had spoken to several people on the telephone, had dug up the files she had on several people in connection with the Rozzini case and still trying to think as to why she felt that Nico's widow, Debra, wanting to know Allison Hudson's address, was suspicious. 'Maybe it's nothing' she softly said to herself, stripping to get ready for bed. Then her phone rang.

Ending the call less than forty seconds later she spoke to herself, 'It's not nothing'.

Donning a dressing gown, she headed back to the lounge, switched on the light, and sat herself down on the couch. On the table in front of her, lay five folders, she had taken these home to be able to read through them undisturbed. They were all labelled. Sandra Rozzini, formerly Pentegrass, wife of Julien who wrote a confession that wrapped everything up, fled to Hawaii and had not been heard from since. This folder she pushed aside, the next was the Rozzini's, Nico and his younger brother, Julien. This she also put to one side, and the third folder as well, which was headed, Phil Madison. That left two, one was labelled 'Harris Police' and the other 'Karina West'. The phone call she had just received was from a colleague in Halifax, informing her that Karina West had escaped. Putting the first three away in a bureau drawer, she then picked up the Karina west folder along with the one about the Harris Police, she left the lounge, turned off the light and headed for her bedroom where she would reread these files.

Had she taken the time to look through her bedroom window at that point, she might have noticed a car parked in the street, a car that was not normally there.

Inside the black Chevrolet Impala, a classic 1972 model, Dusty Kerr, whose nickname was Slim, despite being rather rotund and considerably overweight, smoked yet another cigarette as he watched the house, having observed the lights in the lounge being turned off and assumed that the detective had now going upstairs to bed. When a room facing the street was lit up a few moments later, his assumption was confirmed. He exhaled a cloud of smoke through the open driver's side window, took another drag on the cigarette, then flicked the butt out on to the street and reached for his phone.

Exhaling the last of the smoke, he smiled, showing uneven and slightly yellow teeth. This would be good, he was thinking, this would satisfy his longing for revenge as he pressed several numbers and waited. His mind went back, back to when she, the detective, had first walked into the police station in Harris. All to do with that troublesome Yank, the Hudson woman, who had come in, demanding they arrested Mr. Nico Rozzini. His chief had set into motion a quick plan to deal with her, deal with this Miss Alison Hudson. A plan, with the full backing of Mr. Rozzini, though organised speedily, had worked out well, or so they had thought.

'She's about to go to bed' he said, after a voice had answered the call, 'I am ready' then after listening for a moment, said, 'Call me when all is in place' and put the phone down.

Again, his thoughts went back to that day, his chief had been out, she, the detective, had come in. It had not been a pleasant experience, she had been confident, had spoken to him sharply and had been almost delighted to report that the internal affairs people would come knocking very soon. He recalled her last words as she wished him a 'nice day' and that he had felt as if being hit by a train. The former deputy shook his head, then, looking up at the room where the light was still on, smiled. Revenge would be sweet. He had lost his job, no pay, no pension. His chief, Faulkner Brown, was found guilty of bribery, of fraud and found to be the main instigator and organiser of the abduction and attempted murder of the American woman and was sentenced to four years in prison. He too lost his pay and pension, moreover, consequently, both their marriages also broke down. Revenge would be sweet he was thinking, licking his lower lip in anticipation and was grateful that he had been approached, for he could never had been in a position to attempt to pull off what had been planned, nor the finances to be able to afford it.

He had been quite surprised as to who it was that had sought him out and had spoken in depth about a two-part plan. The first part was about to be executed. Twenty minutes later the lights went out and four minutes after that the clock in the car showed it to be midnight.

Just waiting was the worst part, Dusty thought, contemplating if he should light another cigarette. But then his phone lit up and a text was showing. Simply, it read, 'come now'.

Switching on the engine, which, he realised, sounding rather loud in the stillness of the night. He drove towards the house, then reversed up the driveway. Getting out of the car he suddenly felt a little nervous, and as he turned around the back corner of the house, he took in a deep breath, puffed out his cheeks and entered through the open door.

THE PAST; Period 7

The year 1957 – San Francisco

Oliver Mantell felt the colour come back to his cheeks. His mind was in a whirl, and he was relieved that his legs were now carrying him steadily and that the trembling of his muscles had stopped. He sensed the young woman who was walking beside him, still holding on to his elbow, still steering him away from the scene. She had questioned him, had been cross with him, then, as he had explained, thankful that he found his voice, she had been different. She had then continued to guide him into the direction he had wanted to go, to get to the monastery, where he had initially been heading for when the young boy, came stumbling out of an alleyway, colliding with him, then collapsing on the street. Bleeding.

Taking a deeper breath, Oliver glanced across at the woman, figuring her to be about the same age as him, in her early twenties. Her very dark hair, tied up in a ponytail, her big brown eyes. His thoughts, still somewhat scrambled, recalled the reason he was here, in the United States, here in San Francisco. He thought briefly about a time when he and his best friend, Roger, had travelled from England to Belgium and northern France, both visiting the graves of their grandfathers and other family members who had been killed in the second world war. How they had walked by the many gravestones, how they had commented on the young age of so many of them, how they had tried to imagine what it would have been like for them, facing death every minute and wondered how they themselves might have coped under those circumstances Not at all well! Oliver thought, almost smiling to himself, he had never seen a dead body before and what had occurred only moments earlier had completed flummoxed him. He had frozen. Completely numb as the young boy, probably around ten years of age, lay bleeding on the ground, had been stabbed, numerous times by the look of it. Dead.

Then he had been whisked away, led away from the scene as other folks were heading towards it. He shot another look at her. She was almost as tall as he and he half smiled as he recalled that she, though quite slim in built, had so easily and forcibly, despite his solid frame, led him away. They had now slowed down, and he heard her speak. 'We're here, the monastery, the Franciscan Brothers.'

Oliver stopped, took in the façade of the old buildings. He turned to look at her, he had, thankfully when his initial dry throat had recovered somewhat, introduced himself and had wondered if he should not go back and talk to the police. She had calmly looked into his eyes, though initially a little angry with him, thinking he was just another one of those tourists who had wandered into this, rough, area of the city either by mistake or because of curiosity, she saw his eyes were kind, and, that he was still in shock. He had replied that he was looking for the monastery and had produced a map, they had not been too far away and were now here.

'I will come with you?' she asked, then, 'why is you want to come here?'

Her name was Mercedes and Oliver again looked into those gorgeous dark brown eyes, momentarily lost in their beauty, before replying, 'Ah, yes, yes please, would you? He answered, then as they continued walking toward the large double wooden door of the entrance, said, 'I have come to look for a painting'.

Little could Oliver even think or imagine that, just as he had witnessed the death of a young boy, six years from now, his, by then wife, Mercedes, and their three-year-old son, would also witness a murder. His.

A Franciscan Brother opened one of the big doors and Mercedes did the talking, explaining the reason for their visit. He let them in and closed the door, which made quite an echoing and reverberating sound.

THE PRESENT; Boston

Early hours of Tuesday morning-2ⁿᵈ March

The sound woke him, and he just noticed the screen of his phone lit up before it went dark again. Reaching over he reached for it, pressed a key, and then read the message. He read it again, then noticed the time, a little after one o'clock. Sam gently pushed the covers aside and got up, in the dimness he saw that Chrissie was fast asleep. Sam smiled briefly, knowing she was a heavy sleeper and had on occasions slept through heavy thunderstorms. He nevertheless quietly slipped into the ensuite bathroom, freshened up, then gathering some clothes he headed downstairs to the kitchen where he set about to make himself a cup of tea, looking again at the text he had received and pondered over its meaning.

The kettle boiled and he wondered how best to proceed with the news he had received. Taking the cup of tea through to the front lounge, he sat down and re read it once more.

'Sam, suspicious car outside my house, being watched, make sure Miss Hudson is all right, will contact you again later, be careful'.

In Moncton detective Karen Saunders had turned off the light, although she had earlier dressed in pyjamas and donned a dressing gown, she now, in the dark, got dressed again, her stomach feeling tight and felt her throat was dry, for she had spotted the car in the street. A car she didn't recognise in her area. From the darkened room she could see that there was someone in the vehicle, every now and then she saw the glow from a cigarette. Making sure she had her service gun at the ready, she pondered a while as to what to do. Making up her mind, feeling this was all to do with the Rozzini woman looking for Miss Hudson, she sent a text to Sam. Deciding then not to stay in the bedroom, Karen went downstairs and to the front room, not turning on any lights she was able to get a clearer view of the car. But then a noise reached her ears, a faint noise, but one that emanated from within the house. Someone was inside! She looked carefully through the window, the person in car, was still there, still smoking. A soft rustling noise made her turn around again, then, gun in hand, she walked towards the kitchen.

In Boston Sam scrolled through the list in his phone, found the right number and pressed a key. It was almost one-thirty, knowing that there was a three-hour time difference, he figured Ally would still be up.

'Hey, Sam?'

'Hi Ally, listen, just had a text from detective Karen, someone is watching her, outside her house, she asked to make sure you are okay, Chrissie spoke to you earlier, just making sure and just be extra careful, okay, also, I've been thinking…'

'You know about that' Ally said, interrupting 'dangerous', smiling and though feeling concerned, trying to lighten the mood.

'Yes, 'Sam answered, breaking into a smile, realising what she was trying to do, figuring he must have sounded like the voice of doom, 'okay, well, anyway, as I was trying to say…' pausing briefly and speaking more in an upbeat manner,' thinking this all through, I wonder if it is you that is of interest, after all, it was Terri that had in the first place been taken, maybe….'

'I hear what you're saying, 'Alison answered, gosh, yes, even now, I don't really know why it was they took her away, goodness, you may be on to something, this is so very….' Trying to find the right word, Sam interrupted, 'disconcerting?'

'The very word Sam' Ally said, then, 'I'll speak with her, we'll be extra careful. What does Chrissie think?'

'She's asleep Ally, doesn't know about the text from Karen yet, so, take care won't you, I will keep you updated on what's going on.'

Sam broke the connection and finished his cup of tea.

In San Francisco Ally sat down, phone in hand and thought about what Sam had suggested. He was right, it didn't really make any sense as to why Debra was so intent on writing to her, it was more likely that she was trying to find out where Terri was. But why? Alison sat back in the chair in lounge of her apartment and closed her eyes, thinking back. It had been Julien, Terri's father, who had, after having left them and not been in touch for over seven years, suddenly returned, wanting to be part of Terri's life. Then, not long after she had told him where to go, it had been him, along with a woman called Sandra, his new wife she found out, who had, with the influential assistance of Julien's brother Nico, taken Terri away. That had been twelve years ago. Then two years ago, on a fresh trail to find her daughter, she had ended up in Moncton. A shiver ran down her back as she recalled the moment, she had been semi-conscious and precariously balanced on the ledge, with a raging river flowing below her. If it hadn't been for Sam….

She stood up and paced the lounge for a bit, recalling that finally, after all those years, she had, with the enormous assistance of Sam and from detective Saunders, got back together with her daughter, she had thought at the time, putting all the puzzle pieces together, that it might have been a revenge on the part of this Sandra woman, that Terri had been taken. Learning that her maiden name was Pentegrass and that, along with two other girls, Alison had often bullied her brother Robert, was this the reason? Revenge? But what if there was another reason, and what reason could that be? Picking up her phone, she sat down again and pressed the number for her daughter to whom she had only spoken earlier in the day. Whilst waiting for Terri to answer, her thoughts turned to Simon and why she hadn't, yet, spoken to him. After a brief conversation with her daughter, explaining what Sam had said, Ally headed upstairs. Though concerned about the current events, she was tired. Turning off the lights, she took a quick look outside, but could see nothing suspicious. The night sky, she noticed, were full of stars.

THE PAST; Period 8

the year 1960 – Ontario Province – Canada

The sky was a vivid blue and the sun stood high pouring down its light and warmth so that the temperature where he stood reached almost thirty degrees centigrade. Wayne had stood on this spot for several moments, wearing sunshades he observed his surroundings. He was on the dockyards of the Upper Lakes Shipping Company at the Port Weller Dry docks and looked at the bow of the ship. Recently refitted, it had been a small icebreaker that had been built in the early fifties, designed to clear light ice build-up from the canal, rivers, and lakes. and was now ready for its new role as an exploration vessel. And he, Wayne, was to be her captain. The diesel-powered ship was around forty-five feet in length had a draught of only 5 feet, making it ideal to go into the shallower coastal waters of the big lake. She was equipped with Gyro stabilizers and its 2000 horsepower engine could produce a speed of close to sixteen knots.

Wayne looked out across the waters of the Welland Canal that would join Lake Ontario to the east and Lake Erie to the west. Then looked back at the bow of the sleek ship with its strengthened hull which had been renamed. Now blessed with the name 'Taciturn' she would soon be away of her first exploration journey, carrying a few scientists to study the coastal waters of the lake. Wayne smiled, then finally set his feet in motion, and headed for the dock building where he was due for a meeting shortly, checking his watch. His first journey as captain, having passed and obtained his master's ticket only four weeks earlier. Entering the lobby, he took his shades off, adjusted to the different light, and took the wide staircase on his left up to the next level. He thought about his wife as he suddenly remembered their fifth anniversary was coming up as well as their son's fourth birthday. They had moved several years ago now, having originally set up house in Buffalo, New York, but not long after and almost commencing a new job, another opportunity arose in

Hamilton, in the province of Ontario, a better offer and a move they both felt was the right thing to do and had subsequently moved there and were expecting their first child.

In the apartment, overlooking the lake, Missy stood by the window and was reminiscing. Their son, Dean, was at kindergarten. She smiled as, looking across the vast lake, she recalled a time when she and Wayne as teenagers, had regularly met in the old barn, a fun time of kissing and canoodling, but also with a hit of adventure as she recalled the time when they had been along the waterfront, in the middle of the night and had witnessed the seaplane landing. Then crawling along to where it moored and was unloaded, for some reason the scene came into her head, recalling taking many photographs with her recently given camera that her parents had bought her. She frowned a little as she wondered why it was that that particular memory came to mind. Looking at the sky, which was a clear and vivid blue, she was pleased, it would be a good day for her husband to be taking out the new ship. She was proud of him, loved him very much and again recalled the times they had snuck away from their parental homes to meet in that old barn. Missy smiled, then turned away from the window. Having thought about it, she decided to dig up the photos that she and Wayne had taken that night. 'Goodness me' she said to herself as she went to a room which she had set up as her work studio, still very much into photography, 'that's getting on for twenty years ago!'. Stopping in the doorway, she thought about where they might be.

Wayne walked briskly down the corridor and reached the large meeting room, opened the door, and entered. A man stood up from a chair behind a long table, moved around and came over towards Wayne. 'Captain Koppell' he greeted, extending his hand, 'Nicholas Robbins, but please, call me Nick'.

Then moved towards a long narrow table upon which were spread several oceanographic charts. 'Now, our aim is to research this area here' he said, looking up at the captain who looked to where he was pointing. 'Now, along this stretch' again pointing his finger on the map, 'the waters are quite shallow, any problems there?'

Wayne took in the chart, read the depths that were noted, then nodded and said to the expedition leader, 'Nothing to worry about'

THE PRESENT; Boston

Tuesday 2nd March-2.30 AM

Sam was worried, after having spoken to Ally in San Francisco, he had not been able to settle, there was no news from Karen Saunders, no texts. This was worrying.

'Chrissie, wake up honey, who was it you called to get Ally from Halifax to Moncton that day? By helicopter.'

'Mmmm, what, Sam?' then sitting up and seeing the look on his face, 'Sam? What's happened?'

'Worried something has happened to Karen, she sent a text a couple of hours ago, that there was someone watching her house, nothing since….'

'Did you say about a helicopter?'

'Yes, who was it you arranged that through?'

'Right, yes, I'm up. I'm up, got the number in my phone, I think, are you saying we should go there?'

'Absolutely, I don't know anyone to call in Moncton, wait, yes I do, see if you can find that number, I have a call to make…' and with that Sam left the bedroom and headed for his study. For the next twenty minutes they got themselves ready, packed and each having made several calls met in the kitchen when the taxi pulled up. Neither of them spoke as they rode in the taxi heading for Logan airport. It was coming up to 3am.

They had given the driver instruction to head for a security entrance gate on the north side of the airport. It was a dark cloudy night, a fresh breeze blowing and rain threatening. Chrissie and Sam exited the cab, walked over to the security cabin and Sam spoke to the guard, showing his credentials.

The guard acknowledged them, and they entered the airfield, not too far away they noticed the helicopter and walked towards it. Sam noticed it was a Bell 505 Jet Ranger. The pilot greeted them both, shaking their hands and indicating for them to be seated and put helmets on. He closed the door, then, after having stored the luggage, walked around to get into the pilot seat and donning his helmet he spoke over the radio com. Turned some keys, pressed some buttons and the rotors began to spin.

Checking her watch Chrissie noted it was ten minutes after three when they lifted off. Having been given clearance by the tower, the pilot rose the craft, then swung it around to then head north. Their destination was Bangor Maine, some 230 miles away.

Sam and Chrissie looked at each other. Sam took hold of her hand and then turned to look out of the window. The lights of Boston were left behind.

Checking his watch he was amazed at how quickly they had, between them, sorted out the transport. His first call had been to Joe, a former railroad man he had met whilst living in Moncton, apologizing waking him in the middle of the night, he told him the importance of speaking with his daughter, Maureen Zimmerman, the current mayoress of Moncton. Joe had asked Sam for his number, then would wake his daughter, and get her to ring him.

Meanwhile Chrissie had found a contact number for the company she had used when hiring a helicopter that had taken Alison Hudson from Halifax to Moncton when she had flown over from San Francisco to help in the search for Sam who had gone missing.

As she was finally speaking to someone, the mayoress had at that time called back and was in conversation with Sam. Chrissie explained the situation and it was the man, a pilot, who came up with the best way to get them both from Boston to Moncton, moreover, it happened to be the same pilot who had transported Ally and even more coincidental, knew the mayoress of Moncton personally.

So, through the wonderful ability of mobile phones and speaker phones the four of them talked and listened and it was the pilot, Edward Munn, who then took control of all the travel arrangements. Hence the availability of the chopper at Boston logan Airport which would fly them to Bangor. He himself would fly there too, pick them up and transport them to Moncton.

Having sorted out all of this, Maureen would then speak to her police department and quietly check out DS Saunders house. A short text reached Sam's phone as they were getting in the taxi that Chrissie had ordered, to say that the house was empty, no sign of Karen.

They flew through the night. Sam and Chrissie holding hands all the way.

It was a little before five am when the pilot informed them over the intercom, that they were approaching the airfield and that their next ride was ready.

It was still quite dark, though the glimmerings of a dawn were beginning to show on the horizon. The rain had stayed away.

Edward greeted Chrissie and Sam, greeted the pilot who had brought them there and informed him fuel for his return journey would arrive soon. Then he ushered Sam and Chrissie into his Robinson R66 Helicopter, took the luggage from the other pilot and stored it, then, nodding a thanks and goodbye to the Boston based pilot, got in and prepared for take-off. Taking into consideration the time difference, they should reach Moncton a little before 8am.

Ten minutes into their flight Sam had another text message from Maureen, saying that they were combing through the town security camera footages for any clues.

She also informed Sam that she was working from home, as she was isolating as she had caught the covid virus. Sam replied, saying he was thankful, wished her a speedy recovery and that they were enroute to Moncton.

THE PAST; Period 9

The year 1963-Lake Ontario

Roger Sutherland stood on the dock and looked up at the ship. They would be on their way soon. He was standing in the very place where three years earlier Wayne Koppel had stood. Taking a last drag on his cigarette, he flicked the butt into the water, then turned and headed for the gangplank. It was early, the sun had only moments ago risen, and Roger thought back to the journey that he had been on to take him to this point. He thought of his friend, Oliver. His death had rocked him hard. Killed in a shooting by thugs who were robbing a store. He thought about the very reason that Oliver had travelled to the States. All to do with the treasure hunt he himself had begun, when discovering an intriguing set of clues about three monks from Florence. But, though the search for this treasure had started well, the excitement petered out. Kim, the third member of his treasure hunt team, met a guy, started a romance, and moved away. Oliver, though successful in tracking down one of the monks' paintings, also fell in love and decided to stay in California. Putting all the obtained clues and artifacts away, Roger continued his studies in graphic art and then several things happened, seemingly in close succession. First, he had been offered an assignment, to be the artist on a scientific experience that would be researching the coastline of Lake Ontario and its flora and fauna and the wildlife that made their home there. Then, his house, in Eastbourne, was broken into and all the notes, clues, keys and a painting, were stolen, a targeted theft. Then, as he was making his way to join the expedition, he literally, ran into the French woman, Natalie Umbrego and to discover that she too had a connection with the mystery of the three monks.

Roger walked up the gangplank, the captain had given strict instruction, no smoking in the cabins, and so his decision to stretch his legs, take in the fresh morning air and have his first smoke of the day. The irony of wanting to take in fresh morning air and then to light up a cigarette didn't escape him, and he smiled as he reboarded the ship. The Taciturn. Due to sail in about an hours' time. Time for a cuddle and a snuggle he thought, delighted that Natalie had insisted on joining him for the expedition, even more delighted that, for the first time in his life, he had truly fallen in love.

'Morning Roger' the captain, Wayne Koppel said, smiling, then' breakfast is ready, we leave in forty-five minutes.'

'Morning Captain, thanks' Roger replied and headed for his cabin. The cuddle and snuggle would have to be short, he thought, suddenly feeling rather hungry after hearing the word breakfast.

'Just a quick cuddle mon cherie' Roger said, entering their cabin, smiling at her. She was sat up in bed, reading some French magazine, smiled back at him, put the magazine aside, 'come here tout suite then' she answered, smiling back at him.

Afterwards Natalie Umbrego thought back to these past few weeks as she showered. Back to the moment she was first aware of the men who were on the trail of a painting, an old painting, that of a monk. The discovery, the flight, the race in the car to reach a man she had heard of, the forger, Roberto Solari. The chase that eventually ended up in a severe crash with a tanker. Not for her, thankfully, but her pursuers. Natalie turned off the shower, stepped from the cubicle and wiped the steam from the mirror. Drying herself she brought back to mind how she then followed up on finding out the very reason for the interest in this painting. A trail that led her to England, to meet with a young woman whom she had briefly met, five years earlier. An investigation that led her to locate a man, and in a coincidence of all coincidences, she bumped into this very man at the railway station. Natalie towelled her hair dry, then proceeded to dress, he was already gone, breakfast was his favourite meal, and he had built up an appetite. She smiled at her own thoughts and was soon ready to head down to the canteen. Come to think of it, she almost softly said to herself, I feel hungry too. Smiling she made her way to the canteen.

Nicholas Robbins, the project leader, looked up as she entered, smiled at her, and resumed reading a set of notes as he drank his first coffee of the day. He had briefly spoken to Roger about the itinerary for the day. Taking a last sip, he stood up, nodded to them both and made his way to the wheelhouse to see Captain Koppel. Not really knowing why, he recalled a letter he had received from his mother, all those years ago, eighteen years to be precise. The letter that had hurt him, had shocked him. What he thought he had, the relationship, the love. It was gone. He remembered, as he climbed the steel stairway up to the wheelhouse, the young girl, the Dutch girl, so pretty, slim, and blonde. It was where he, thinking back, must have dropped the letter. Did she read it? What did she do with it?

'Morning Captain,' Nicholas greeted, 'weather looks good today?'

'Yes sir,' Wayne turned and answered,' looking good, weighing anchor very soon'.

The wind was from the north, and it was sharp. She could feel her face stinging from the cold. Yet the water was calm, almost like a mirror. Natalie shivered, but it was not from the cold. It was as if something wasn't quite right. It was as if something was about to happen. Puffing out her cheeks, she stood by the railing near the bow of the ship. It was late afternoon, and the sky was a strange blue and orange colour.

All the others were inside. Taking in a deep breath, she shook away this strange feeling that now seemed the be in the pit of her stomach.

She was about to turn and head inside for warmth and for her dinner when she sensed somebody behind her.

'Hey' Roger said, 'I wondered where you'd got to'.

Turning her head, she then said, 'Look at that sky Roger, it's so different and rather strange, don't you think?'

'Oh, my goodness!' Roger exclaimed, 'what's even more strange, is that!' he finished, pointing.

Natalie looked.

Ahead was a white cloud, a low cloud, like a mist, which settled upon the water. It was bright white, and as they approached it, or as it approached them, it began to blot out everything around it.

'Get inside' Roger said, grabbing Natalie and taking her with him to the door, 'That looks like some sort of ice storm'.

'But there seems to be not much wind, the water is so calm' Natalie managed to say, as he reached and opened the door for her.

Roger took a last look before he entered the interior of the ship.

The whiteness was rapidly nearing. He shut the door, then shot past Natalie and headed for the wheelhouse. She followed right on his tail.

Captain Wayne Koppell didn't even turn his head as they both entered, totally focused on the whiteness that was now engulfing the bow of the Taciturn.

'What is it?' Roger asked, Natalie now beside him.

'I have no idea' Wayne replied. He reduced the ships speed and set the handle on the control to 'slow'.

The white cloud reached the windows of the wheelhouse, and everything turned to white. Wayne stared straight ahead, Natalie had put an arm around Roger's waist, he responded by putting his arm around her shoulder. The three of them stood there, silently.

In the main lounge of the ship Nicolas Robbins was sipping a coffee, the smell from the kitchen reaching his nostrils and making him realise how hungry he was. It wasn't until her looked up from some notes he was reading that he saw the whiteness. Puzzled, he placed the papers on the table in front of him, stood up to investigate, but then a dizziness came over him.

In the kitchen the female chef suddenly just collapsed on the floor, the two gas rings on the cooker went out. In a cabin adjacent the lounge, a woman was writing notes and checking several maps when she too suddenly realised, she couldn't breathe and very quickly toppled to the floor.

In the wheelhouse Wayne, Roger and Natalie looked in horror as each struggled for breath and were perplexed as to why. Wayne was the first to collapse, however, he did manage to crawl over to the speed controls and with effort, pulled the lever to a 'Stop', position, before totally succumbing and collapsing on the floor.

Roger and Natalie, who still held each other, also crumpled to the floor and passed out. The last of the crew, both in the engine room at the time, in unison, crumpled to the floor. The turbine engine still spinning but beginning to slow.

The exploration ship, the Taciturn, was enveloped in the white cloud. The engines stopped fully and within the confines of the mysterious whiteness, all became very still.

THE PRESENT; Moncton

Tuesday 2nd March 07:55 am

Breaking the stillness of the morning, the helicopter landed on the helipad adjacent the fire station.

It was upon seeing the river, that Sam spoke, saying 'I wonder…'

A police car arrived and Sam took control as he left the helicopter, 'Chrissie, please, go with the police, then tell them to go the Ravine road, to the place where they lowered Ally's body that night, they'll know where that is, I will go on the river, I see that the fire station has a rubber dinghy there…' giving Chrissie a quick kiss on the cheek he ran towards the fireman who had come out to investigate.

Chrissie thanked the pilot for all his arrangement, told him she would pay him well and walked quickly towards the police car. A young police officer got out and awaited her. She could see the concern on his face as he greeted her and held the door open for her to get in. The driver, a policewoman, turned and nodded a greeting. 'Sam says to go to the Ravine Road, where they had lowered Alison's body onto the ledge…?' Chrissie said, as she found her seat belt.

'Okay…' the driver said, after a moment, 'Yes, of course, I remember, that's where they found miss Hudson's car! Damn! Should have thought of that…'. The police car sped off, turning around and now with light flashing and sirens blaring, headed away from the fire station and towards the bridge.

Detective Sergeant Karen Saunders shivered. She was cold and wet. Realised, as she slowly regained consciousness, that her wrists were bound behind her back and that her mouth was covered by tape. Hearing the sound of the river, she understood where she was. The very same spot where they had placed Alison Hudson. The very same spot where Sam Price had driven to and had, that night, rescued the woman. Her head was spinning a little, she was struggling to breathe properly, and she shivered again. She had a pain in her stomach, was trying hard not to be sick, which would cause a huge problem, given that her mouth was taped.

Her neck hurt; this is where she had been injected. Trying hard to stay as calm as possible, she focused on what she needed to do. Firstly, any movement would not be good, she felt that as she careful looked around her, that she was already on the very edge of the shelf and in a precarious position. Other sounds came to her ears, the sound of a siren, also the sound of an engine.

Her stomach cramped and she began to convulse, gagging and struggling now to breathe, she felt herself sliding off the shelf.

08:05 am

Daniel Houseman, the fireman, with the help of a colleague and Sam, slithered the rubber dinghy over to the river and then he and Sam got in. The second fireman handing Sam a lifejacket to put on as Daniel pulled the cord and started the small outboard motor. Then opening the throttle, he pointed the orange-coloured dinghy upstream.

Meanwhile Chrissie held on the best she could as the police car sped through the town, lights flashing and sirens blaring. The Ravine Road, where Miss Hudson's red Triumph Stag had been found that day, nearly two years ago, the driver knew the place. Neither she nor the young officer spoke, and Chrissie could see the face of the driver in the rear-view mirror, totally focused but also still annoyed with herself for not even considering this possibility.

Being shaken about as the car sped around bends, zigzagging through some traffic, and bravely crossing through intersections, Chrissie thought about Detective Karen Saunders, recalling the time she had first met her, at the police station, remembering how she too had been so concerned for Sam's welfare that day. She knew the story of how Sam had found

Ally, how he had rescued her, from a narrow ledge overhanging the river. Had someone really placed the detective in that same spot? Were they going to be too late?

Feeling the wind in his face as the dinghy bounced on the water, Sam wondered the same thing, feeling sure, that the ledge was the place where they, whoever they were, had placed Karen. Revenge? They were getting closer, would they be too late, was she there at all?

On the narrow ledge, which ran some twelve feet in length, with no more than five feet at its widest, tapering at both ends, Karen felt she was losing her balance, she could feel the edge of the shelf under her back, she looked up. The road was about ten feet above her. No-one would see her unless they actually peered over the edge. Her ears once again picked up sounds, a siren. Seemingly coming closer. And the sound of, what she thought might be an outboard engine. Was someone on the river below?

Dare she look, dare she hope?

She decided to carefully turn her head, to see below, briefly she saw the river, saw the fast flower water. Then she shivered again. She lost her balance.

Sam was peering ahead, remembering the time he had clambered down to discover the woman, the soaking wet scarf, the soaking wet and heavy winter coat....

'There!' he shouted, then 'Noo! she's just fallen!'

Daniel saw her too, pointed the dinghy towards the place where the woman had fallen and before he could say anything, the man, who had arrived by helicopter, who had been so urgently commanding, who's determination was extremely obvious, jumped into the water.

Sam, in a quick motion, took his glasses off, throwing them down, then jumped. He ignored the sudden coldness of the water, totally focusing on the place where the detective had gone into the water. He was relieved to see her bob up on the surface. He too then saw her mouth was taped, and it seemed her hands were tied. He reached her, grabbed her, turned her over just before she was about to go under again, then managed to keep her head above water. Somehow, he managed to rip the tape from her mouth. He heard her gasp. Meanwhile Daniel, having by now gone past them, turned the boat around, then aimed to come alongside them, thinking that the current would sweep them both downstream, he successfully got the dinghy in front of them and moments later Sam bumped up against it. He could see the exhaustion on the man's face as he struggled to keep himself and the woman afloat. But, needing to hold on to the tiller and engine, there was nothing he could do to help him get on board, it took all his efforts to maintain the dinghy in position.

The police car screeched to a halt, Chrissie and the young officer leapt from the car and headed for the steel barrier at the edge of the road. Reaching it, they both gasped as they saw what was happening on the river.

'Sam's got her!' Chrissie managed to say, watching the scene unfold.

Sam, beginning to struggle in the current, but relieved to know that she was alive, let himself hit the rubber dinghy. He then also realised he had to somehow get Karen aboard on his own. Holding on to the detective with his left hand, his right hand reached over the side of the boat, managed to grab something to hold on to, then, as he saw that the fireman was doing everything to control the small engine against the rapid flow of the river, he heaved and pulled Karen towards the dinghy.

Daniel saw that there was no way the man could get the woman and himself out of the water, he had to help. Waiting briefly for the right moment, het let go of the tiller, moved forward, and took hold of the woman. With all the strength he could muster he pulled her aboard. The boat, now rudderless, began to turn and pick up speed from the current. But the woman was inside the boat. Sam was relieved, managed to gasp,

'Got this' looking up at the fireman. Daniel understood, jumped back toward the tiller and engine and after some manoeuvring, managed to get the dinghy on an even keel, and facing the boat upstream, slowed it right down.

'They've got her' the second policeman, having joined them on the road's edge, said, then, grabbing her communications phone, 'need paramedics to go down to the fire station, DS Saunders is alive, but injured'.

Sam, now that the boat was going much slower and steadier, with the aid of the current, managed to pull himself into the dinghy. For the first time, seeing Karen lying on her side, noticed her hands tied behind her back.

From somewhere the fireman had pulled a knife out, handing it to the dripping wet man. Sam nodded his thanks, still trying to regain control of his own breathing and ignoring the cold, then set about to cut the ropes. He heard Karen moan. She too was dripping wet; she too must be so cold.

Chrissie and the two officers got back in the car. She was relieved and as the car tuned to head back into town, she allowed herself to cry.

Sam finally cut the ropes that tied her wrists, then half turned, and half lifted Karen to hold her in his arms. She opened her eyes. He saw her recognition, saw that she was tried to comprehend, trying to speak.

'Shh, don't speak, ambulance on the way'.

Holding her tightly, he then noticed his glasses that he had discarded, reached them and put them back on. His mind went back to when he had done the same, taken his, then steamed up, glasses off. At the time he thought about either contact lenses or have laser surgery. He had done neither. He ignored the cold, suppressed a shiver and held the woman tight as the fireman turned and steered the dinghy back towards the fire station. He heard a siren, then, as they went under one of the bridges that crossed over the river, saw the ambulance go over.

'Hold on Karen, ambulance will be there when we get there'.

'How?' she managed to say, her voice hoarse, just a whisper.

'Shh, not now, later…' Sam said, placing a hand on her cheek.

Daniel steered the rubber dinghy towards the shore and slithered it up a short wooden platform from where they had, less than twenty minutes earlier, departed from. He cut the engine then, also noticing others heading their way, helped to get the man and the woman out. Two paramedics with a stretcher came and detective Karen Saunders was gently placed upon it and wheeled into the ambulance. She had taken hold of Sam's hand and refused to let go of him. Sam walked alongside until they reached the ambulance, then pried himself loose, kissed her forehead and said, 'See you soon' As the men closed the doors Sam turned and was suddenly embraced by Chrissie who had coming running up to him.

'Are you okay?' she asked, pulling back, and taking hold of his face with both hands, then planting a kiss on his lips.

'I'm okay, really, just wet, and a little cold, must go and see this fireman chap,' and arm in arm they walked towards the fire station.

'Thank you, sir,' Sam said, releasing himself from Chrissie and extending his hand, 'I am Sam Price, brilliant seaman ship there…'

'No no, quite alright, 'I'm Daniel, Daniel Houseman, chief of this station, and thank you, you saved her…' then finding no voice to speak, just looked at Sam.

'This is my fiancé, Chrissie, and the woman is Detective Sergeant Karen Saunders…'

'I, I know.' Daniel said, his voice breaking up, he cleared his throat, the said, 'she came and got a winter coat from me, that I found on the riverbank, what, couple of years ago? oh my goodness, I recall the story now, that woman, an American, had been left on a ledge….'

Both Sam and Chrissie smiled at the man as he put two and two together. 'I wonder, Daniel, any chance I could change somewhere in your station....

10:50 am

They arrived at Karen's house, Sam and Chrissie in the back, Karen in the front passenger seat, driven by the same officer who earlier sped to the scene. She had informed her on route from the hospital, that the forensics had been at her house and had concluded a thorough check.

Karen thanked her, got out and walked up the driveway, another colleague was there and gave her the keys. Sam retrieved their luggage from the trunk and Chrissie was right beside Karen as they entered the house.

In the hallway Karen looked at Chrissie, saw Sam arriving, then speaking to them both, 'Upstairs, to the right, guestroom, I'll, I'll just get some fresh clothes and get out of these hospital garments.... I...'

Chrissie pulled herself towards Karen, briefly hugged and said, 'Go, take your time, we're fine, we'll make ourselves at home.'

Chrissie followed Karen up the stairs, Sam following with two small cases.

Once in their appointed guestroom, Chrissie placed herself into Sam's arms and held him tight, having until then, had no time to show any emotion.

Sam held her firmly and after a few moments of quietness, they pulled apart and kissed.

Whilst at the hospital, Joe had appeared, he and Sam embracing and Sam thanking him for his assistance. He was introduced to Chrissie and gave his apologies from his daughter, who was isolating at home. Sam got her number from Joe and spoke at length with the current mayor of Moncton, thanking her and wishing her well.

It was when they were all downstairs, drinking coffee and tea, that a call came through for Karen. She listened, frowned, the nodded and ended the call.

Still quite pale, she sat down opposite Sam and Chrissie and said,' they have found a car, a black Chevrolet Impala, old model, off the road to Harris, apparently lost control and flipped over a barrier, then rolled several times down the embankment.

Two passengers, the driver, Dusty Kerr, former deputy at Harris, and Karina West, you know who that is, both dead.' Standing up, the detective moved over to the window, just wanting to gather her thoughts.

THE PAST; Period 10

1973 – Hamilton Ontario Canada

Missy Koppell stood by the window. She had been standing there for some time. The sun shone on the lake. How often had she stood by the window, how often had she just stopped and looked out this window. The water shimmered in the spring sunshine. Today was even more poignant, even more emotional. It was Monday, 4th of June. Ten years to the date. Ten years to the date her husband went missing. The ship, the crew, a total of five men and three women. Gone, vanished. Into thin air.

Searches made, by ship, by air. Deep sea divers and sonar equipment was used, and satellite images were poured over. Nothing, no sign, no debris. No sonar detection, no radio signals received. It was as if they never existed. Last known position was around the Rochester Basin where the seafloor is over 800 feet from the surface, the deepest part of the lake, only Lake Superior was deeper in places. Last known weather report in that area. Fresh breeze, calm seas. Yet, gone, disappeared, vanished, into thin air.

Tears welled up. Missy took in a deep breath and then let the tears roll down her cheeks. Ten years. Their son, Dean, had been seven.

There was going to be a small ceremony today, a memorial service, at the Port Weller Dry Dock. To be held in one of the large construction hangars of the Upper Lakes Shipping Company. Missy checked her watch and took another deep breath before she turned and headed for the door. A driver was coming to collect her.

A little later, in the courtesy car, Missy smiled, for she had something, despite the memory of her husband, to smile about. Their son, her son, Dean, would be there. The first years bringing up the boy without a father, was hard. Even more so, when, at the age of thirteen, he began to act out, got disruptive, started failing his grades at school, got into fights and some trouble with the law.

His grandparents, Wayne's mum and dad, came to the rescue when Missy finally broke down with exhaustion and spoke to them over the phone. They took him with them to where they now lived, having long ago moved from Rochester to Portland.

Dean calmed down, started to improve at the new school he now went to and as well as writing her a long letter of apology, he spoke to her regularly. Surely something to smile about this day, moreover, he had some news he was going to share when he saw her today.

Mr and Mrs Koppell and their grandson Dean were on the last leg of their journey by air. They had flown from Portland to Chicago and after a two hour wait, boarded a flight to Buffalo. Here they would travel by car to the Port Weller docks where the Taciturn had been rebuilt from an ice breaker to an expedition ship. It was from here the ship had set off from, on that fateful journey, ten years ago.

Seventeen-year-old Dean sat quietly in the back of the car beside his grandmother, his grandfather in the front beside the driver. The news he had promised his mother he had, was certainly not what she might expect.

She was easily the tallest woman there. Standing a little over five foot ten inches, she was blonde, her hair cascading halfway down her back. She wore a dark green top over faded jeans and under a light tan leather jacket. Her feet in tan coloured ankle boots with a one and half inch heel which made her ever taller. Her blue eyes were watchful, scanning the room slowly, methodically. There was a dark brown satchel slung over one shoulder and in her right hand she held a small writing pad. The left held a silver-coloured pen. She had arrived later than most of the people there, placed herself near the back and watched and listened, every now and then making a note in the writing pad.

A small, sort of platform or dais, had been set up in what appeared to be a hanger of sorts. The floor was concrete and there were racks of equipment along two sides. Upon the dais stood a noticeboard, and upon the noticeboard were pinned several photographs, a large print of the ship, The Taciturn, was in the middle, at the top, and below, in a row, eight photos, eight faces. Their names clearly stencilled below each photo's. Five men and three women. The second photograph along from the left, was that of Nicholas Robbins. Even from where she stood at the back, she recognised the man he had become. The man she had, almost twenty-eight years ago, slept with. She had comforted and cuddled him. Kissed him. Had lain in his arms as she fell asleep.

Her marriage of sixteen years had fallen apart four years ago. She was lost in thought for a moment, as she thought back and how often she had spoken the words of the Beatles song, we can work it out.

'Try to see it my way, do I have to keep on talking till I can't go on, while you see it your way, run the risk of knowing that our love may soon be gone'…

She had been steadfast, adamant, she had stood her ground. He had been stubborn, hadn't given an inch. They couldn't work it out.

It was then, shortly after her divorce, when one day she went through her possessions getting settled into a new apartment, when she found the letter.

Someone, on the left end of the platform began to speak. The memorial was short, there was some music played, there were tears and sobs. A minister prayed. To one side of the large hangar, three long tables had been set up, coffee, tea, fruit juices and an assortment of sandwiches and cakes were available. Paper plates and serviettes, drinking glasses and cups and mugs placed by a jug of milk and two bowls of sugar. Spoons and stirrers completed the array.

The forty-six-year-old, tall blonde Katja Wiersma, began to mingle. Young Dean Koppel couldn't help but notice the tall woman and was momentarily distracted as he was speaking with his mother. Missy noticed, looked at the blonde woman, figured her to be not much younger than herself, but appreciated her fine figure and smiled at her son, who, noticing his mother's look, felt himself colour.

The news had not at all what she had expected or hoped for. But seeing her son, there before her, seeing his eyes. She was grateful that he had grown up well. Through letters written by her parents in law, she had followed his progress, from a troubled and angry teenager, to a steady and settled young man. But was he old enough for what he intended to do? He had a girlfriend, he loved her. Her name was Melanie, Melanie Wright, 'She is the right girl for me mother' he said, emphasising the word 'right'. Missy smiled, but as she was about to point out his young age and trying to formulate in her mind what to say, he said to her' She's pregnant, and I am going to marry her, not just because I believe it is the right thing to do, but because I love her, and she loves me, and well, it is right'.

It took a moment for Missy to take this in, she looked over his shoulder to see Wayne's mum and dad standing together, both with a cup and a plate in hand, and she caught their eyes. Both nodded. They approved of his decision. She smiled at her son, took hold of his shoulders, and said, 'I support your decision' her voice barely above a whisper. Her hugged her tightly. 'Thank you, mother,' then, pulling back, he smiled, his eyes tearful, and said, 'We are getting married next month'.

Ten minutes later, as some of the assembled folks were already starting to leave, Missy heard a voice behind her.

'You are Mrs. Koppell?' the voice accented, definitely European, she thought, turning to face the tall woman. 'I am'

'Hello, sorry for your loss, I know, it is a long time now, but, well, I am Katja, Katja Wiersma, Dutch. The man Nicholas Robbins, he was one of the many Canadian men who liberated my city, this is Leeuwarden, in 1945, I met him then' she said, then, giving a brief smile, 'I would like to speak with you?'

Missy sensed that this woman might know something that she didn't, just in the way she spoke and had so intensely looked at her with those, rather piercing, blue eyes.

'I, I must spend a little time with my son, and with my in-laws, they are travelling back today, can I give you my address and could you come tomorrow? I live in Hamilton, not very far from here…'

'Tomorrow will be fine' Katja answered, 'then with a pen poised over her notepad waited for the address. 'Thank you, see you tomorrow' the Dutch woman said with a smile.

Tuesday evening – 2ⁿᵈ March

Sophie put her phone down and smiled. His voice couldn't hide the excitement. He said he was all packed, Froukje was due back at work next week and then he would move to be with her. Thinking about what to make herself for dinner, she checked what the time would be in New York. She, Tammy, and young Terri had bonded so well in their adventure chasing the clues of the three monks, and Sophie felt she wanted to share what Martijn had told her, about the letter to the Canadian soldier. She dialled the number.

In New York.
It was 12:45.

Tamara Wilson stood in front of the full-length mirror in her spacious bedroom. She twisted a little to the left, then a little to the right, studying her figure. Her petite figure that easily fitted within the frame of the full-length mirror. Standing at five foot three inches, she wore snug blue jeans, her feet were bare upon the soft carpet. Her top was equally snug, a white plain t-shirt. Her blond hair was tied into a ponytail and not wearing a scrap of make-up she looked to be in her mid-twenties.

She was in fact thirty-eight. New York born and bred she now owned a fabulous apartment overlooking Central Park and was the chef and owner of a French restaurant called La Petite Tresure. The Covid restrictions were beginning to ease, and they were once more able to open. Tammy, as she was known to her friends, stepped up closer to the mirror, studied her face, then stepped back and reflected on her life. Her best friend Chrissie, from Boston, was going to be married this year to Sam, the Dutchman. Sophie, her friend in Paris was in a relationship with Martijn, the Dutch detective. Young Terri Hudson, with whom she had an interesting adventure involving the three monks from Florence, had gone back to San Francisco and her mother Alison, whom she had yet to meet, was apparently in a relationship with a chap from Albuquerque named Simon. Then, of course, there was the handsome pilot, Thomas, from Portland. He was now romantically involved with Cynthia. Why was she still single?

Had she been too busy, with her studies, with her business. Had she been too un-approachable? Walking away from the mirror, down the corridor of her luxurious 28th floor apartment, she passed the three seascapes that hung on the wall and entered her kitchen. It was time for lunch, then time to head for work and prepare for the evening service.

Her phone rang.

'Sophie!' she said, recognising the caller.

After a lengthy conversation Tammy put her phone down, then, having already gathered her notepad, she scribbled down all that Sophie had told her about a man named Nicholas Robbins and the connection to Roger Sutherland and Natalie Umbrego. Knowing about Claire who worked on the mystery of the three monks from her home in Myrtle Creek, it was her she was going to call. But first, some lunch.

Myrtle Creek
1:30 PM

'Hello?'

'Hi, Claire? This is Tammy, from New York…'

'Oh, hello, yes, I know who you are, is everything okay?'

'Yes, yes, I have earlier spoken to Sophie, from Paris, you will know who she is?'

'I do, from Thomas and Tia, goodness, it's not about them is it, are they alright?'

'Eh, yes, why, aren't they there?'

'No, they've gone to help that Spanish woman.'

'Really, yes, I know about her, anyway, no, it's not about that, Sophie had some information from that Dutch police chap, Martijn, not met him yet, nor you, look forward to that one day, no, the information I have, is with regard to a guy named Nicholas Robbins, apparently he was in the exploration ship that went missing? I know you and Sam investigated that ship in connection with that French woman and the Englishman, somewhere I picked up on the information that you found out whilst you were looking into the disappearance of someone?'

Claire took in all that Tammy said, then, 'Yes, I was looking into a certain Holly Koppell, she was the girlfriend of Robert… do you know about Robert?'

'He was the guy, sadly passed away now, who was good at finding missing people wasn't he?'

'Yes, well, he began all this, searching stuff, when he found out that his girlfriend went missing, sadly he never found her, I, well I wanted to look into that, see if I couldn't find her, for Robert, you know… anyway, that's when I found out about her grandfather, trying to establish a timeline connection, his name was Wayne, it was then when I discovered that he had been the captain on that ship, and when I looked further, found that among the people also missing, were the French woman, Natalie Umbrego, and the Englishman Roger Sutherland, I do recall some of the other names, Nicholas Robbins, does ring a bell, what information do you have?'

In New York Tammy decided that she really liked this Claire and made a mental note to go and see her one day, ' Goodness, yes, you have a good memory, so, this has nothing to do with this ship just disappearing, it's just that he was in the Canadian army, very much involved in the liberating of several towns and cities in the northern part of The Netherlands. As Sophie was telling me about a letter which Marijn's colleague found in an antique shop, whilst she was visiting her brother, and the coincidence of it all, I was wondering whether researching him, might be of help in your search for this Holly woman.'

Claire was in thought for a moment, then answered, 'Thank you Tammy, you know, the more I think about it, I wonder if this all does connect, the disappearance of that ship, it was called The Taciturn, could well be connected?'

'Yes, I don't know if you have ever met Sam, but he would say that it is likely, not a coincidence. Anyway, leave this with you, I must get to work now, but listen, with Thomas and Tia away, if there is anything you need, you call me, okay, do you have my number?'

Tammy gave Claire her number and ended the call.

Claire smiled, she had heard Thomas speak of this Tammy, knew it had been her that had paid for and organised all the travel when they, along with Terri, the daughter of Alison, had flown to Paris. 'Nicholas Robbins, well, let's see what we can find out about you mister' Claire softly said to herself.

Over the nearly two decades that Robert Pentegrass had delved into finding missing persons, being dubbed the 'Searcher' by the Portland Police Department, he had installed on his computer system, that he named his 'Search Engine', many programs that would enable him to delve deeper. Giving access to more secure files and reports. Claire spent the best part of the afternoon, after the call from Tammy, snooping and researching in many directions. Then came across what she audibly called out, 'Jackpot!'

For nearly ten minutes, she was totally engrossed in what she was reading, then reading it through a second time. She sat back, not only flushed with the excitement of having discovered this report, but also from the seriousness of what she had read.

Claire placed her right hand over her mouth. What should she do now? She wondered, then taking a deep breath, decided she need to speak to Thomas first. Getting up she crossed the room to the window, then crossed back again. This was big, this was disturbing.

the year 2000 – New Year's Eve.

Holly crossed the road and headed for the Rozzini mansion. She had been invited, so had Robert, but this wasn't his thing, she knew, she understood that. He had insisted she go. When she was just about to go up the path to the house, she turned, waved at Robert, who, she could see, smiled, and waved back. Little did she consider that she would never see him again as she was let into the house.

There were lots of people there and Holly mingled and chatted, ate, and drank and she thought how Robert, who she now considered to be her boyfriend, would not have been able to cope in this situation. She smiled to herself, got herself another drink and checked her watch, not long before midnight. Not long before the start of another year. The year 2001, what would it bring, she briefly wondered, then began chatting to a school friend.

Despite the rain, though fortunately it had eased a little, the firework display was going ahead, and the party had all come out to the back veranda of the large mansion house. The church bells had chimed, the hugs and kisses and well wishes had been done, drinks were still flowing, and the buffet table still had ample goodies to tuck into. Holly moved with the others and waited. She decided she would watch the display then cross the road to see and wish Robert a happy new year. She knew he would be waiting. She felt a little dizzy, realised she probably had a little too much to drink, despite telling herself to be careful.

The host, Nico Rozzini, had spoken in a loud voice and had called everyone out to the veranda. The fireworks began. Then there was a woman who was suddenly there beside her, her shoulder pressed against hers. She leaned closer and spoke in her ear, a loud whisper, so as to be heard above the noise of the sparklers and rockets which were fired into the night sky.

'I know what happened to your grandfather' the voice said.

Holly turned to look at the woman beside her, looked straight into her eyes, frowning, and was about to say something, but the woman spoke. 'Very confidential, you need to come with me'.

Then Holly felt the gun press into her ribs. As she registered this, she sensed someone else, another woman, on her others side.

'Don't try anything silly. Just come with us, all will be explained'. A voice whispered.

A woman either side of her Holly was led around the side of the mansion house around to the front, then along the path onto the street and a car approached.

Holly noticed that Robert must have gone inside, no doubt to wish his father and mother a happy new year. One of her captors opened the rear door, made her get inside and slid in beside her, the second woman got in the front.

The driver then turned around.

'Daddy?'

'Hey honey,' the driver replied, then accelerating away, said, 'I will explain everything, soon, we must go, see your grandmother.'

'Grandma? In Hamilton?' Holly asked, still in quite a shock, glancing at the woman sat next to her, the one who had pressed the gun to her side. Shortish dark blond hair, around thirty years old, she guessed, wearing a floral dress that came to below her knees, funky looking purple boots, and a lightweight leather jacket, she very much looked the part for going to a party. Holly guessed her to be a little taller than herself, but sizing her up, had she not had the gun, which was held firmly in her lap, she could easily take her. She focused briefly on the back of her dad's head, what was going on? Why did they have to see grandma?

Switching her focus, she took in the other woman, sat next to her father in the front, also around thirty years old she estimated, her hair slightly blonder and longer, also about the same height and weight as her other captor. She wore light blue jeans, leather ankle boots and a colourful blue and white squared patterned sweater over a white blouse. Who were these women? What was going on? She felt her stomach muscles tighten as they drove along, seemingly, she thought, heading for the airfield.

A clock tower as they drove past showed it to be a little before half past midnight. The light rain that had fallen earlier had briefly stopped, but it once more began to rain, heavier now. 'Okay, not far from your place now Holly' her father said, quickly turning his head around, then said, 'get some stuff, passport is important, some other personal belonging, but quickly, okay? '

'And I'm coming with you, to help' the woman in the passenger seat said.

'Just follow the instructions honey' her father said to her, briefly turning around before once again concentrating on his driving. They pulled up by Holly's apartment, that she shared this with two other girls. Both were, thankfully, Holly thought, not in, like her they had gone to a new year's party somewhere.

It was coming up to ten minutes to one o'clock, when the two women returned to the car. Her father had got out of the vehicle and stood by the open trunk, taking a suitcase and a leather holdall from his daughter, then, quickly giving her a hug, said, 'right, me must go, a plane to catch'.

It wasn't too much longer, the rain having eased off again now, that they reached the outer perimeter of the airport and approached a security gate.

There was a security guard box, a security guard. The woman in the front had rolled down the window and showed some credentials. The guard perused them, threw a quick look into the car at the passengers and driver, then handed back the document and pressed a button. The gate slid open.

'Just follow your father, say nothing, do nothing, understood?' the woman next to her said, lifting her gun slightly and looking directly into Holly's eyes.

Holly nodded. The car stopped and her father got out. There was a small aircraft, the steps were down, a man stood in the doorway. Holly opened the car door and followed her dad. Up the steps, briefly looking at the man as he had stepped aside to let them in. She sensed the woman with the gun, right behind her.

It wasn't until, after they had sat down, side by side on the front row of seats, and after the door was closed and told to fasten the seatbelts, that Holly's father began to speak. The man in the doorway was the pilot, and the woman with the gun was sat a few rows behind them. The second woman had not entered the plane, she had taken Holly's luggage, had placed it into a small hold in the side of the plane, closed the hatch and had walked back to the car that had brought them there.

The rain eased a little and Holly was pressed back into her seat as the small plane accelerated and lifted off into a dark night. Seeing the few lights that were still on at this time of the morning, Holly trying to gather her thoughts as she wondered what on earth was going on? She thought of Robert, had so wanted to see him, to wish him a happy new year. Flying to see her grandmother? Now? Why? She remained focused on looking out of the window as the plane rose in altitude. Her father beside her had begun to speak, had started to say that this journey was necessary, but she had held her hand up, gesturing for him to be silent. 'Not yet' she said to him, looking him in the eye for a moment, then turning her head to look out the window.

She needed to think, needed to calm herself down. Her heart was still beating way to fast. The two women, the gun, the urgency, the car ride, now on board a plane heading for Hamilton in Canada.

She began by collecting her thoughts, by putting them in some sort of order, thinking back about what she knew, about her grandfather, who had gone missing, along with several others on board a ship. Decades ago, now, thirty? Forty years? She was asking herself. Before she was born anyway. Her own life had been often unpleasant recalling the many times she had to endure her mother and father arguing. Her mother had left when she was fifteen. Her relationship with her father was often trying. But she immersed herself into school, and into her sport, loving to play field hockey. Perhaps the physicality helped her destress. A fake yawn helped her ears to unblock from the altitude pressure. Beginning to relax a little, Holly continued her reflections, leaving school, starting work, getting a lovely apartment which she shared with two others. All good, and now being a key member of the hockey team, she had truly begun to be her own person. Had begun to be less angry, more content. Meeting the very shy Robert and beginning a friendship with him had given her much pleasure.

Now, suddenly, when she had been looking forward to the new year with a boyfriend, with new adventures and challenges ahead, here was her father, and here she was, in an aircraft, flying in the middle of the night, to see her grandmother. Why? It was time for answers!

Turning away from then window, Holly faced her father, 'Okay, shoot, what is all this about? Why the urgency? Why the gun?'

'When I was seven years old, my father, he was the captain of this, exploration vessel, doing scientific research on Lake Ontario, well, you have heard the story, the ship, called 'Taciturn', disappeared. It was not a small ship, a refurbished icebreaker, around 45 feet long, had a shallow draught of about 5 feet, which meant it could do its research closer to the shoreline, plus it had a 2000 horsepower diesel engine, gyro stabilisers and could easily do 16knots. A substantial vessel. Yet, gone, not a trace, vanished into thin air. Last known location was close to what is referred to as the Rochester Basin, where the depth is over 800 feet, over the past few hundred years, over 500 ships have been lost in the lake, many of them, around this, Rochester Basin. Anyway, as I said, I was seven years old, but I remember when mother was told......'

Dean Koppell, who had been looking into his daughters al this time, turned to face forward, he closed his eyes, remembering.

Holly was silent for a moment, again taking in the story, though it had not been told to her in such detail, the size of the ship, the depth of the sea, all those lost ships over the centuries, she felt that her father had researched this incident.

As if guessing what his daughter was thinking, Dean turned again to her, 'Yes, I have done some research on this, however, I know most from mother, but, she has more, a lot more, so, we are going to see her, her health is failing, and she insists on speaking to me, and to you…'

'So, 'Holly said, after some moments of silence and turning around to look at the woman who sat two rows behind her on this eight-passenger jet. 'How long will it take to get there, and how bad is grandmas' health?'

Dean turned to look at her, then had a quick look around the plane, then said, 'This is a Lear Jet, pretty fast, apparently, we are flying to Winnipeg to refuel, then on to Hamilton, according to the pilot, we'll be there around six in the morning, 'looking at his watch, 'coming up to twenty minutes past one am, I suggest we get some sleep'.

The woman behind them, got up and handed Holly a blanket, 'your dad is right, best get some sleep'.

THE PRESENT; Moncton

Tuesday 2nd March – Moncton

'After all this excitement, you'd better get some sleep' Sam said to Karen, smiling at her as she lay on the bed. The doctor had not recommended she went home, but the detective had insisted.

Sam bent down and kissed her forehead. She took hold of his hand, 'Be careful' she whispered, her voice barely audible after all the talking she had done earlier.

Sam nodded and then following Chrissie, left the room.

There had been several people by her bedside at the hospital not long ago, after the doctor had checked her over and said they could talk with her, but not for long.' She's dehydrated, close to exhaustion, she is stable, but needs rest, she insists on speaking with you, she also insists on going home, I'll think about that. So, but keep it as short as possibly, okay'.

Sam had nodded and together with Chrissie had entered the room, followed by one of her police colleagues and the fireman, Daniel. The railwayman, Joe, waited outside and Sam had already spoken briefly to his daughter, the mayoress, Maureen, who had been anxiously waiting at home, not being able to come in person as she was isolating from the virus.

'Hey,' Sam began… but Karen spoke, 'No time, got to tell you what I know, while I have the strength, you can tell me later how you and Chrissie got here so quickly, and, of course, thank you, for….'

'It's fine, and yes, tell us what you know, your colleague here will write it all down' Sam interrupted, throwing a sideways glance at the young officer who had been there when they arrived by helicopter, who had his notebook and pen at the ready.

Less than ten minutes later they left the room. The constable left, Daniel, the fireman, shook Sam's hand vigorously, then nodded to Chrissie and left, not saying a word.

'I think he and Karen…' Chrissie said, her voice soft, she had seen the emotion in his eyes.

'Yes, I'm sure you're right, I picked up on a look that Karen gave him as he entered the room. He never mentioned a word when we were out on the river, it must have been hard on him to witness once he recognised who it was.

Joe walked up to them. 'I'll speak to your daughter next Joe, she wanted to be fully updated.

Sam pressed some numbers on his phone.

'Hello Mrs. Zimmerman, it's Sam…' he began, but was interrupted, 'please, call me Maureen Sam, thank you, I'm listening'.

Sam began, totally recalling what Karen had said only minutes ago….

'When I realised that someone was watching me, I started to take precautions, I sent you that text first of all, then, having turned my bedroom lights off, I then went downstairs, foolishly I was too confident, perhaps having my gun at the ready made me so, when I got to the kitchen and chanced a peep through the window at that car that was parked there, I heard a noise. Someone was already in the house, then I turned, and in the semi – darkness was this figure, dressed all in black, a black tightfitting outfit, head to toe, black boots, gloves, a hood that had only opening for the eyes. It was a woman, a little bigger than me, particularly her top half, however, she said nothing, didn't speak, just stood there, but then lifted both arms and she had a gun, a small gun, but she levelled it firmly and directly at me. I raised my own gun, levelled it at her, wanted to speak, but then, from a different part of the kitchen, Karina West arrived, walked straight up to me, and injected my neck. It all happened very quickly really; I was stunned. I then felt myself sway and starting to collapse. I felt that Karina had taken hold of me, lowered me to the floor, but after that…nothing'.

Here Karen stopped for a moment, her face pale, her eyes tearful. Then went on, 'Next thing I felt pain, in my neck where she had injected me, but also my wrists, realising that my hands were tied behind my back, also, I was gagged, as you know Sam, and…well, '…

'Thank you, Sam,' Mrs Zimmerman said on the phone, having carefully listened to Sam's account, 'I will get as many officers on this as possible, with this former deputy, Dusty Kerr, and Karina West now both dead, it seems this woman in black is the leader, in command, with an agenda, but what? Also, as you mentioned, this friend of yours in San Francisco, may well be in danger too, I have already contacted a counterpart there, they will, as of now, get some protection in place, also, I will text you a contact number, again, thank you so much for your assistance.' she managed to say before breaking into a coughing bout.

Sam said, 'You get back to bed, rest, thank you and we will keep you posted.'

Chrissie left Sam and Joe to chat together and rang Alison.

'Hi,'

'Is Karen alright?' Alison wanted to know, before Chrissie could even get a word in.

'Yes, she'll be fine, it is all quite confusing as to what is going on, Karen was left for dead, placed on that same ledge as you were, but then, we have found out, that Karina, that nurse, and the former deputy from Harris, both involved in this, are now dead, car crash, suspicious, and there is now a woman in black. Apparently, a new leader, so, who is she? and, what is going on. I mean, the police have already checked out Nico's widow, Debra, but she is home, Sam and I feel that it is all about Terri, and you.…'

'Take a breath Chrissie, ' Alison interrupted, ' I know this is all, well, upsetting, I am so glad that you and Sam got there in time, and, I have had the local police come around, telling me that a security detail is going to put in place, but, well, yes, you're right, I agree, it could be to do with Terri, but, why?'

'Did you tell the police about Terri?'

'No, their job is my protection, do you think I should?

'I'll talk with Sam shortly, Karen insists on going home, currently trying to persuade her doctor, but just thinking, how about we send Terri to be with Tammy in New York, she'll be safer there, I feel, what do you think?'

'I haven't said anything to Terri yet, didn't want to worry her, I like your suggestion, but won't that put Tammy in danger?'

'Let me speak to Sam, we'll talk to Tammy, ring back soon, okay?'

Terri Hudson sat herself down in the staff cafeteria of the museum. A well-known and long-established art museum in the southeast district of San Francisco. Taking a sip from the bottle of water she carried around with practically everywhere, she was about to tuck into the lunch she had prepared, when here phone rang.

'Mother?' she answered, recognising the caller number.

Terri spoke and mostly listened for several minutes before ending the call with, 'I'll be careful and think about what you said'.

Two minutes after that, tucking into her first sandwich, a staff member entered and said that a woman was wanting to speak to you personally. Almost then and there getting up, Terri changed her mind, said, 'Thanks Kathy, but bit of an emergency at home, get her number and I'll call back, must go, thanks.'

The receptionist, Kathy, headed back to her desk and Terri packed her lunch back in the container, picked up her water bottle, then left, heading for a part of the museum un accessible to the public, took some stairs to the next floor and got to a window just in time to see a woman leave. Using her phone, she took several photos and watched her get into a car. Taking a picture of the vehicle, she then called her mother.

'Mum, your call came at the right time, a woman has just been, asking for me, I didn't see her to speak to, but have taken some pictures, including one of the car she drove away in, I'll forward these to you, can you show them to the police and, can you forward these to Sam? I have this strange gut feeling about this woman, so, yes, I'll take the offer of staying with Tammy, is she alright with this?'

'Yes, Chrissie had spoken with her, will you call her? I guess you've got her number?'

'I've got her number; I'll call her now.'

THE PAST; Period 11 - Part 2

New Year's Day – 2001 – Hamilton – Ontario Province

"I've got her number, once I have told you everything, please call her' Missy said, her voice strong and upbeat. Yes, she was ailing, yes, she hadn't long to live, but she had accepted that, and so, with a smile on her face, she looked at her son and Granddaughter and continued, 'pin back your ears and listen'.

Dean and Holly were all concentration. They had landed at just after 6am, were driven to the apartment and greeted Missy in the lounge, where she stood by the window. The woman with the gun had remained outside the apartment.

'This is an adventure that I share with a woman called Katja' she had started, then told them she had her number,'

Once again standing by the window, she looked out over the lake, then turned, faced them as they sat, side by side in the three-seater couch, their faces a picture of concentration as they looked up at her.

'Back in 1973, we had the ten-year memorial service, at the docks, that day I met someone, a Dutch woman, her name, Katja Wiersma, she said she had something to share with me, regarding the disappearance of the ship. You, Dean, had come over that day, with grandpa and grandma, a day forever in my thoughts, as that was the day you told me about Melanie, and, about her being pregnant with you Holly….'

Missy said, looking at each in turn, she then turned again and walked back towards the large window, a window with a panoramic view of the lake, a window she had stood by countless times. 'She, Katja, came the following day, right here, and we talked, right here, in this very room.'

Missy turned again, strode towards them, and began to tell of that day, and of what followed…

Missy placed the two mugs of coffee on the table and looked at the tall woman who stood by the window.

'You have stood here many times, I think' she said, turning and smiling, her English was good, with only a slight accent. She had on the same faded jeans as the day before, also wearing ankle boots and the light tan jacket, which was now slung over the back of one of the armchairs, along with the brown satchel she had carried. The top she wore was different, it was dark blue. Her blond hair was not tied back and hung down over her shoulders and back in several curls. Her blue eyes set in a slightly tanned face. She wore minimal make-up, Missy noted, didn't need to, she was quite beautiful.

'Yes, yes I have' Missy answered, please, sit, you have, something to tell, I can sense that.'

Katja took up the offer and taking the satchel away, sat in the chair, then proceeded to open the bag and took out a folder which she placed on the low table, taking care not to knock the mug of steaming coffee.

'I slept with Nicholas Robbins' she began, then sat back, crossed her long legs, and continued, 'I didn't know his name then, well, he said, call me Nick, he was one of the soldiers, from a Canadian Regiment, who liberated my hometown, 1945. He looked, well, a little sad, I thought, when I first saw him, it was a party, many of my friends and neighbours in a local school hall. Many Canadian service men too, drinking, dancing, very happy, the Germans were on the run, the town was free. I saw him, and he saw me. I smiled and, well, as I said, I took him back to my place. He was kind, he was soft spoken, he was a little nervous, but he was a gentleman, we talked, we kissed and cuddled, but, although we did sleep together, we ....well, he had been drinking a bit too much, fell asleep, I fell asleep, in his arms, it was, it was nice' Katja said, a smile on her face as she reached for her coffee.

'When I woke up, he was gone, his regiment had to pull out heading for a town called Franeker, about fifteen kilometres to the west, where there were still some Germans. It wasn't until several days later, that I found the letter. It was, I think you call it, Dear John, but it was from his mother, informing him of his girlfriend now being with another man…I think he must have received it that day. Anyway, time goes on. I was seventeen at the time.'

'Gosh, seventeen, same as…' Missy interrupted, 'sorry, please, go on' briefly having thought of her son and his pregnant girlfriend.

'A lot of time passed' Katja continued, 'When I was twenty-one, I got married, we had a son the following year, then, when he was four, he contracted polio, sadly died, we tried for more children, but didn't have any. I began to focus on my work, started as a copy writer for a magazine, but I wanted to find my own stories, went out, went away following up on stories, the marriage, already quite strained, suffered and we split. Anyway, moving on from that, one day when I was going through my stuff when I moved to my own apartment, I came across some notes I had scribbled in a dairy, I'd forgotten I had, when I began reading, then, I had written that I had found the letter that had belonged to Nicholas Robbins. You see, as I grew older and when I was getting ready to get married, I cleared much of my stuff, and the letter, well, I remembered that I had taped it to the back of an second world war photograph, one that showed the Canadians liberating my city, I put it in a frame and away it went with other stuff, old clothes, books and so on. But as I read his name, I wanted to know more. It made me stop. I wanted to know, whatever happened to Nick. This was back in 1964, and following clues and searching records, I discovered all about the Taciturn exploration ship, he, Nicholas Robbins, was the exploration leader.' Katja paused, remembering that day, and how, sitting amongst her various packing boxes, she had cried. Wishing she had never given away that letter.

'I quit my job and became a freelance journalist, wanting to hopefully obtain a story about this ship's disappearance. Anyway, over several years I covered a number of stories, learning my craft, learning how to research records and so on, obtaining useful contacts and managed to pay my bills, managed to establish a good career.'

Katja took a few sips of coffee, then put the mug down and continued, 'all my findings are in there, you can read it later, hopefully you can help me in some further investigation. So, it wasn't until early last year, that I was able to afford to spend some time here, that is, in the States more than Canada, I also had some newspaper contacts now to sell any stories to, I went to Rochester, I had found out a few things about Nicholas, like me, he too had a failed marriage, found out that he was now working as a scientist in a naval facility in Thunder Bay. This made me think about the exploration, it was supposed be to study the flora and fauna along the shorelines of Lake Ontario, there was a graphic artist on board to sketch the wildlife, there was journalist on board, French, she was a late addition, but I found out something that made me think that all was not as it seemed.'

Missy finished her coffee and placed the mug on the table, fascinated with the story that was being told. Sitting back again, she looked at Katja and waited for her to continue.

'The ship, Taciturn, used to be an icebreaker, it was refurbished to be used for explorations, but I found a detailed worksheet of this refurbishment. Among it, a very sophisticate piece of deep-sea sonar equipment. On the face of it, maybe necessary to check on deep sea life, but, the ship also had a more standard sonar fitted, to register the depth of the ocean floor so as not to run aground, but this other equipment, having delved into more deeply, was far more than that, it could sound out and record the ocean floor to a high level of accuracy, but more than that, it could detect and record what lay beneath, what was under the floor of the ocean, or lake.'

'Wow, that is very interesting, so, what do you think was going on?' Missy asked, impressed by what Katja had found out, as she herself had also tried to follow up on why the ship had gone missing, but had been unable to find out anything useful. This information was quite the revelation, and moreover, put a new slant on this whole, expedition, what was really going on?

'What was going on indeed!' Katja replied, 'Well, this gave me a new direction to go in, I began to feel that this was maybe a military expedition, but, to what end, what could be so important at the bottom of Lake Ontario, particularly around the Rochester Basin?'

'Oh, my goodness!' Missy exclaimed, and leapt from her chair, 'back in a minute!' she said, leaving the room.

Katja stood up, wondered what had triggered the woman's recollection, going over to the window again, she looked out, thankful that she had sought out this woman, the wife of the captain of this ship, was he involved? Did he know what was going on?

'Here we are' Missy said, re-entering the lounge, she placed several photographs on the table. Sitting down again, she watched as Katja came back from the window, sat down, and picked the photo's up. After some moments, having looked at them intently, she raised her head and looked at Missy.

Missy smiled, ' These were taken, most of them by me, I was, nearly seventeen, this was in 1941, I had a boyfriend, Wayne, he was the one who had discovered this facility, had been curious, because of all the security surrounding it, had snuck out from his house at night, many nights, for several years, had found this old dilapidated barn and from there had observed the comings and goings. Then, one night when we were there together, in the old barn, we decided to go down to the shoreline, sneak up closer, it was exciting. Then we heard the plane, Wayne took a few photos then, I then took more as the plane docked at the back of this facility.'

'These are amazing,' Katja said, relooking at each one, then said, 'This is what I found too, this facility, US Naval Facility, set up in 1938.' Then looking at Missy, 'these are good, you didn't follow up?'

'We were kids Katja, other teenage things to do other than sneaking up of Naval Facilities'

'Of course,' Katja said, smiling, 'well done for taking these though'.

'There was something else, something Wayne came across, a label, it had come off one of the crates, had blown away in the wind one night, I don't know where it is, it might still be in one of the boxes of Wayne's stuff, down in the basement lockup, but it read, Ontario Project.'

Missy stopped speaking, Dean and Holly had been hanging on to her every word, having been transported to that day and time as she relived the account in detail.

'Wow, Grandma,' Holly said, 'did you ever find that label?'

'Why yes Holly, it is now with all the other documents I have'.

Dean stood up, he too now took time to look out of the window, recalling he had done so many times when he was a child.

'Why the urgency now mother?' he asked, turning around.

Missy looked up at her son, then across to her granddaughter. 'It is because of something Katja found out, only days ago.'

It was all quiet for a few moments, Holly stood up, taking in all that she had heard so far, but, she knew, there was more to come, she turned and looked at her grandmother. She was pale, looked tired. She felt a little guilty for not having spent much time with her in the years gone by.

'Katja and I came up with a plan' Missy said. Holly returned to sit next to her father who had also returned from the widow and they both again looked at Missy.

'We decided to visit this naval base, the one near Rochester, the one in the photographs that I took, and Wayne…. I was going to be the photographer, she, Katja, the journalist, she had good credentials, we sourced a place to stay, organised travel and Katja searched, found the right connection and, yes, she was allowed to come and visit the base.'

We were here, in this apartment, Katja stayed for several days, and I remember how we were so pleased with each other to have received the invitation.'

Missy smiled at the memory, then refocused and continued, 'so, yes, we headed for Rochester, settled into a motel and duly arrived one morning for our visit to the Naval Base, the sign by the large gates still read, US Naval Facility, as it had, way back in 1938.' After another brief pause, Missy went on, 'A man in uniform met us once we were past the security gate an on to the station itself. He greeted us, took us inside and introduced us to another man, you know, I can't remember either of their names, anyway, I was to leave the camera I had, at the reception, strictly no photos!'

We also had to leave our handbags, Katja kept her pen and pad, and' Missy said, now with a broad grin on her face, she leaned forward a little, 'and I had a small pocket camera, hidden in the pocket of my jacket!'

'Grandma!' Holly said, also smiling.

'Yes, I have always liked photography, and this was a new model, about a year old I think, it was a Kodak 110, goodness, about the size of a packet of cigarettes, with a film cartridge that would take 24 pictures.' Leaning back in the chair again, Missy continued, 'Katja spoke most of the time, listening and asking questions, my role, as the man was being distracted, not only by her questions, but, Katja was a stunning beauty, we had hoped it would be a man that would assist us, and he was most definitely attracted to her, so my role was to, surreptitiously take photos, trying to muffle the sound of the clicks as I did so' stopping again and smiling at the thoughts of that day. Then came the moment we both had worked towards, the question, Katja turned to look at me, so that I could also watch for any reaction, then asked, 'I have some information, from before the war, 'Katja had begun, 'about some research, called the Ontario Project?'

We both noticed it. He was momentarily stunned. He coloured ever so slightly, but we noticed. He then found his composure, frowned, looked at us both and said, 'Ah, yes, I recall, back in 1938 or 39, it was to do with sound. As you may know, sound travels faster in water than in air, it was to do with researching a way to improve detection, but it was abandoned not long after the war, '… then he carried on with the tour, of what we were allowed to see,'

Missy had fallen silent again and Dean broke it, 'So, did you see or found out anything, well, suspicious?' he asked, rather impressed with his mother and this friend Katja, whom he remembered having seen at the memorial that day. A stunning beauty indeed.

Missy took up the story once more, 'We thanked him, then headed back to the motel I had managed to take fourteen photos, which we would get developed and we talked through what we had seen and heard, Katja making a report of it all.'

Standing up, Missy went over to a dresser, opened a drawer, took out a folder and came back, flicking through, she pulled a few sheets out and handed them to her son, 'This was Katjas' report, read it.'

'But Grandma, why the urgency? Why did you need to see us, and, at gunpoint, on a private jet? What is going on?'

Missy looked at her granddaughter, then at her son, then back to Holly,' I'm so sorry my dear, Katja's report will help to give you both a clearer picture, but, as I said earlier, it is what Katja discovered only a few days ago, we have, put your lives in danger, please Holly dear, read the report, then I'll explain further'.

Holly could see her grandmother was suddenly very emotional, she got up from the couch, went up to her, put her arms around her and kissed her cheek. 'It's okay grandmother, really, whatever is going on, we'll deal with it'.

Dean in the meantime had picked up the report and began reading. Holly rejoined him and leaned across to also read the report. Noticing the title that Katja had given it; 'Soldier-Sailor-Spy'.

Holly and her father read the report, Katja's report that was based around the same information written by Nicholas Robbins that Claire would discover over two decades later.

After some time in silence as Holly and her father were reading and Missy was watching them, it was Holly who looked up and spoke.

'I still don't understand Grandma, why the urgency, why did I have to come here?'

Missy voice softened, her eyes were tearful, she was starting to look very tired. 'The photographs I took, that day, at the facility,' she said, then managing to stand up from her chair, she walked over to the window. 'Katja recently found someone, met someone, who was a scientist. Our research had not really led anywhere, over time we forgot about it, though something was nagging at us, we could not move forward with it. Then, as I said' Missy said, turning briefly to look at her son and granddaughter, before turning back to gaze over the lake and continuing, 'this scientist, well Katja spoke to her about what she and I had done, it came up, and she showed her the photos. She apparently frowned, according to Katja, was silent for a long time, then asked for pen and paper, made some calculations, there is a photo, among them on the table there, it showed some equipment, like a storage corner, some gas cylinders, some other tools, and a small chalk board, or noticeboard, upon which were a lot of scribbles, partly obscured by one of the cylinder…'

Dean sifted through the pictures, found the one his mother was talking about, showed it to Holly, 'we have it here…' he said.

Missy turned, looked at them holding the photograph, then again turned to the window, 'this lady worked it out, deciphered the formula, apparently, she was somewhat shaken and spoke to Katja at length again where this photo was taken.

It was then when a mistake was made. After she left, Katja spoke to someone in Rochester, a man who had been helpful in the past, a man who had also made enquiries, was curious, connected with a regional newspaper, looking for a good story. Anyway, Katja told him what the scientist had told her, when he asked about her, Katja mentioned that she was a well-studied scientist, from Portland……. her name was Holly……

Somehow the man then made a mistake to talk to the wrong people, upon realising this, only recently, on boxing day, he spoke to Katja, telling her that this scientist friend, this Holly from Portland, was possibly in danger. She rang me…' Missy turned, walked back to her chair and looked at them both, ' I am so sorry, the coincidence of it all, Katjas' friend, the scientist, was from Portland, Maine, but those who have been involved in keeping a cover up, well, keeping it covered up, joined the dots, tracked Katja to me, then to Dean, and….'

'To me?' Holly finished.

'Yes, to you, hence the urgency, get you to safety, Katja is also on her way here, she is so sorry Holly….

'Not her fault', Holly said, then standing up and giving her grandma quick cuddle before then walking toward the window and looking out over the lake.

'So, what is it, that this other Holly, discovered?' she asked.

'The formula was, or rather is, for a compound, that when mixed with air, de – oxygenises it, so it becomes extremely thin, like when on a very high altitude. It forms a vivid white cloud. A deadly white cloud.'

'Would…' Holly began, '…would it have taken time, I mean, to, well you know, work?'

Missy answered,' A question I asked as well, Holly dear, the answer, a blessing in a way, it would have taken no time at all'

Tuesday 2nd March

Claire checked the time, checked the time in Spain where Thomas and Tia had gone to help Letitia and saw that it would be close to midnight there, still, this was important, she needed to know what to do next. Standing up from behind the desk in what Thomas had renamed the search engine room as Robert had named his computer that same name, even having made a wooden sign that said so.

She pressed the number for Thomas's phone and heard it ring.

'Claire?' Thomas asked, recognising the number.

'Sorry to disturb you so late….' Claire began.

'No problem…what up?'

'Okay, now, listen okay, this will take a little time….'

'Talk to me Claire, 'Thomas interrupted, 'take your time…'

'Okay, well, I was looking into a man named Nicholas Robbins, he was the expedition leader on board that ship that vanished, the one that Roger Sutherland and Natalie Umbrego were also on, all to hopefully help me in the search for Robert's girlfriend Holly, whose father was the captain of that ship…' Claire paused for a moment, ' are you with me so far?' she asked.

'Absolutely, carry on…' Thomas answered, looking across at Tia who was now sitting up in the bed beside him, quizzically looking at him. 'It's Claire' he whispered, covered the mouthpiece of his phone. Tia then leant across and put the phone on speaker.

'Well, I came across a report, about this Nicholas, written by a journalist, a Dutch Journalist, her name was Katja Wiersma, and she wrote a piece she titled, 'Soldier-Sailor-Spy'… It is fascinating reading, she knew

Nicholas, and she worked together in trying to uncover the disappearance of the ship, along with a woman named Missy Koppell, which in itself was of great interest to me, for that was Holly's grandmother, anyway, I will read your this, quite lengthy report, okay?'

'Sound very intriguing Claire …,' said Tia.

'Hi Tia, sorry for the late call….'

'Don't be silly, sounds as if you have discovered something interesting.'

Claire took in a deep breath, loosened her shoulders, and began to read…

Despite it being now after midnight and they had been close to both falling asleep, Thomas and Tia were now fully awake, moreover, they were drawn into the story that Claire was telling……

Once having returned from the war, it hadn't taken Nicholas long to put aside the memories of his previous girlfriend, the one about whom his mother had written, the one who had chosen not to wait, but had gone into the arms of another. The woman who was now by his side as they stood by the railing of the cruise ship that was soon to sail into the Bay of San Francisco, sailing beneath the famous Golden gate Bridge and doing a circular tour taking in the Island of Alcatraz, and all of it including a dinner, was his former girlfriend's younger sister. They were on holiday, celebrating ten years of marriage. They had been greeted aboard by the captain, who stood not far from them, greeting more guests as they boarded. But then a woman came up the ramp. For a moment Nicholas tuned out of what his wife was saying and picked up a little of the conversation. It seemed this woman was the captain's wife and when she mentioned something about the Ontario Project, his ears totally pricked up and trying very hard to tune out of all others sounds, he focused on them. When more guest arrived, and the captain again turned his attention to greeting them aboard. Nicholas had heard enough to create in him a sense of intrigue and his wife, realising he hadn't paid much attention to her, shook his arm, and then dragged him away to find their seats.

The Ontario Project. At first Nicholas had assumed that it might be to do with the city, his city, his hometown, but from what he had picked up, it had to do with a secret mission on the lake.

It was 1956. Eleven years ago, he had returned from the war in Europe. Ten years ago, he had married Rita, who had been the one that had started their romance, had flirted with him, had paid him all the attention. It had been good; he saw that it gave her pleasure to be now with her sister's former boyfriend. He had to admit, that it gave him pleasure too, now and then, seeing the look on the face of the sister he had once dated, he had once thought of, as, the one, and who's fling with another had not lasted long. But the years rolled along. He had started work for the Upper Lakes Shipping company based at the Port Weller dry docks. Children had come along, a boy first, followed by a girl and then another girl. Three children. All was well. This ten-year anniversary a welcome holiday, a week by themselves. He smiled as he gave his wife full attention, though somewhere in the back of his mind, was the conversation he had partly picked up. The captain, a former pilot for the US Navy, had, apparently flown a secret mission, to Lake Ontario, back in the early forties, in fact, in 1941, shortly after the Japanese had bombed Pearl Harbour. What sort of mission, why the secret, and what was happening in Lake Ontario? He would investigate, he would research and find out, he was intrigued.

…. Claire took a moment, then recapped to say that that was when Nicholas had first heard of this project, by chance really, but he didn't start to fully investigate for another five years. Then, taking a quick drink of water, she resumed to read the account she had found….

It was late in the year 1961. November. It was cold and Nicholas, or Nick as he preferred to be called, was in a sombre mood. It seemed that this was surely going to be a winter of discontent. His mother had passed. His father had not been around for many years, had left the family home before the war, apparently heading for California, had not been heard from since. His marriage was over. Rita taking the three children away to Vancouver. He had strayed, he had foolishly, one day, flirted with his former girlfriend, his wife's sister, she had responded, an affair ensued. He looked through the dusty windowpane of the workshop at the docks, looked at the grey sky, the choppy water on the lake. It was then he thought back to the conversation he had heard in San Francisco, the story of the captain, who had been a pilot. He needed a distraction, he needed to focus on something. What was it, that this secret mission had been called? Yes. He remembered, The Ontario Project!

Throughout that winter and well into the new year, Nick researched and travelled. By now also an accomplished sailor, he rented a boat, a small cruiser, around fifteen feet. He also rented some diving equipment and armed with some other instruments, cameras, and sonar detectors. It was in the April of the year 1962, that he set out on this adventure....

...again, Claire took a sip of water, then asked, 'are you guys still with me, awake?'

'Absolutely, very awake, do carry on, 'Tia answered.

'Best bit coming up' Claire responded, then, taking another sip of water, cleared her throat and continued....

I first sailed out of the Welland Canal, into the lake and headed for the Naval facility near Rochester...Nicholas Robbins wrote, in his very detailed account...

It was raining lightly, the wind was from the east and Nick sailed close by the large hangar like building that was the naval facility, built, he had researched, back in 1938. He noticed the small dock on the lakeside and assumed that this was where the captain, then pilot, who's name, he knew, was Zoltina Huanca, must have landed that night, in 1941, delivering some cargo that he had picked up from Portland. Nick slowly motored past, the engine barely above an idle. Two long fishing rods attached on the back deck would show to the casual observer that here was a chap out fishing. Nick took a series of photos of the facility, then headed towards the east, into the wind which had picked up a little, heading for an area he knew to be the Rochester Basin. Forty minutes later he threw the fishing lines from the two rods into the water, switched the engine off and let the boat just drift with the wind and the current. A small anchor acting as a weight to minimise the movement. Then went to the port side of his boat, set up various boxes of equipment and lowered the sonar device.

Looking at a portable satellite navigational reader, he saw the longitude and latitude reference on the screen, exactly where he wanted to be. Months and months of meticulous research, had at last proved rewarding. He had discovered that there had been a trial, of a small submersible, a torpedo shaped submarine, able to accommodate two people. And with a sophisticated and advanced sonar system capable of detecting at a range of over 5000 metres. He had also discovered that a trial run had taken place, the intention was to travel through the lake and partly up the St. Lawrence River, testing out its equipment, speed, and ability to move smoothly throughout the waters. The trial was partly successful, but the submersible was lost on its return. Nick had the coordinates.

He lowered the sonar device. Thinking about all he had learned. What were the Americans doing in this trial, this research, and, in Canadian waters. There had been no information found on any form of rescue of the two people who had been on this trial, who were these, presumable, men? And why wasn't any rescue attempt made?

Nick checked the readings, then donned some headphones and listened. The boat meanwhile drifted slowly in the wind. There was no other vessel in the vicinity.

Making notes he is listening for over twenty minutes. But then realised that the wind had picked up. Rain began to fall, and he needed to control the boat. Reeling in the device, he began to pack up, pulled the fishing lines in, winched in the small anchor, looked at the sky and headed for the wheelhouse. Starting the engine, he set off for home. He would need to come back another day, and, he realised, there was no way that he could dive alone, he needed someone else. Thinking this all through he steered for home....

Claire stopped speaking.

'Did he go back? 'Thomas asked, thinking the whole story through.

'No, not then, but, fourteen months later, he was on the Taciturn, and you know what happened then, it has to be connected...' Claire said.

'I agree, what a good bit of research you have done Claire, but what do we do about it? Was Nicholas, or Nick, was he on a mission different from what was announced, not studying the coastal flora and fauna?'

'Yes, because he had installed very high-tech sonar on the ship, which already had a sonar system, the thing is, such costly equipment. Surely, he was not alone, there must be others who knew why this exploration was taking place?'

'Yes, I agree Claire, it sure smell a lot like a cover up, and you were right to bring it to our attention, I also think that we, all of us, need to tread very carefully'.

'We'll sleep on it, Claire, talk to you tomorrow, okay?' Tia said, looking for confirmation at Thomas who nodded.

Claire ended the call.

Meanwhile in New York.

Tammy wasted no time. She organised staff to make sure her restaurant would have all the personnel needed, then called around to locate a private yet to take her to San Fransico. She then called Terri back, told her to get a taxi and go straight to the small airport to which she gave the address.

Leaving her apartment, checking the time, she then decided, as it seemed to be an international situation, to call the man from Interpol, the hunk, as Terri had described him, and rightly so, Tammy thought, smiling to herself as she rang Sophie who would have his number.

In the taxi to the airport, she spoke to her French friend, and having got his number, rang Walther.'

Forty minutes later, she was on board the private jet, one she had chartered before, leaving from a small, secluded airfield near Yonkers. Terri was in danger, Terri, daughter of Alison, whom she still yet had to meet, had become such a close friend, the youngsters showing her mettle and determination in a case they were involved in.

In San Francisco, Terri had packed and had then first gone over to her mother's house. Ally took in all that Terri had told her, so appreciative of Tammy's help to get her daughter to New York. She then looked closely at the photos Terri had on her phone. 'I'm sure I know her!' Ally exclaimed, looking at Terri, then finding her own phone, she dialled a number, again looking at the photos Terri had taken.

'Chrissie' she said, then went on, 'Terri will shortly send you a photo, this is of a woman who was asking to see Terri at the museum, only a little while ago, she had just received my call to be careful, so, she made an excuse to see her another time, then ran around to where she could see the woman, took a few shots, I'm sure I know who it is, hang on, I'll give Terri your details, one moment….Terri deftly manoeuvred her fingers on the keypad, checking as to where to send them, then nodded to her mother.

In Moncton Chrissie look at her phone, saw the pictures arrive and opened them up, then as she was looking, she too exclaimed, 'Oh yes! I know her too.!'

Sam came up alongside Chrissie and looked, then looked at her. Chrissie spoke on her phone to Ally, 'Without a doubt, that is Bella Madison, Phil Madison's wife!'

'Agreed, Ally said, I thought so too, who should we call?'

'You've got that policeman friend in Albuquerque, Roger....'

'Roger Mantell? yes, he'll have connections here, can I give him your number too, he might want to liaise with the Canadian police, in fact I'm sure he will...'

'Good thinking, you ring him, I'll pass this information onto the police here, well done Terri, and? Is she going to stay with Tammy?'

'Oh yes, we are about to get a taxi, I wanted to make sure she gets to that plane, Tammy is already on her way down here, having never met her yet, I wanted to see her, thank her, you know.'

'Of course, be careful, okay?'

Bella Madison was puzzled. Having failed to get an appointment with the girl, with Terri Hudson, at the museum, she first decided to get some lunch as she realised, she hadn't eaten since breakfast. Having managed to find out the place of work for this Terri girl, she had thought it best to go there first. She now had to adapt her plans, she had the address of Alison Hudson, she would go there, after having something to eat, and, with a bit of persuasion she would get the girl. But here is where she became puzzled.

She arrived at the address, after only briefly having stopped for a drink and a sandwich, only to see a taxi pull up, then a blonde woman appeared form the house, Alison Hudson. But then, right behind her, a young woman, with a suitcase and a holdall bag appeared. This had to be Terri. They got into the cab; luggage was put in the trunk. There was nothing else for it, but to follow the taxi. She was going somewhere, but where, more importantly, why? Had she been rumbled; had they been warned?

Making sure she kept a safe distance, she followed the cab, it was heading towards an airfield, according to what she could see on the navigational system in her car. She spotted an incoming aircraft. A private jet. Making sure she kept her distance; she then found a spot to pull over and stop. Watching it land, she got out of her car, grabbed a camera from the passenger seat and started taking shots. Of the plane, of the young woman who must surely be this Terri, and of Alison.

The sleek jet landed, taxied, turned, and headed for a small terminal where Alison and her daughter had walked to, after clearing through the security gate. The taxi they had arrived in, was waiting. Some traffic went by and Bella, suddenly feeling that she may have indeed been rumbled, decided to get back in the car, and take more pictures from inside, rather than stand so exposed. The jet had stopped, the door had opened, and steps had come out. A woman appeared. A blond woman. Bella took photos. She bounded down the steps and the young woman, practically ran up towards her, dragging her suitcase and still holding the large bag. Her mother followed.

Who was this woman? Arriving on a private jet? Bella was thinking, taking a few more shots. She then watched as young Terri introduced the blond woman from the plane to her mother, they too then hugged before the newcomer and Terri entered the plane. Alison then returned to the waiting taxi. The jet taxied to the other side of the airfield. No doubt awaiting instructions. Bella was more than puzzled now. Had she been identified? One thing was for sure, her visit to the art museum had no doubt set all this in motion. But how was it, that the girl had been wary, there must have been a warning given, but, by whom? The nurse and the deputy were both dead, she had made sure of that. The policewoman as good as, tied and gagged on the ledge, she couldn't have survived.

Terri was flying away. Bella knew that first she needed to return the rental, turning the ignition on, she began to re-think her strategy, it was no point in seeing Alison now, in fact, as she turned and headed for the international airport from where she had rented the car, she became wary that she might even already, be under surveillance. A lot of planning had been done. There was a lot at stake. First, the revenge abduction of the policewoman, the Detective sergeant who had been the driving force that had put Julien Rozzini and her husband Phil, in jail. Karina, the nurse also involved had managed to escape, with a little help. She had needed the nurse, and the deputy, who was more than willing to help plot a revenge against the detective. They had planned and executed it well, had left the detective for dead, tied up and gagged, on the ravine ledge. That part of the plan having been concluded, she then had no further use for the nurse and the deputy. She knew they were dead, no loose ends there. So, how had they found out about her? It baffled her, but first things first, get rid of the rental. The young girl Terri would have to wait a little longer, there was another person she needed to take care of. Sandra Pentegrass, Julien wife, who, she had been told, had made the confession that had all the details of her husbands and Julien's involvement, as well as Nico, Julien's brother, who, cowardly, had shot himself.

But how to find her, when the police had so far not been able to. Bella was arguing all these things in her minds, not really knowing how to proceed, now that she knew she was likely being sought by the police. But one thing she did know, she realised the light lunch she had wasn't enough, her belly was rumbling.

Cynthia Barnes made her way through the field on her belly. Slithering smoothly through the cornfield every now and then raising her upper body to gauge how far she was away from the ranch. It was early in the morning and the dew began to seep into her clothes, but she ignored the wetness. It wasn't cold. Before the sun had even risen, she had ridden her horse, borrowed from a friendly farmer where she had stayed for the past two days, had followed the Sacramento River for about half a mile and had then tethered her horse to a small tree. She then walked for a while, but as she got closer, she then began to crawl and slither as the sun had now barely risen above the horizon. Dressed in denim jeans, a cotton shirt underneath a light brown leather jacket and her feet in short length leather boots she got closer and closer. Dragging a satchel with her which contained a pair of binoculars, a camera and a stun gun, as well as a hunting knife and a photograph. A photograph of a young woman. She reached the boundary of the field and was now only yards away from a nearby barn. With the binoculars she checked all around, no sounds or sight of anyone. It being a Sunday, Cynthia had figured, they might not get up as early as during the week and likely the best time to come. Putting the binoculars away, she slung the satchel over her shoulder and stood up, then jogged over to the barn. Entering through a side door she closed it behind her and looked around. The usual farming equipment, a tractor and an open topped small jeep. Very much like the ones used by the military in the second world war. Going over to it, she noticed that the key was in the ignition. A plan began to form. But first she had to find the woman. Find Claire Symonds.

An open hatch door where a pulley system was set up let in plenty of light and Cynthia walked her five-foot eight-inch frame towards the big double doors. She saw how these would easily open, pondered a moment about the jeep and whether or not it would start, she then pulled out her phone from her jacket pocket and dialled a number.

'I'm on the property, stand by' she said. Tucking a few strands of her dark brown hair behind her ear, she headed back to the door she had entered by. Took in a deep breath, pictured the layout of the ranch house in her mind, then opened the door.

Her fortieth birthday was only weeks away, but she was physically in good shape. She saw or heard no one, quickly covered the ground between the barn and the house and headed around to the far side where, according to the plans she had secured and perused, were the bedrooms. She bent low to pass by three windows and reached the corner. She now heard a radio, likely coming from the kitchen which was in the centre of the ranch at the back. Slowly turning the corner, she reached the first window. In her observations a day ago, having then very slowly crawled around the ranch, almost a hundred and eighty degrees, keeping a good distance and using the binoculars, she had seen the woman. She knew her details, twenty-two years of age, standing around five foot four inches, slim in built and her hair medium blond and cut quite short. A description from three years earlier, when she had gone missing, from Portland Oregon. Robert Pentegrass, who had been given the nickname 'The Searcher' by the Portland police, had been searching for missing persons for over sixteen years now. Cynthia, though preferring to be called Tia, had been assisting him for the past six years.

She walked up to the window, the curtain was closed. She tapped softly on the glass.

The curtain opened, a face appeared, Cynthia pressed her forefinger to her lips in a sign to be quiet. The woman, Claire, stepped back in surprise, but then came forward and opened the window. Cat like Cynthia entered the room.

Immediately she noticed the bracelet on Claire foot. A monitor, very much like prisoners on parole might be fitted with. 'Hi, police are around the corner, well, close by' she whispered to the young woman, who was quite pale, but nodding her head in understanding. 'Come with me'

Tia then grabbed a chair which she pushed tight under the doorknob. Then went back through the window, helping Claire out and wondering how far she would be able to go before the bracelet would sound the alarm. As Tia led the way, she pulled out her phone and spoke briefly.' I've got her, confirm, come now, 'Then, grabbing hold of Claire's hand, pulled her and they both ran towards the barn. Once again entering through the side door, 'Get into the jeep, stay low.'

The barn doors opened and there was still no action from the house. Tia ran to the jeep, jumped in the driver's seat and turned the key. The engine kicked in straight away. Pressing the accelerator the jeep shot forward, exited the barn and sped past the house. From the corner of her eye, she noticed that Claire's bracelet had started to beep, and a light was flashing. In the rearview mirror she saw a man, followed by two other men, come bounding from the house, the first had a shotgun.

'Stay low!' Tia warned, going as fast as she could on the dirt road. A shot rang out, but it didn't hit the vehicle. She knew there were other vehicles on the ranch, on the nearside, powerful vehicles, new vehicles, fast vehicles. With still many miles to go to safety Tia focused on the dirt road, slipping and sliding around a couple of bends like a rally driver. But then she heard the sound. A helicopter appeared, flying low and directly toward them. Tia briefly took one hand of the wheel and waved. In her rear-view mirror, she saw a car appear, but then slither to a stop, the driver getting out and grabbing the gun. But the helicopter was on the scene, the FBI called a warning on the loudspeaker and from the side door of the chopper one of them fired a shot which shattered the windscreen of the car.

Tia drove on. She could see there was no more danger from behind, but also knew that there were neighbouring families who were in cahoots with these human traffickers. She noticed the helicopter landing and men pouring out. The ranch, at least, was secured. Keeping the speed up, Tia drove on, towards the place where she had been staying these past days, A haven. But there was one rancher in between, would they have contacted them? Beside her Claire sat quietly, still quite pale.

In the distance to her right, she saw her horse. She would arrange for it to be returned. Then, coming from a track further along, Tia noticing the dust the vehicle was kicking up, a large vehicle, some sort of land rover. She estimated that she would pass the entrance before he got to the road, but would then be behind her, and much faster. 'Bit more trouble ahead' stay low' Tia said, then pressed the accelerator to the floor. It would be close. The driver of the vehicle coming from the farm road was going very fast, aiming to sideswipe them. But Cynthia had the situation in hand, she knew that at the speed she was going, she wouldn't be able to stop in time, but could also see, that she would pass by the farm road just ahead of the rancher coming out. The driver of the other vehicle calculated that he would be too late, and as he approached the main road he pressed hard on the brakes, the vehicle slid from side to side, the dust from the farm road creating a billowing cloud.

Tia shot past the entrance, notice the look of concern and fury on the driver and then watched in her rearview mirror. The land Rover shot onto the road and though able to slow down to a degree and turn, the vehicle slipped over to the far side of the road and into the verge. However, the four-wheel drive coped with the ground, and it wasn't long before it was back on the road and in pursuit. The road was quiet, early Sunday morning and though Tia was going as fast as she could, the vehicle behind them was now beginning to gain. Still about three miles to go to safety.

Claire, recovering from the initial shock of all, took in their situation, looked at the woman beside her, her rescuer, saw the determination on her face, understood the danger she had risked getting her, and began to think how she could help, also seeing in the mirror on her side of the jeep that the car behind was coming up fast. Looking behind her in the back of the military jeep, she saw something that could help, hopefully, it was a jerry can. Leaning over and reaching, she grabbed it, looked at the approaching car, then lifted the jerry can. It wasn't full, but not empty either for she felt some liquid sloshing around as she handled it. Then with all her strength, she lifted it, then threw it into the air.

The timing was great. The jerry can arched through the air, then came down on the road, only yards away from the speeding pursuer, then bounced and smashed into the front grill of the car with a loud bang. The jerrycan flew upwards from the impact, then before the driver could do anything to avoid it, it hit the windscreen, then flew over the top to land behind it on the road. The driver had braked, slowed dramatically and nearly lost control. The windscreen was cracked.

'Great job Claire!' Tia called out as they were still travelling at speed, the wind creating havoc with her hair, 'that will take care of him' noticing that he was now slowing down and she eased a bit on the accelerator as she could see he had stopped altogether, then watched as he made a turn to head back where he had come from.

'Only about a mile to go' Tia said, turning to Claire and giving her a smile, reducing the speed even more and beginning to relax.

Ahead of her, lights flashing and sirens wailing, the police were heading towards her. Tia waved at them as they passed, two cars in succession. The road to the farm was just up ahead and she slowed and turned into it. Her heartbeat was slowing down to normal, and she was thankfully that she had rescued young Claire.

'Well done, Robert' she whispered, and thought back about a time when she had not been so nice to him. A time she would often think about, though a time she wished she could forget.

Looking across at her briefly as she slowed even further to turn into the farm road, then, remembering she had a bottle of water placed in the cup holder and said, 'Claire, there is some water there, please, take a sip, we are nearly there.'

Tuesday 2ⁿᵈ March

It was early evening, and it was getting dark. Claire sipped some water from a bottle and recapped the day in her mind. What she had found out had been most intriguing, though she was glad that she had called Thomas and Tia. Thomas was already on his way back home, most likely flying across the Atlantic at this point. Tia, after she had told them all her findings and Thomas had asked her to hold on as he was coming home, had then said that she was nearly ready in her work to assist Letitia and would be going to the courthouse the next day.

Tia. Taking another sip of water as she headed downstairs to the kitchen, she recalled the time she was in the old jeep. The time when a tap at the window and seeing her face for the first time, a woman set to risk herself to assist in her rescue. The drive along the road, when thinking about it later, had been exhilarating. Claire smiled to herself, and she remembered throwing that jerrycan. Goodness, already over five years ago!

Meanwhile Thomas was indeed somewhere over the Atlantic jetting towards New York. From there he had sourced a connection to Portland. He too was reminiscing, thinking back to when he had first arrived at Roberts house in Myrtle Creek and young Claire so defiantly challenging him. He could, of course, understand her wariness, after what she had been through, though not, as yet, having heard the full story from her, he had picked up some information from Tia and her involvement in her rescue. What a fine young lady she was, he thought, and resourceful, having done the major work on the investigation regarding the missing Eddie Philpott. But what she had uncovered this time, in her search for Holly Koppell, now that was not only complicated, but bordering on a difficult legal minefield. He checked his watch and calculated he would arrive in New York in less than an hour.

✤

THE PAST; Period 13

The year 2019 – the town of Harris Monday 6th of May

Nico Rozzini entered the foyer of the CP Holdings mining company where a large clock on the wall showed it to be a few minutes after half past eight. His company, a company he had purchased just about ten years ago. A silver mine once belonging to the Boston Parker family. He strode up to the first floor, passed by his secretary who said, 'Good morning Mr. Rozzini' and continued along the passageway to his office after uttering an acknowledging grunt.

He entered his office, closed the door and just stood there for a moment. He looked at his desk, noticed the very empty space behind his desk on the wall, where, not long ago, had hung a large oil painting. A seascape. A wonderfully painted scene and it had come with the company, which he had purchased lock stock and barrel, from Joshua Parker. Still standing just inside the large office, he visualised the scene, of seamen struggling on board a sailing ship, with turbulent waters. He closed his eyes. The turbulence of the last few days had been very much like what those sailors must have been going through, he thought.

He had panicked. But reasoned that he had been careful and had efficiently come up with a plan when that Hudson woman had walked into the police station asking for them to arrest him. The sheriff had called him, and he had been rather pleased with himself to have so quickly come up with a plan. The sheriff and his deputy would do as he asked, he was in no doubt about that.

But the game was up. The American woman, Julien's ex-wife, had not been dealt with as hoped. The detective from Moncton had become involved and the plan had unravelled very quickly from that point. Internal affairs were about to enter the police station. The nurse, Karina,

125

had been arrested just as she was about to fly out from Halifax. Julien decided to go on the run and his friend Phil had also been arrested and held for questioning.

The game was up, and he knew it. Nico opened his eyes, got his legs to move and headed for his desk. No time to ponder, no time to think, there was no way out. He sat down in the leather desk chair, pulled open a drawer, retrieved a gun.

Moments later a shot rang throughout the building. His secretary came running from her desk, opened the door to the office, saw what had occurred, tutted and went back to her desk to call for an ambulance. Though she knew for sure that her boss was dead. The wall behind him, where once the beautiful seascape had hung was now splattered with blood.

Epilogue; Moncton

Wednesday 3ʳᵈ March

The three of them sat in the front room of Karen's apartment. They had recently finished their breakfast and were about to recap the events of the past few days when Karen's phone rang.

Answering it, the detective managed to say' Oh, hello Mayoress, how….'

Listening for some time, both Sam and Chrissie noticed that Karen, still a little pale from her ordeal, showed a look of concern on her face, before eventually saying, 'Gosh, okay, thank you,' a pause, then' yes, I'll get onto that as soon as I can, and yes, I will make sure that I am well rested before I do, I have Sam and Chrissie still here, may I share what you have told me?'

'Okay, thank you again, and you get better soon also' Karen said, then, still with a rather concerned look on her face, ended the call.

Then, turning to Sam and Chrissie who sat side by side on the three-seater couch, she put a smile on her face, then began to say,' Well, as we were about to recap, some more information to consider…'

'Are you okay Karen, that, we assume, was Maureen Zimmerman?'

'Yes, yes it was, still not altogether well, but improving… anyway, rather disturbing news, so, let me fill you in, she said I could share this with you, so, neither of you have ever seen my boss, have you? Well, with staff shortages in both stations here in Moncton, he was very much based at the station on the south side, anyway, he is detective inspector Murray Canney. That is to say, he was, turns out, he may well have been in cahoots with the Harris police, involving bribes. When internal affair started looking into the sheriff there and his deputy, well, it led to some anomalies regarding Inspector Canney. Anyway, he probably had an inkling, because he has scarpered, gone, last known to have boarded a plane to Toronto and from there to Miami, no further contact. So, not good news, also, was he in any way involved in the abduction of Alison, or me?' Karen paused momentarily,' The thing is, as well as following up on what we know, I have been promoted, detective inspector Saunders if you please' she finished, smiling a little now.

Neither Sam nor Chrissie spoke, taking in what Karen had just told them. It was the newly appointed inspector, who again spoke,' Okay then, come on, let's get positive here, you have already told me of how you got here so quickly, I know from you Chrissie, how Sam, with the help of Daniel…..' noticing Chrissie look, then added, ' and yes, he and I have been out a couple of times, so, anyway, I can't ever thank you enough Sam, but, we must continue to find this Bella Madison, thankfully, you have told me that Terri is now in New York, which is great, but it still leaves a few questions, why was Debra Rozzini so keen to get Alison's address, and how is Bella connected? '

'The police in San Francisco are keeping an eye on Alison, they also have details of Bella, and an all-points bulletin is out on her, we still don't know as to why it is Terri that she was after, having gone directly to the art museum to see her, having got that information from somewhere…' Sam said.

'This is the question, why Terri?' Karen agreed, 'I will try and get to see both Julien and Phil, who are in prison in Halifax, might get something out of them, though doubtful, also we will keep an eye on Debra Rozzini, she has to be part of this, I'm sure'.

'Agreed, I think that Sam and I should go to New York, be with Tammy and Terri' Chrissie said, looking across to Sam for confirmation.

'Yes, I don't think you are now in any danger, and, as inspector, you will need to follow up on the deaths of the deputy and the nurse, as well as now digging into the involvement of your ex-boss' Sam said, following this with, ' So, yes, Chrissie is right, Terri seems to be the main target, but, I also think Alison could still be in danger too, what do you think?'

'I agree Sam, 'Karen answered, 'This Bella might still somehow get to her, use her as leverage maybe?'

'Of course, you are both right, so, how do we proceed?' Chrissie asked.

'There is someone else, who very possibly, might know the reason why Terri is so important.' Karen said, then looking at both Sam and Chrissie in turn, 'Sandra Pentegrass'.

BOOK 2
OUT OF THE
BLUE

Prologue

Wednesday – 3ʳᵈ of March – 2021

Sandra Pentegrass had made up her mind. It was time to come clean, time to face the music. First however, a matter of justice. At least justice according to her. After having written that confession, having then flown to San Francisco and couriered it to the school, she had then boarded the flight to Hawaii. Hoping that she would safely land there before the proverbial hammer came down. Before the police would arrest her. There had been no sign of the police. Recalling the sense of relief she had felt upon arrival, she knew however that there were a few things to still put right at some time in the future. But that was for the future, maybe. She made a point of looking for transport to another island and once there she settled down, looked and found work, had finances in place to get an apartment and the days grew into weeks and the weeks became months. But a nagging sensation, she would often refer to it as that stupid conscious, would not go away.

The sun shone brightly. The water was smooth and the wind in her face warm, as she stood by the railing on the port side of a small cutter. A fishing vessel. She was going to return, the time in the future, was now, no maybe about it, she was going to give herself up. For although she had written that detailed confession, concerning the abduction and the consequent deceitfulness, when she and her husband had taken Terri from school. Had promptly flown her to San Francisco, had enrolled her in a girl's boarding school and had created a false story about the girl's biological mother having been killed in an accident. Writing down the full details as to who was involved. Then more details confessing her part, though minor, in the abduction and subsequent attempted murder on Alison Hudson. Also naming furthers suspects, in the form of the nurse, Karina West, and her husband's friend, Phil Madison. What she didn't put in her report, was why it was that the girl, Terri, was so important. Something that Julien had told her, many years ago.

When she had carefully planned her escape and planned the confession to be delivered to the boarding school, she had been just in time. She had been worried, had not been happy with what she had heard was going to be happening regarding Alison Hudson. Though certainly not in any way was she her favourite person, but this was going too far. She wanted out, began to form a plan in her mind, then set about to execute it. She was almost too late, for the police were on to them far quicker than anyone thought possible. Alison Hudson had been rescued. The police arrested Phil Madison, searched, and found Julien, her husband. She told Bella, Phil's wife, that she was heading for friends in Portland, but in reality, set out for San Francisco, then on to Hawaii. She no longer trusted Bella and had seen a change in her over the past few years.

Feeling extremely relieved that day upon arrival in Honolulu, she had then organised transport to Maui, there to re-invest herself, keep low, stay out of the limelight.

But over time, she began to think, began to look back, began to wonder how it had been that she had so readily assisted and agreed with Julien to take his daughter away from Alison. Had so readily stepped into a whole new lifestyle in Halifax, had so easily bonded with Julien's friend Phil and his wife Bella. But when the sudden appearance of Alison Hudson brought about a frantic plan to ensure the disappearance of the woman who was in search of her daughter, she began to feel uncertain, began to feel almost ill with what was planned. It was then that she began to see things in a new light, began to see a different side of Julien, a different side of his friend Phil and what was even more disturbing, was a different side to Bella, who she had considered a friend. A ruthless and selfish side.

Standing on the port side of the cutter, the wind soft and warm, she knew what she had to do. The engine of the old fishing boat chugged rhythmically over the calm seas, heading for Seattle. Before giving herself up to the police though there was something else, she needed to do. Two things in fact, the first was to say sorry, the second was to say thank you.

THE PAST; Period 1

The year 1762 – Oswego

Christoffer Rosenborg was thankful to the captain of the 'Antoinette' who had secured a place for him to travel with a small wagon train across to Boston. He would travel in the covered wagon which formed the middle part of the train, with an open buckboard wagon at the front and rear. Each wagon had two drivers, a further five men rode on horseback and Christoffer shared the wagon with three women. There were two spare horses making a total of thirteen and Christoffer noticed all the men were armed with revolvers and several shotguns were also present to deal with any form of assault that might come their way.

Just as the group were leaving the harbour area, Christoffer noticed the cargo on the dockside that was ready to be loaded onto the ship that had brought him here. He frowned, he knew cargo, he knew ships, and though the twin master looked fine in the morning light with its tall centre mast, he felt the cargo looked too much and too heavy for the ship. The wagons set in motion and as one of the three women he was with began to talk to him, he turned towards her, smiled and forgot about his concern.

A concern that the crew of the Antoinette didn't have. Several of them were new on board, had never been to Oswego before and whilst there were one or two that were, to some degree, interested in the town history, learning about the Dutch who had occupied it, followed by the French and then, currently, the British who had built the fort on the east side of the river, most were drawn to one of the three saloons. This late-night revelry was possibly a factor in not noticing that the cargo on the dock was more than the ship could handle. But in it went and the captain was happy with a well-paid shipment and the ship left the port mid-afternoon on a sunny day with a clear sky and a mild breeze.

The sun had not long gone down, but there was still light on the waters of the lake when a watchman, sat halfway up the centre mast as he was dealing with some mainsail issues, noticed a change. A dark cloud had appeared, and the sea was becoming choppy. He yelled his sighting to a deck hand below who in turn passed it on. But no one seemed particularly worried, until the cloud robbed the remaining daylight, rain came down and the wind increased dramatically within minutes.

The mainsail had to be lowered. Already it was beginning to billow and causing a rocking motion. The men scrambled, a crew trying to man handle the big sail, another set of men working on the forward sail and the captain, suddenly aware that all was not well, was shouting orders. He also became aware at that point that his ship was not performing as it should, not only was the rocking now much heavier and though the helmsman was strenuously trying to turn the ship into the wind, but it also just wasn't reacting well. The rocking became more a rolling and though several times the ship did roll back to an even keel, it was sluggish, it was slow, and it still wasn't directly facing into the wind. The captain realised the problem. They were too heavy laden, there was too much cargo.

In the next twenty minutes the darkness overwhelmed the remaining light. The rain increased in strength and the wind came in and whirled about, like a tornado. The ship wallowed in the waves. The mainsail was torn from the grip of three of the men taking two men with it over the side as they had become entangled in the ropes. The captain no longer shouted any orders, he watched, hanging on the starboard rail as the ship rolled over onto the port side, it was a slow roll. He and two other men nearby him, watched as the tall mast swayed and all of them just knew, the ship would not roll back as both masts hit the water. One man lost his grip and slipped across the deck and into the water. The captain clung on to the rail and watched as the ship took on water, as it slipped beneath the by now very choppy waters. Then the starboard side slipped down, strangely as the ship sank beneath the waters, it righted itself and then sank down, in an upright position. The waters were cold, many of the crew were unable to swim, though even if they could, as some of them did, they were too far out, there was no way to swim to safety. The captain clung on to the rail as the waters reached and overcame him. He was going to die, this he knew, but he was not letting go of the rail, was not letting go of his ship. Once most of the Antoinette was under the water, it steadied and then slowly sank straight down, the tall mast came right back out of the water. Totally upright now and the last piece of the ship to vanish beneath the waves.

The captain and his crew did not survive long in the cold waters and by the time the ship had sank straight down and then settled on top of a previous shipwreck, they all had died, the captain still, at least for a while, clung to the portside rail amidships. Other bodies were trapped inside and still others began to float back up to the surface. Loose ropes and cables swayed and swirled in the cold and dark waters and just over a hundred and eighty years later, these would cause trouble for a submersible, tangling and twisting it, ensnaring it like a prey of the deep.

THE PRESENT; Myrtle Creek

Thursday 4ᵗʰ of March

It was raining and it seemed apt, it was how she felt as she stood, holding an umbrella that had been in the boot of the rental vehicle, and let the tears just roll down her cheeks. She looked at the tombstone, and smiled through her tears, for not only was his name neatly carved in the marble, but in brackets at the bottom, the word 'The Searcher' had been chiselled in.

Since her arrival in Hawaii, having successfully made her escape, she had, after settling down into a new apartment, begun to re-evaluate her life, in particular, how she had drifted so far away from her family, how had it been she had become who she was. Determined to put her past behind her in so much her behaviour and direction, she still wanted to put down in words, a report, she thought to herself. Like a school report, she had mused and smiled. Settling herself down at the dining table one evening, she began, and took herself back to when she was at high school. Bringing to mind recollections and reflections of that time, a lifetime ago, yet, when she began to write down these thoughts, they came to her as if they only recently occurred. High school. Lincoln High school, situated in the northwest of Portland, Oregon. She was a year behind her brother. Robert. It wasn't until he had been at high school for nearly a year, that a caring teacher realised that it might be wise to get some medical prognosis for him. Not that he was rude, or abusive, or disruptive, on the contrary, he was mostly quiet, very rarely showed any emotion, but often his mind would not be able to concentrate on the subject taught. Yet he was smart, able to focus intently on some matters. His parents agreed and so it was discovered he had a form of Aspergers.

She stood by his grave. Still crying. 'Sorry Robert' she whispered, letting the tears just flow.

She had not been able to bond well with him. Once at the high school, she did hear of him being bullied, yet, ashamedly, did not care then. There was quite a bit of bullying around at that time. She recalls the tyranny of the ABC girls. But had decided to not team up with any group, not to get involved, but to keep her head down and study. A boy in her class was also a victim of bullying. Standing there, in the rain, she wondered, had there been times, when she could have stood by him, supported him? She had not.

It was a shock, to her, to the whole school when the boy had committed suicide. A note he had written was read out. There were many tears, many red faces, guilty faces. She had, she recalled, been both sad and angry. But had she been angry with herself? She had not been one of those bullies, but she had also done nothing to stop them. Sandra, spoke in a whisper again, 'Sorry Robert, but I'll try and make up for my behaviour'.

With that she turned and headed back to her rental car. With her own name very likely still being in the police system as being wanted, she had very cleverly, she thought, although with the help of this new friend she had bonded with over these past few years in Hawaii, made an agreement to use her credit card and identity to be able to travel back to the mainland. A temporary arrangement, she assured her friend as she had also told her of what she had done and was now going to do. Starting the engine, she put her seatbelt on and checked the satnav having punched in the next address. Roberts house, though having done careful research, she knew it now belonged to Roberts high school friend, Thomas Klaassen. She faintly recalled him but would not have recognised him if she fell over him. She also knew about a young woman, named Claire, who also lived there. Would she be home, would he be home. She drove the short distance and parked the car. 'Right' she said to herself, getting out and heading for the path, 'time to set things straight, time for amends. Time to say thank you. She walked up the path toward the front door.

Claire, having not long ago returned from the store and shaking out her umbrella, had noticed the car arriving, taking her face mask off she watched a woman getting out and heading towards the house. In the light rain she huddled into her raincoat and came up the path. Claire opened the front door and watched the woman walk up the path. She seemed familiar, but she didn't know why. Saying nothing, she stood and waited, thinking about the day when Thomas had walked up the path, seemingly a lifetime ago now.

Sandra suddenly noticed, looking up towards the door, that a woman stood there. 'Hi, you must be Claire' she said, then stopped at the bottom of the steps that led to the small front porch. Then, deciding to carry on speaking, 'I'm Roberts sister, Sandra, I really need to talk with you, first of all to thank you, but also, I have some important information to share.'

Claire saw the family likeness, also noticed her red eyes, she had been crying. 'Come in, out of the rain' she said, wondering what kind of information she might have.

Claire stepped aside to let her in, then closed the door and led the way to the kitchen. 'It looks like you could do with a coffee?' she asked, turning to face Sandra.

'Please, yes, thank you, I… I have just visited my brothers grave…. thank you, for being there…'

Claire proceeded to fill two cups from the prepared coffee jug, 'Milk?' she asked.

'As it is, that's fine, thanks, listen, there is a lot I would like to know, but the important things first, do you know about a girl called Terri?'

'Terri? Alison's daughter?' Claire asked, then, without waiting for an answer, 'I know the story of what happened, I mean, with you and…'

'Me and Julien, Terri's father? but no, I mean, wait, you know about that?'

Sandra answered, then without giving Claire a chance to say anything, went on,' Gosh, I figured that you may have heard something, perhaps through Robert who knew about Terri being taken from Portland, but you seem to know more?'

'A little, I know about Sam, Sam Price, the man who helped Alison get her daughter back…and about your confession letter…' Claire said, looking directly into Sandras's eyes. She noticed they were tearful and couldn't help seeing the look of guilt on her face.

'I don't know anything about a Sam,' Sandra said, then continued,' but do you have any idea why it was that we took Terri away?' Sandra asked, her voice sounding a little broken. Then, in that same broken voice said, 'I think that Terri could still be in some sort of danger….'

Claire frowned, then, thinking quickly, she immediately acted. She grabbed her phone which was on the kitchen counter and pressed some keys.

'I'm ringing Tammy, she is from New York, she knows Terri, would know how to get hold of her, I only spoke to her recently, so I have her…. Hi, Tammy, …yes, it's Claire, sorry to trouble you, but would you know how to get hold of Terri?'

After listening for only a moment, 'What? really, I, well, she's okay?'

In New York, Tammy answered, 'Yes, she is, has something happened Claire?'

'Robert's sister, Sandra, is here, sort of out of the blue, she was married to Julien, and I think you know the story?'

'I do, isn't she wanted by the police? be careful Claire'.

'Oh yes, I'm fine, but Sandra thinks that Terri might be in danger.'

'May I speak with her?' Tammy asked, feeling concerned.

Claire passed the phone over to Sandra.

'What do you know, why are you there, better not harm Claire….' Tammy began, with Terri now having arrived in the lounge where Tammy stood by the panoramic window overlooking Central Park.

'No no, I'm here to make things right, and, well, I will turn myself in the police soon, but I came here to visit my brother's grave, I also have never told anyone as to why, at least I'm pretty sure I know, me and Julien took Terri away from Alison…'

'Do you know about Bella Madison?' Tammy interrupted.

'Bella?' Sandra asked puzzled, 'yes, I thought her a friend once, why?'

Tammy related the events, the attempted murder of the Canadian detective, the death of the former deputy sheriff of Harris and the death of Karina West, finishing with the sighting of Bella in San Francisco when she had attempted to see Terri at work.

Sandra took in all that was told, then said, ' I am so sorry, I should have mentioned this in my confession statement, I didn't think of it when I was writing this confession, didn't consider that it mattered anymore, but it sounds as if Bella is quite desperate! But I don't know why she should be…goodness, I am glad Terri is safe, but Bella is still out there?'

Tammy calmed down a little beckoned Terri over, put her arm around her and said to her, 'This is Sandra, Robert's sister, she with Claire, 'then to Sandra, 'I have Terri here with me, you are on speaker phone now ….'

For a moment there was silence, then 'Oh Terri, I am so sorry, for….well, I can't apologise enough, but hearing about what has now happened, well, I think I know why she wants you, I believe it must be for the same reason that Julien wanted to take you away from your mother, his brother Nico helped, so did I of course, and I will face whatever punishment comes my way, that's why I left Hawaii, came over to hand myself into the police and to tell the whole story'

It was Terri, slightly blushing, but hearing the emotion in Sandra's words, answered, 'I got a call from mum, she had a call from Sam, saying that it had been this Bella woman who had been behind the abduction of the police detective, and it was Nico's wife, Debra, who started the suspicious activity when she asked about the whereabouts of my mother, she, that is this Bella woman, appeared at my work, I was suspicious, didn't meet with her, but managed to take a few photos of her, that's how mum knew who it was, and so, Tammy offered a safe place here, she came and got me… but why is it then, what do you think the reason is that she wants me?'

THE PAST; Period 2

The year 1938 – Rochester – New York State-USA

It was coming up to half an hour past midnight. The Ford drop-side truck, drove slowly over the gravel road and stopped when a man stepped in front of the vehicle with his hand raised. The windscreen wipers were working hard to clear the heavy rain and the driver applied the brakes and awaited further instructions. A face appeared at the driver's door, and he was told by signals to remain in the truck and turn the engine off. Two men then unbolted the right-hand drop-side and lowered it. There was a line of overhead lamps that swung slightly through the force of the rain. A light was placed about every ten feet and before the driver lost all visibility through the windscreen, he noticed the row of lights led to a building some sixty feet or so further down.

The two men, wearing heavy rain-jackets, with hoods, wearing strong gloves and heavy boots, worked in unison, not saying a word, manhandling the various crates onto a flat-bed trolley that stood on steel rails. The boxes were of different sizes and shapes and a total of fourteen were placed on the trolley. One of the men then released a brake-lever, gave a push and the trolley moved smoothly on the gleaming rails, descending slightly towards the building.

On the other side of the large roller door, two men awaited the next trolley. Pleased they were on the indoor shift, rather than to be out there in the rain and wind.

The rails ran on for some eighteen feet to where sturdy buffers would end the run. The men heard it coming, then it appeared, the wet boxes gleaming in the many overhead lights that hung on the curved ceiling of the vast hangar. The men slowed the trolley down, then moved quickly to unload, before rolling it back towards the roller door, where now, two men were awaiting to heave the flatbed back up the slight gradient to receive more goods from the next lorry to arrive.

The vast corrugated iron building was divided into three sections. The main hangar, where the goods would come in and where on either side of the steel tracks men and women were busy along long tables and benches unpacking, sorting, and then marking the goods to reach the right department, where further work would be carried out to assemble the many components that were arriving. This was all done in the second section of the large building, where many tools were hung on racks and some heavy machinery was set up. This was the side of the building that led to the lake. thirty feet or so from the large outer roller door, was a deep trench, it was six meters wide and nearly five metres deep, filled with the water from the lake, much like a boathouse, but more on an industrial scale. The third part of the building ran along the left side, it housed offices, a canteen, a boardroom and five sleeping quarters, each with four bunks, plus two further quarters, a twin and a single.

Even at this hour, having now gone well past midnight, there was activity everywhere, not only with goods coming in and being sorted, but there were acetylene gas torches working away, there was hammering and assembling.

Commander Vernon Webster was on duty during the night shift. This was their busiest time at present, with so many deliveries coming in, so much to unpack, to check, then to prepare for assembly. Standing upon a metal gantry that ran practically the whole length of the hangar section, he would pace up and down, often smoking a small cheroot as he watched his team working below, checking a schedule he had on a clipboard he carried, he would be in regular contact with the chief petty officer, Billy Cartwright, who was on the floor below, also with a clipboard and also walking everywhere and keeping a check on progress. Every now and then looking up to give a nod to the commander.

Due to the secretive nature of the project that they were working on, it had been decided that to minimise disruption in the nearby towns, that shipments would arrive at night, and that work would be carried out during the period between around eight in the evening and six in the morning. Later, it would also be at this time, when tests would be carried out. On the waterside of the building, where crews were building a vessel, Master Chief Ben Cutter was in charge. He had a desk in one corner, with filing cabinets and drawing boards. Here he would sit, study the plans, then check on the progress. A detailed form had been prepared. A time schedule. Lighting another cigarette, he was happy to place a tick in another box. It was all going to plan.

Come daybreak, most of the work would stop. The crew would eat and sleep. A crew that was divided into teams of four. Four that would be on the unloading shift, outside, not a shift to be on this night with such heavy rain and cold wind. Then a team of four would be accepting the goods through the roller door and place them on the benches on either side. A third team of four, with two on either side of the rail tracks, would unpack, check the components, and deliver them to the right area. Then a fourth team, these were always in the assembly section, constructing. They were skilled in this area, unlike the first three teams who would rotate. Finally, there was a team of four who were the brains, the scientist, the engineers, and the developers of what it was they were assembling. The commander had his own quarters, and the Master Chief and chief petty officer shared the last quarters.

Not all the crew were based inside the large, corrugated iron structure. In Nearby Rochester, though a little to the northwest of the town, close by a small settlement of a group of Mennonites, stood a large mansion near the lakeside. Here were based a support team, including cooks to prepare meals, a cleaning crew, and a medical team of three. Also, there were two female divers, both extremely well trained in their craft, brought in from Hawaii, they would be needed later in the project. All of them, as well as those on base, all having signed documents that they were not to disclose any information whatsoever, this covered in the espionage act, the US version of an official secret act.

It would be during the daytime that a special dedicated team would be allowed on base, to bring food and bedding and towels and any needed cleaning equipment.

1938 rolled into 1939 and the tension in Europe grew, the fears of war being imminent spurring the commander and his team on to get the project to a point of testing. It was all action during the night shift, hardly a moments let up, the teams worked well in unison and without exception, everyone would be glad when morning arrived, and they could get to their bunks and rest.

Thursday 4ᵗʰ March

Constance Shelton returned to her cell after the lunch time meal and lay down on her bunk. Relieved, safe, at least for a while. She had made good an arrangement she had made some time ago, a financial arrangement for those who would help her escape. The escape had gone well. Her goal at that time had been to silence a young man named Eddie. Eddie Philpott, who was heading for Albuquerque to give himself to the police, but also, to share some vital information regarding the stolen golden coins. She had heard of this news from one of the inmates. She had made a deal then, a reward for getting her out. She had been successful, had been ready, was awaiting the bus that would bring him from Flagstaff. But the police were there also. She thought she had outsmarted them, thought she was well disguised, but she had been spotted. By miss Alison Hudson. She thought back to that scene, shivering slightly when she recalled that she had been ever so quick in response, had been so close in stabbing the woman, but a hand had grabbed her hand. A powerful grip. Mr. Simon Lightfoot. Closing her eyes she visualised them. They had, between them and with the help from a man in Oregon, a Robert Pentegrass, and a man from New York, a medical examiner, named Raphael Morton, put together a case of the actual events surrounding that tornado strike on the archaeological group. It was in fact, after hearing the full report, that for the first time she had realised that all had not been as she had been told it was by her son, by Conrad.

Knowing the whole story now, of what had happened back in 1988, she felt, for the first time, ashamed. Turning onto her side in her bunk, she sighed and though she had been ill several times, after hearing the full story and receiving a new prison sentence for her part in it, almost two years ago, she tried very hard to get on with life. Occasionally crying herself to sleep, most unlike her as she thought herself a strong and commandeering woman. But now, now that the inmates who helped her escape that day, had been paid, receiving funds after their release, having served their time, it was time to plan again. Her son, Conrad, who had lied to her, who had merely enticed her with the easy opportunity to obtain a vast amount of gold coins, and who had already drawn in the Dean of the college, a man she had been having an affair with, persuaded her. Too easily. In hindsight, she knew now that her son knew of the affair, knew how to manipulate people. She also knew, from friends, who had warned her that she was too easy on him, that he was spoilt and arrogant, but she had not cared. Her marriage was not at all going well, her husband had strayed, she knew this, but she had the money, she had the wealth, family money. So, she played around, began an affair, and the opportunity of obtaining these gold coins was too good to pass up.

Constance turned over on to her other side. She was glad she was in a cell by herself. Having paid her debt, having by doing so kept her standing within the in-mates, of a rich woman who paid her dues, no one would bother her. Constance now began a new plan, what to do next, for later today she would be in court, she had a lawyer, a good one, and felt sure that she would likely be set free, and her punishment would be time served, plus a fee, court costs and the like. Fine, it would be better than serving another two years.

With the help of a close friend, one she trusted and had known since school days, the very one who had admonished her for being too lenient with her son, she had secured her finances. Her husband was no longer her husband. The freight and removal company she owned, was sold, further finances in a secure bank. She had no other children. Her son was dead. It was now, just her, and again shivering at the thought that she nearly stabbed that woman that day at the bus terminal, she once again turned onto her back. Time to repay, time to do something right. She had not always been this selfish, this greedy, this arrogant person. She closed her eyes and again tried to stop the tears from coming. It had been her son that had killed the professor, it had been her son that had killed his fellow student, it had been her son who had coerced others to do the things they did. She opened her eyes, got up from her bunk and thought of the professor's family, of her daughter Millie, who had been part of solving the mystery, she thought of the parents of the student that was killed. She knew that her, one time lover, the dean, had fled to Spain, but had succumbed to the covid virus. Yes, she thought, sitting up and swinging her legs from the bed, she got up and sat down on a chair by a small desk, it was time. And her first stop was going to see Miss Alison Hudson. Checking her watch, it was less than an hour before the court hearing.

Meanwhile in San Francisco Bella Madison had to re-think her plans. She knew now that she was a wanted person. Yesterday, driving back to the international airport, she had thought about her options. How to discover where it was that Terri had flown to. Who was that blond woman who had embraced her so familiarly, where was she from? But Alison had not gone with them, that meant she could still be a good leverage, however, having then changed her mind about returning the rental, she had headed for the address she had for miss Hudson, only to find, that when she arrived in the street, she saw Alison up ahead, talking with two people, a man and a woman. Bella just knew, these were undercover cops. There was obviously a security detail on her. Quickly stopping by the curb, she watched for a moment, thinking through what her next action should be. It was very probable that her rental car was in the system. Somehow, she had been discovered, but must not dwell on how, she admonished herself softly, think!

Seeing an opportunity, she reversed the car into a driveway, then drove away. Get rid of the rental, get a new identity, and wait for an opportunity. She still had some contacts here in the city from when she and her husband Phil had lived here.

Whilst in Moncton.

Detective inspector Karen Saunders was driving. Sam was in the front passenger seat and Chrissie sat in the back. They were heading for the town of Harris. Sam was recalling, as they drove, when he first arrived and settled in Moncton, when he had a call from the auction house to visit a potential client in Harris. What a mystery and adventure had unravelled since that day. They were on their way to visit Debra Rozzini. Having now identified the woman who had been the leader in the abduction and attempted murder on the detective as being Bella Madison, having now also had it confirmed that both the ex-deputy, Dusty Kerr, and the nurse, Karina West had died in the car accident, which, was caused by a small explosion that had been placed under the driver's seat. An explosion that had to have been detonated within a small range. It was undoubtedly Bella Madison who had done that. They found an abandoned car near a field where witnesses say a helicopter had landed in the evening. Karen's weapon, that she had held and had pointed at the intruder, was also found in the wreckage. Further investigations were under way, and it was discovered that a woman had boarded the helicopter and had been flown to Toronto.

They reached the top of the pass from where the road wound itself down towards the town. Sam noticed the police tape was still up where the car had gone over the barrier and into the ravine below. In the back, Chrissie saw it too, and thought how ruthless this Bella Madsion was. She was glad that Terri was now safely in New York, but Alison could still be in danger. She hoped that they could get some answers from this Debra woman.

At Karen's request, Sam and Chrissie were accompanying her. There was a shortage of staff, the crew at the southern police station very much involved alongside a person from internal affair, delving through old cases and looking for further evidence against the detective inspector that had suddenly disappeared from the radar. Of Murray Canney there was no sign, last known sighting was now confirmed as Miami. Her own team, as well as with the day to day running, were investigating the car explosion, the manner in which Karina west had managed to escape from prison and tracing back the movements of former deputy Dusty Kerr to better establish the link between them all. An officer had also travelled to Halifax, to talk with both Julien Rozzini and Phil Madison. As she had thought it unwise to see Debra alone, Sam, who had met the woman previously, had offered to come. Chrissie insisted on coming too. The newly appointed detective inspector was glad of their company. She was still trying to shake of the ordeal on the ledge, focusing on what needed to be done and not on the fact that she nearly died. Yes, she was glad they were with her, as she drove into the town of Harris, recalling the last time she had been here. Checking the sat nav she followed the instruction to get to where Debra Rozzini lived. Throwing a glance at Sam beside here and catching a glimpse of Chrissie in her rear vision mirror, she smiled. Yes, she was sure glad they were with her. With their company she didn't feel out of her depth, once again pushing the thoughts of her ordeal to the back of her mind.

THE PAST; Period 3

the year 1941 – Lake Ontario

'Depth 350 feet' Chief Petty Officer Billy Cartwright called out, using the microphone attached to his helmet. He sat in pilot's seat. The cigar shaped submersible, a little under five metres in length and only one and a half metres at its widest was on a test run, it's second. It looked much like an underwater zeppelin. It had a weighted keel and two small wings near both the aft and bow to keep it level.

Divided into two compartments, the pilot seat was in the rear section, accessible via a hutch that could be accessed from the outside by a countersunk wheel in case of emergencies. As the submersible had a wide turning circle, the battery powered engine was able to quickly reverse. The pilot seat was able to swivel and by the action on a single lever, the pilot would be able to reverse the engines, turn around and steer in the other direction, again with all the relevant screen and equipment to hand, mirrored on both sides. The pilot controlled the speed, the descent, and the direction, guided by the various instruments on the panel that was in front of him, regardless of which way he was facing. The front compartment was also accessible via a hatch. The seat here was fixed and the instruments all in front and to each side of the occupant, in this case seaman Albert Green, provided a huge ray of information as well as the controls for the weapons. Sonar, radar, and radio providing a range of information. The armament on board this small submersible were two torpedoes, one lined on each side in an encased tube. These could reach a range of between a thousand and twelve hundred metres, depending on sea conditions. '350' check' was his reply.

They had launched less than thirty minutes ago and once free from the interior dock built into the large naval building, they had turned east and had begun a slow descent, heading for the lake's deepest part, the Rochester Basin.

'Air pressure, hull pressure and engine power all reading normal' the pilot, like his colleague in the front wearing full navy uniform, reported.

'All instrument readings normal' was the reply. They were each in their own compartment, unable to see or let alone reach each other, for the centre of the submersible housed the engine and a variety of other systems including the top-secret long range underwater sonar that could anything in or on or even above the water with a range of an estimated ten miles.

'Depth 375, levelling out' Billy reported.

'375, check' came the reply over the headset.

Back at the naval facility, Master Chief Ben Cutter sat behind an instrument panel in a room that had been built above the docking bay. With him, this night, the clock on the wall showing it to be twenty past three o'clock in the morning, sat the chief engineer, the Frenchman Alain Dupuis. A fifty-two-year-old from Marseille with a vast knowledge of underwater salvage and exploration work, droughted in for this specific assignment. The first test had been two days earlier, again in the middle of the night, to test the engine, the manoeuvrability, the depth pressure, and battery performance.

This night's test was for the sonar and radar equipment, as a plane was due to arrive in the next hour or so, the task was to detect it. On the screens before them the two men could see that the 'Ontario One', the submersible having been officially dubbed with that name, a second was currently under construction, was indeed level at 375 feet, moving now at four knots and heading in a north-easterly direction. The crew on board knew of a plane that was to arrive but had not been told of its time of arrival, or from which direction it would come, it would be up their instruments to find out.

Both in the submersible and in the main hangar control room, the men were focused. It had only been a week ago that the Japanese had bombed Pearl Harbour. It seemed war was imminent.

It was two minutes before four am, when seaman Albert called out, 'Detecting a plane, small craft, coming in from the southwest, flying low'

'Copy that' the pilot, Billy, answered. 'Now at 180 feet, heading north, will turn and head back to base, keep an eye on the plane Billy'. Albert reported.

'Copy that, it's turning, coming in lower, looks like it might be aiming to land on the water'.

Back in the control room the two men watched the instrument panels and then looked at each other. They gave each other a nod of approval. Then Ben picked up the phone, pressed a number, then spoke to his commander. 'All systems check, the Portland cargo is incoming'.

Commander Vernon Webster acknowledged the call, then headed down to the dock area where he noticed a member of the incoming and despatch team, ready with torches to guide the incoming seaplane in. He nodded and checking his watch left to head to his quarters. The last compound arriving. A special number of ingredients from the Portland Chemical plant. Ingredients necessary to complete the weapon.

Meanwhile the Curtis Seagull plane descended and touched down on the calm waters of the lake. Zoltina Huanca, pleased to have reached his destination with the secret cargo, spotted the two torchlights, made a few adjustments and steered the plane towards them. Less than a hundred feet below from where he touched down, the Ontario One was also heading back to base. A second test run where all systems functioned to specifications.

THE PRESENT; Moncton

Thursday 4th March

The detective stopped the car. They were outside the house of Debra Rozzini. She opened the door and got out, donning her face mask. Sam also got out and Chrissie was about to when she got a call.

'Wait a minute' she said, getting out of the car and answering the call. 'It's Tammy'

Sam, now also having put his facemask on, and Karen, waited as they could see Chrissie was intently listening. 'right' Chrissie said, after ending the call,' interesting information, Sandra Pentegrass has turned up, out of the blue, she is with Claire, let me tell you what she has revealed….'

Less than five minutes later detective inspector Karen Saunders knocked on the door and moments later all three were sat down in Debra's lounge, Sam and Chrissie on a leather two-seater, Karen on a matching single chair and Debra Rozzini perched herself on the edge of the fourth chair. 'Please, no need for the masks' she had said upon inviting them in. She was slightly red in her face and her eyes were almost staring as she waited for the detective to speak.

'First of all, Mrs. Rozzini, why did you visit your health club and ask for the address of Miss Hudson, and secondly, we are aware that Bella Madsion is in San Francisco and a warrant is out for her arrest, so, do make sure that you tell us the truth. Sam here, you know, Miss Small is here as she has knowledge of this case and has just heard from Terri Hudson, Julien's daughter, who is safely in New York. So, in your own interest, talk.'

There were a few moments of silence as Debra looked from one to the other, then, the redness in her face having gone and beginning to look rather pale, said, her voice quite shaly, ' Bella asked me, she rang me, she said on behalf of Julien, that could I get the address of Miss Hudson in

San Francisco, she said the health club, where I am a member, was sure to have it. She said it was important to Julien, said he wanted to write her an apology… well, I, thought, okay, I can do that, but I didn't get it, rightly so of course, and rang her back that very day, said I would have to go to the police station and enquire, I said I didn't think that such a good idea… she said, that's okay, thank you and hung up.'

There were some more moments of stillness in the room, three pair of eyes focused on the Rozzini woman. She then, again briefly looking at each of them, finally focusing on the detective, said, 'I, well, I heard the news this morning, of what happened, to you detective, and, I knew you would call, but, truthfully, I had no idea, I had nothing to do with it, when Bella rang off, I thought that was the last of it, I honestly don't know anything, and, you say Bella is in San Francisco? Is, is Miss Hudson all right? '

Before answering that question, detective Karen said, 'Do you know why it was that Julien Rozzini, with the help of your late husband Nico, and a woman called Sandra Pentegrass took Miss Hudson's daughter away from her when she was in Portland? Mr. Price here told me that at the time, when he came to see you, said you were not aware of this event?'

'No, I didn't know about any of it, I met Nico in San Francisco, but not long after we moved up here when he purchased the mining company, until, until it all happened, I had never heard of Miss Hudson, or even knew that Julien had a daughter'.

'Was it in San Francisco that you then met Phil Madison and his wife Bella?' the detective asked.

'Yes, they were friends, well more Nico's friends really, they moved up here because Nico offered Phil a job with the company.'

'How old are your children?' Karen asked, having made a few notes on a jotter pad as the conversation had taken place.

Debra frowned briefly, then answered, 'Peter is sixteen and Martha is fourteen'.

Are they Nico's children?' was the next question.

'No, Nico is, was, my second husband…why?' Debra sked, her face going from pale to slightly red again.

Karen looked at Chrissie, then back at Debra and said, 'Miss Small here has only moments ago spoken to her friend in New York and also to Terri, I'll let her tell you what this is all about.'

Chrissie gave a nod to the detective, then looked at Mrs. Rozzini and related to her all that she had moments earlier related to Sam and Karen.

Meanwhile Tammy and Terri were in a cab driving from Tammy's apartment to Yonkers, to see a man. A medical man, a forensic scientist, a medical examiner based in Yonkers. Raphael Morton.

'Mr. Morton? My name is Tamara Wilson, I am a friend of Alison Hudson and her daughter Theresa,' Tammy had begun when connected and the call was answered, 'Now miss Alison Hudson knows a Simon Lightfoot and a miss Millie Parker, who is the daughter of the late professor Emily Parker, who, as you will know, died back in 1988, along with your sister Josie. I have read the full report of what really happened that day Mr Morton, including your findings, it is because of your knowledge that I am calling you'.

After the quite lengthy conversation Raphael had asked then to come on over and he would see Theresa. The cab reached the address and as they got out of the cab a voice said' Tamara Wilson?'

Tammy turned, looked at the man before here, somehow, from somewhere, recognised him, despite the coloured facemask covering the lower half of his face and was momentarily stunned, flushed a little, then found her voice, 'Yes, but please call me Tammy and this is Terri' she added as the young woman came to stand next to Tammy and had noticed the exchanging look, 'okay, you seem to know each other?' she asked.

Raphael Morton also blushed a little, held out and shook hands with both women, said, 'please, follow me, and' turning to Tammy, briefly studying her face although, like him she was wearing a mask, one with a range of psychedelic colours, then said, 'I think we may have met, though I cannot think where' then turned and continued his way.

'Yes, I think you are right, but I can't place you' Tammy said, smiling and following Raphael into the building. After having walked through a vast foyer and along two corridors Raphael suddenly stopped, turned, faced Tammy, looked at her intently for a moment, then said, 'bright coloured top, faded jeans, brown boots and a denim jacket too long in the sleeves.

Tammy looked up into his lovely brown eyes. He stood nearly six foot tall, his brown skin was smooth, his eyes warm and his smile was infectious. She remembered, had only briefly seen him, never actually spoke to him, but she now recalled, had brought him into her mind not that long ago, 'Stratford, Strauss and Helpin' the law firm, right here in Yonkers!' she said, blushing now and this to the amusement of Terri who was enjoying this scene.

Tammy felt her presence beside her, nudged her softly with her elbow.

'Wow, yes, that was, back in...' Raphael began, quite taken with this attractive woman before him, though also noticing the elbow movement.

'Six years ago, 2005!' Tammy answered, composing herself, she continued, 'may we chat later? Sorry, but... Terri...'

'Of course, yes, yes, Terri, you need some answers, so, come on, we are nearly there' and with that he turned, walked along a short corridor and then reached a door above which a sign read 'Forensics'. 'Once inside here we can take these blessed masks off' he said, opening the door, 'though please wash your hands with the anti bac liquid there' heading for the table and using the pump action bottle washed his own hands.

Quite some time later and some two thousand miles to the west in Albuquerque when Tammy and Terri were on their way back to Tammy's apartment, Constance Shelton was free and wasted no time. With finances to hand, she chartered a helicopter to take her to San Francisco. Her court appearance had been short, her lawyer had been good, and she was free to go. It was late afternoon when she reached the small airfield after having been to her house, had showered, changed and packed.

Meanwhile around nine hundred miles away as the crow flies, Alison Hudson had been adamant. Her house in a quiet suburban area of San Francisco, had secure windows and doors. She agreed with the policewoman that she would indeed dial a specific number that she had put into her phone, in case she heard, saw, or even smelled anything out of the ordinary. Anything at all. The policewoman had sternly said, with her eyes piercingly focused on hers. Though she was at least an inch shorter, Alison had seen the seriousness and promised, she would call. Closing and locking the door after she let the policewoman out, she then went into her lounge, watched her get into the unmarked car and drive away. Terri was safe with Tammy, she reasoned, though still not understanding, or knowing why it was she was a target. Why it was that she was so important.

She recalled the time when she was with Sam, in his apartment in Moncton, when she had pulled up the article on the laptop, the article showing that photograph of Julien and Phil, with their wives, Sandra and Bella. Alison smiled remembering that she had teased Sam as he had stared at the women in the photo dressed in skimpy dresses. Sandra being the one who had written that lengthy confession and had subsequently flown to Hawaii, not to be heard of again, and Bella, now identified as the woman who was behind the attempted murder of the detective, who was behind the explosion that had caused the car crash, killing the deputy and the nurse. The nurse who had injected and drugged her and had been part of the team that had left her to die on that ridge. A lifetime ago? No, just over two years ago! Why was this Bella woman after Terri?

Moving to the kitchen she wondered what she would make herself for dinner and again thought as to why she hadn't called Simon. Their last meeting had been wonderful, she had taken a train to Albuquerque, had been a little uncertain about how she felt, moreover, how he felt about her. But it had been good. Natural, no friction, no tension. Yet, that had been in April last year, she had stayed for a week, and though the parting was relaxed, with a promise to call and see him again, the calls had become less frequent, and she hadn't spoken to him since Christmas, when she had decided she couldn't see him for the festive season, that she wanted to spend Christmas with her daughter. He said he had understood. But neither had contacted the other since that day.

She had started a bookkeeping business from home, in view of the many restrictions due to the covid pandemic, she had easily found several clients who had been impressed with her accountancy diplomas and the work was steady. Preparing her dinner, she wondered why she hadn't told Chrissie she hadn't spoken to Simon for all this time, perhaps it was so as not to spoil her happiness with the upcoming marriage to Sam.

Sam. Had it been because she had fallen in love with him, and had given him over to Chrissie who, she knew, loved him so much, that she had not been able to, perhaps, fully commit to Simon? Still, she was reasoning in her mind, why hadn't he called?

Was he unsure, was there someone else, she knew that there had been, was he over her, totally, or not at all?

Little did she know that not two hundred yards away Bella Madison was watching her house.

Constance was in the air, flying a first leg to Phoenix, Arizona. From there, the pilot told her, they would head to Bakersfield, before the last leg into San Francisco. Estimated time of arrival, around midnight. Whilst in the air she made several calls and arrangements.

Back in Albuquerque Simon Lightfoot stood by the window in the lounge, watching the flow of the river that was a mere ten metres away and the traffic that was on the bridge to the left of his vision. Behind him, in the kitchen, Felicity Smith was preparing dinner.

THE PAST; Period 4

The year 1943 – Lake Ontario

Half a moon shone on the lake. It was a little after two am. A steady breeze from the east caused a moderate swell on the water. Four hundred feet below the surface, it was calm. Billy Cartwright was relaxed and pleased. Another good night of testing, this time with a full complement of missiles and the four new cylinders, attached to each side of the submersible both fore and aft. Small narrow canisters, that, when released, would ascend to the surface where the difference in pressure would activate a valve that would emit the gas into the air. A gas that would quickly grow into a cloud which would consume the air and create an almost vacuum less space where the air would be so thin as to be unbreathable.

His fellow submariner was again seaman Albert Green who sat in the forward compartment, also relaxed and happy with all the readings from his array of instrument. 'Ready to….' Began Billy, speaking on his helmet microphone, but a sudden movement stopped him, and he checked the dials. 'Al… we're descending, slowly, down now to four hundred and twenty feet, and…'

'Slowing down.' Albert finished, 'yes, also the cabin pressure is going up, what's happening Sir?'

'Not sure….' Chief Petty officer Billy replied, 'okay, we have stopped movement, except slowly going further down, four hundred and forty feet now'.

'Sir, 'seaman Green said, 'I can see an object on the radar, its narrow and we seem to be heading down to it, some hundred feet below us'

'Trying to increase power to the engines, 'came the reply. But the submersible could only slowly turn in a circle and still descending. 'It's like we have caught on a line or cable or something, we seem to be winding around it, trying to reverse engines…'

Back at the command centre on the base Commander Vernon Webster was puzzled, he saw the details on the screen before him, had heard their conversation and picked up on the worry in their voice. Had something snagged them? Had the submersible been caught in a net of sorts, a discarded or broken fishing net? He would wait a few more minutes before contacted them, feeling they needed to fully concentrate on what it was they were entangled in.

But it was they who opened the contact with base.

'Ontario One to base, we have a problem'.

'What do you think it might be?' the commander asked.

'I don't know sir, 'Billy answered, 'But we seem to be slowly turning, like a corkscrew and still descending, now at… four hundred and seventy feet.

The commander could see the details on the various screen at base. Then called them, 'You seem to be in a static position, but going down. It seems from our reading that one of the engines had now stopped?'

'Yes sir, …okay, the second engine also stopped now sir, still slowly turning in a circle, still descending, now at… nearly five hundred feet.'

'A reading on the engine mode reads high, something must have caught in the blades, snagged, then, causing that turning motion' Billy said.

'Nothing showing on any of my reading, Albert responded, 'but the thin shaft is now only about fifty feet below us, more shape is coming over the sonar readings now, I'm sure it's the mast of a sunken ship sir'.

'Understood Al' Billy said, we are at an almost standstill now, depth, five hundred and ten' The dials for the engine mode are decreasing, maybe we could try and restart them when the dial drops to normal?'

Commander Webster heard the question and looked over to the Frenchman Alain Dupuis, for any guidance.

'Yes, if a thin cable or rope has been caught on the blades, then a reverse thrust may unravel this, but wait until the dials are in the green, and then try just one engine first' was his answer, and over the speaker system Billy heard and understood the instruction.

'Understood sir, in the meantime Al can try and manoeuvre the cameras in the hope of spotting something that may be of help'

'Already on it' Al replied, focused on a screen in front of him and slowly turning the knobs that controlled the forward and aft cameras. Unfortunately, when the engine cut out, one of the search lights, the one situated on the keel near the aft had stopped working. Trying to direct the forward searchlight beam towards the rear, Albert Green had some light available, but the water at this depth was black and somewhat murky, and though trying for nearly ten minutes, with a hushed silence both in the sub and on the base, there was nothing to be seen that showed how the blades had been entangled.

The Ontario One just hung there, as if held by some invisible string, suspended in the dark waters, some fifty feet above a sunken sail ship. On his screen Albert could make out a lot more detail of the ship below them, it was the shape of a large sailing vessel and it seemed to be in an upright position, but, if his readings were accurately interpreter, it seems the vessel was sat atop another wreck. The mast of the top ship was now merely no more than ten feet below them.

'Just been doing some research' Commander Webster said, speaking over the com system, 'You seem to be right above the spot where, back in 1762, a sailing vessel, a twin master, named the Antoinette, sank in a violent storm, no survivors' As soon as he said about the survivors, he inwardly cursed at himself for being insensitive as it was now likely that his men on board the Ontario One would suffer the same fate.

'Sorry' he said, immediately after,' didn't…'

'It's okay Sir,' Billy interrupted, realising why it was that he apologised. It certainly seems to be looking like they would join their gravesite.

On the base the commander, the master chief and the French engineer could but look at the various screens and feel a sense of helplessness and fear that there might not be anything they could do.

Billy watched the dials for the engines and sat in silence. He wondered how something, that was obviously very small, could have caused them such a big trouble. A fishing line, a cable? But how would it have been there, hanging as if in mid-air? He failed to understand. After several moments he then spoke to Albert,' Seeing as we corkscrewed around whatever it is that ensnared us, most likely being some sailing ropes from the vessel below us, in a clockwise direction, I am going to give the starboard engine a big thrust in a moment, see if we can reverse ourselves out of it'

'Understood sir' Albert replied, still trying to see on the cameras if he could spot anything that might be of help. There was no communication from base for a few moments, then the voice of the French engineer came through the speaker system, 'Engine mode at normal, your plan is sound, go ahead and let's see what, if anything, happens'

'Understood' Billy replied, then' here goes.' He closed his eyes for a second, then pressed a knob and turned a dial on his instrument panel.

There was a humming noise for a moment, then a short burst of a whirring noise that began to vibrate the vessel. Then it all stopped. The blades on the starboard propellors ceased, the dial on the engine temperature mode rose quickly.

'No go,' Billy replied, will try the port engine' and without confirmation set about to do the same procedure. This time the humming was softer, and the whirring sound was not as loud. This time it seemed the propellor was turning smoothly and the engine dial remained on normal. But then the submersible began to move, very slowly, but going clockwise and descending. Billy switched the engine off and watched the depth meter show that they were now another five feet deeper.

Once again, the Ontario One stopped and hung in the water.

'Just over forty feet to the vessel below us sir' Albert said, his voice and tone soft and sombre.' If I'm reading this right, it seems that we have landed right on top the main mast of the sail ship below us.

'Understood Al, sorry my friend' Billy answered and at the base the three men glanced at each other. 'We can't get a spotlight down there, not that it would be of use, we can't get divers down there and the Ontario Two is not operational.' The commander said to no one in particular.

'An explosion perhaps?' Master Chief Ben Cutter suggested, 'The sub can take the vibrations, maybe this can break it free from whatever it is that's holding them?'

The commander thought this through for a moment, then replied, 'We do have some depth charges, but to accurately set it at the right depth, close enough to hope to break the sub free, not recommended, and though maybe the vessel can take it, an explosion at that depth would increase the hull pressure too much, I fear it could cause the sub to implode.'

'Yes, 'Alain agreed, 'the hull, already at that depth, would not take much extra pressure'

'Al?' Billy Cartwright asked.

'Sir?'

'Did you bring your bible?'

'Yes sir, always, just flicked it open, Ecclesiastes three, to everything there is a season, a time for every purpose under heaven….'

'…a time to die' Billy answered.

Both men fell silent.

THE PRESENT; San Francisco

Friday 5ᵗʰ March

Sixty-eight-year-old Constance Shelton picked up the rental car from the small airfield where the previous day Tammy's chartered jet had arrived to collect Terri and fly her to New York. Though it was a little after midnight, Constance punched in the co-ordinates that she had for Alison Hudson's address and headed there. Something was worrying her, was it a premonition, was it just anxiousness in meeting the woman she had tried to stab, was it because she wanted this meeting to be over with. She didn't know but drove steadily through very light traffic.

When she reached the correct street, she stopped the car to try and visually how the street numbers worked, and it was then that she caught a movement. A dark figure was stealthily walking by the side of a house three houses away from where she had stopped. The figure then disappeared around the back. Constance noted there were no lights on in the house, though there was a lamp on the porch that shone dimly. She then saw the number on the door frame. This was the house! This was where Alison Hudson lived. In her research to obtain the relevant information she wanted, thanks to a connection she had in the police force, she was aware of the incident that had occurred in Canada, was aware that the police were on the lookout for a Bella Madison, all this in connection with Alison Hudson. How it all connected, she didn't know, but at this very moment she was strongly aware, that it was right for her to be here, at this time. She felt strongly that Alison was in danger. She switched of the engine, got out and practically ran across the street, also snuck alongside the house where she had spotted the figure and reached the corner, peering around to observe the fully in black dressed figure, now obviously female by her form, hunched down and opening the back door with some kind of instrument.

Waiting, her heart beating loudly in her chest, she watched, then, as the woman went inside the house, she turned the corner and as quietly as she could walked quickly towards the back door. Listening for a moment, Constance then tried the handle of the door. She opened it, smoothly entered, and softly closed the door behind her. Whilst she might be heading toward seventy, she was proud of her fitness, the time in prison had made her stronger, both mentally and physically. In the dimness she saw the woman ahead of her, a glint showed that she had a knife in her hand.

Constance tried to see where light switches might be, then knowing they were within reach, she yelled out,' Alison! Wake up! Intruder!' then switched on the light in the hallway as the figure in black was on the staircase going up, startled at the sound of the yelling and the light.

Bella was not only startled, but confused and uncertain as to what to do. Her mind tried to frantically work out what was going on and what to do next. She saw the woman by the light switch, who was she, she wasn't from the police, that was for sure. Then another light came on, on the upstairs landing and Alison appeared, dressed in a dressing gown she looked down at the woman on the stairs, with a knife in hand, Bella! 'Well, so here we are Bella'! Alison said, her voice strong, with an edge to it and Bella could see the determination in the eyes of the woman she had come to coerce into reaching the girl Terri. It was when she was looking up the stairs, that Constance moved, she ran up and around the woman that Alison had identified as Bella, grabbed her black top just below her neckline and pulled with all her might.

Bella saw the movement, but wasn't quick enough to respond, felt herself been dragged backwards, tried to slash her knife arm around, failed and tumbled down the few steps, landing in a crumpled heap on the bottom of the stairs, having hit her head hard against the wall. Alison came running down and Constance stomped on the woman's arm which still held the knife, then lost her balance a little and stumble back into the hallway, relieved to see that the knife was no longer in the intruders' hand and that she seemed quite dazed. Constance reached into the pocket of her jacket and pulled out a phone, 'Here, call the police' she said, her breathing laboured and feeling rather shaky she handed the phone over to Alison who had come all the way down the stairs and had stepped over the semi-conscious Bella. Taking the phone, she realised who it was that was handing it to her. 'You?'

'Call the police, I know they can't be far away,'

'I will use my own phone' Alison answered, handing back the phone to whom she knew to be Constance Shelton, reaching into the pocket of her dressing gown, 'I have a direct number for my detail, '

Bella was moaning and started to get to a sitting position. Constance walked over to her and spoke' Make any more move to get up, and I will hurt you'! she said, her voice menacing, and Bella could see, that whoever this was, she was not to be messed with. Her head was throbbing, and her arm was hurting where the woman had stomped upon it.

'She is here! In the house! Under control but come quickly!' Alison said, her face was flushed, and she looked at the woman who was closely watching Bella. Sensing she was being watched, Constance turned her head, 'I will explain why I am here shortly' then turned to face the still shaken Bella.

Less than an hour later, the time now being just after one o'clock in the morning, Alison, relieved, sat down with a mug of tea. It was all very quiet. The police had come and gone. Bella had been arrested and taken away, and after a brief conversation with Constance, who had explained her presence and who had profusely apologised for her attempt at harming Alison, the pair had hugged and Constance had departed, in need of sleep.

Despite the hour, being around four o'clock in the morning in New York, Alison contacted her daughter Terri, who was instantly wide awake when her mother told of Bella intruding into her house. Then told the full story of what had occurred and that all the danger was now gone. 'Goodness mother, I'm so glad you are safe, I was going to tell you later, but I have lots of news to tell, especially why this Bella wanted to get hold of me…

Terri then told her of the conversation she had with Sandra Pentegrass, who had showed up in Myrtle Creek and met with Claire and told her the reason she and her husband Julien had taken her when she was seven, also telling her that Chrissie had been told as well as she and Sam and the detective were going to visit Debra, Nico's widow in the town of Harris. Then, not stopping for breath and gushing the whole story out, went on to inform her of her trip to Yonkers, the opportunity was there, all Tammy's idea, then shared her experience of the various tests she had done, and blood samples taken, from which the result would be given in a few days.

Finally finishing her story and saying how much she loved her.

Alison, phone in hand, then absorbed all that had happened, put her phone on the bedside table, lay back on the bed and began to cry. After a few moments she got up, refreshed herself in the bathroom and smiled. The mystery was solved. The culprit arrested. All was well. Stripping down she then pulled back the covers and slipped into bed. She decided that she would ring Simon later this morning.

Much later in Myrtle Creek, on Friday 5th March

Lea Vaughn drove into the street, checked the numbers, and stopped the car. She switched off the engine, grabbed her notepad and got out of the car.

Claire had heard the car, saw it drive slowly and stop. Well, she thought to herself, who is next to come walking up the pathway. Closing the door to the engine room, she headed downstairs and got to the front door and opened it.

She recalled the time Thomas had arrived, recalled just yesterday, Sandra Pentegrass arriving, and now, someone else she didn't know. She guessed the brunette that was heading towards her to be in her late thirties of early forties.

'May I help you?' she asked as the woman looked up to realise, she was there, in the doorway, having not noticed her before as she was trying to figure out in her mind as to what to say.

'Oh, hello, hi, I am looking for Robert Pentegrass?'

'And you are?'

The brunette stopped at the bottom of the three steps that led up to the porch, and answered, 'Hi, I'm Lea, Lea Vaughn, and a long time ago, I shared an apartment with Holly, who was, at the time, Robert's girlfriend?'

Claire didn't hesitate, she believed in timing, a time for everything, how timely was this woman's appearing, 'Please, come in, my name is Claire, and I have questions.'

'Okay, thank you, 'Lea replied, stepped on to the porch and passing by Claire to enter the house.

Claire closed the front door, said, 'please, follow me' and led the way into the kitchen, 'Coffee?' she asked heading for where a ready-made jug was standing on a hotplate.

'Please, just black, thank you,' Lea answered, placing her notepad on the kitchen counter.

'Robert passed,' Claire said, poring two mugs, 'almost two years ago'.

'I, I'm so sorry, I hadn't picked that upon my investigations, so, Claire? How are you....'

'Connected?' Claire interrupted, pushing one of the mugs towards the newcomer.

THE PAST; Period 5

Monday 4ᵗʰ June 1963 – Lake Ontario

Ahead was a white cloud, a low cloud, like a mist, which settled upon the water. It was bright white, and as they approached it, or as it approached them, it began to blot out everything around it.

'Get inside' Roger said, grabbing Natalie and taking her with him to the door, 'That looks like some sort of ice storm'.

'But there seems to be not much wind, the water is so calm' Natalie managed to say, as he reached and opened the door for her.

Roger took a last look before he entered the interior of the ship.

The whiteness was rapidly nearing. He shut the door, then shot past Natalie and headed for the wheelhouse. She followed right on his tail.

Captain Wayne Koppell didn't even turn his head as they both entered, totally focused on the whiteness that was now engulfing the bow of the Taciturn.

'What is it?' Roger asked, Natalie now beside him.

'I have no idea' Wayne replied. He reduced the ships speed and set the handle on the control to 'slow'.

The cloud reached the windows of the wheelhouse, and everything turned to white. Wayne stared straight ahead, Natalie had put an arm around Roger's waist, he responded by putting his arm around her shoulder. The three of them stood there, silently.

In the main lounge of the ship Nicolas Robbins was sipping a coffee, the smell from the kitchen reaching his nostrils and making him realise how hungry he was. It wasn't until her looked up from some notes he was reading that he saw the whiteness. Puzzled, he placed the papers on the table in front of him, stood up to investigate, but then a dizziness came over him.

In the kitchen the female chef and her young assistant suddenly just collapsed on the floor, the two gas rings on the cooker went out.

In the wheelhouse Wayne, Roger and Natalie looked in horror as each struggled for breath and were perplexed as to why. Wayne was the first to collapse, however, he did manage to crawl over to the speed controls and with effort, pulled the lever to a 'Stop', position, before totally succumbing and collapsing on the floor.

 Roger and Natalie, who still held each other, also crumpled to the floor and passed out.

In the lounge Nicholas lay on the floor, struggling to breathe.

The exploration ship, the Taciturn, was enveloped in the white cloud.

Less than forty nautical miles to the west, at the US Naval Service base, Kingston Carmichael was in the command centre on the second level. He was the only one present, watching the various monitors that were set out in an arch before him.

The facility had changed enormously over the past twenty years. The previous commander and crew were no longer present. The large machinery area, were once the Ontario One and Two were designed and built, now had a different array of equipment, various tables, electronic equipment and rows of racks containing a vast number of tools. The loading bay on the waterside was still there. The wooden jetty which had been there when Zoltina Huanca moored back in 1941, had been removed and the dock had been slightly enlarged with a new canopy built extending over the waters of the lake. The large trench now held two boats. There was no sign of the second submersible that had been near completion.

Kingston had graduated top honours from the Naval Academy in Annapolis two years ago and was given the rank of Master Chief to oversee the naval facility with the express role to ensure the protection of the Ontario Project.

Special agent Adam Holborn, from the Naval Investigative Service, sat behind his desk in his office next to the command centre. Four years now. He had been wounded in action and given this desk job, charged with perusing all the known details of the Ontario Project, all the personnel involved, all the equipment used, from its concept through to the test runs. Concluding with the accident of the first submersible.

The second world war had been at its height in Europe. The US were battling the Japanese in the Pacific. Thousands of men were sent across the Atlantic. Due to the accident, the facility at Rochester was closed, all the people were moved, and a small team of maintenance men kept the facility running.

When Adam had first reached the base, had first looked at his assignment, he had started his investigation from the point of its concept. The dossiers on the Commander, the crew, the engineers. He had walked through the vast hanger like structure, took in all the equipment and knew there was a lot to deal with. The project, though thought to be successful at one point and with potential to assist in the war effort, proved wrong once the submersible, the Ontario One, had been entwined and dragged down.

It had taken him nearly two months to study the first set of documents. He then opened the dossier on the attempted rescue. It was written in detail and Adam couldn't help but be drawn into the account. A steaming mug of coffee was left to cool down as he began to read the words written by Commander Vernon Webster.

'We have a problem' Chief Petty officer said. It was seven minutes past two am, it was August 17th, Tuesday. At the base command post, Master Chief Ben Cutter watched the various screens. The radar, the sonar, the tv screen that showed images from the four cameras built into the submersible. Ben cutter could see the images as Billy Cartwright swivelled the cameras around to see what it was that was causing their forward movement and what was causing their gradual descent. The light from two forward facing beams searching in the dimness of the cold water of the Rochester Basin. There was nothing captured in the lights that would identify the cause. In the rear of the submersible, seaman Albert Green checked and double checked the various instrument at his disposal. The gauges reading depth. The screens, two of them, that were lit up green and showed no sign of any radar contact. The sonar sounds pinging in his ears on the headphones showed only one cause, according to his expertise, this was the single structure, thin, tall, that lay some two hundred feet below them. But there was nothing that showed why the sub was now slowly going in a circle, and why it was descending.

At nine minutes past two am, the question was asked if any cause was known. A minute later the port engine cut out, another minute after that the starboard side engine also stopped.

The commander and master chief looked at each other, then back at the screens.

'Ontario One to base' Billy Cartwright spoke. In the forward compartment Albert listened in as the report was made, the finding confirmed.

'Go ahead Billy' Commander Vernon said, his voice with a hint of emotion, he had seen the screen, seen what the camera had picked up.

'A small cable, sir, quite thin, no more than a half an inch in diameter, it is anchored below us, likely from one of the wrecks down there, somehow, the cable was plied loose and was pulled upwards, we guess some four or five hundred feet, perhaps a large fish might have got entangled, tried to free itself and swam upwards with the cable, which then, at some point came loose, yet didn't sink immediately back to the bottom, but hung there, until we ran into it, it snagged on us somewhere near or on the tail fins. As we moved it became more entangled, ensnaring the craft and we have been winding around it, twisting tighter and tighter, and subsequently then also pulling us downward. Both engines had stopped, we don't know the reason why. The batteries will not last forever, we are still being drawn down, currently at….530 feet. Pressure is building sir, without power to the engines, we can't free ourselves, we have no way of cutting ourselves free either'. Billy Cartwright paused a moment, then continued, 'we are already too deep for divers, the second submersible isn't ready, we can only hope that we might get the engine powered up to try and pull us free, however, this might also put us in a worse position, the power of the engines could well accelerate our descent.'

Adam looked up from the dossier, noticed his mug of coffee and took a sip. Then, standing up, he walked around his office, through a window he could see the large bay beneath. The workshop where the submersibles had been built. He knew the outcome, knew the time spent, divers sent anyway. But to no avail. The engines had not been able to be restarted, divers had not been able to even dive close enough to affect a rescue. Air was running out. Adam returned to his desk, so many other dossiers to read though, to follow up on. But as he reached for his mug of coffee again, hoping to drink the las bit, Kingston Carmichael burst into his office.

'We have a problem! Huge problem! One of the canisters on the sunken sub has worked loose, has reached the surface, there is a ship, the one we have been monitoring, right above, the canister…

'Released the gas?' Adam asked coming towards him and together they went to the command centre. He knew about the Taciturn, knew who was on board, knew that the sinking of the Ontario One was being investigated, his orders were to follow and observe, there was little chance, according to his bosses, that they would discover anything, but observe.

'Look,' Master Chief pointed to the screens, 'the ship slowed and is now dead in the water, our sonars detect no engine noise.

'Any other vessels in the neighbourhood?' Adam asked, scrutinising the various screens.

'No, we have no eyes on the ship, it's, roughly forty nautical miles away, but, if the cylinder reached the surface, well, we know what it is supposed to do.'

'Yes, I am familiar with the workings, familiar with the outcome, you're sure it released from the submersible?'

'Yes sir, shortly after the sub was lost, they made sure that we had a monitor in place to make sure that if the canisters moved for some reason, we would know. According to the reports I've read, it took several attempts to guide these monitors down there, all with the help of the two deep sea divers that were part of the team. They were able to go down to a certain depth, then with lines and weights and magnet, secured these monitors. Just now, it was the one on the forward port side, which detached, a signal was received, only moments ago, tracking the movement of both the time of the canister release and the movements of the ship, I can see that it reduced speed, then slowed ever further, and is now in a dead stop. The position of the ship is very close to where I believe the canister hit the surface.

'Action?' Adam asked, looking at the young man before him.

'We need to get a boat out there, secure the ship, recover the bodies.'

Friday 5th March

'The bodies were recovered' Lea said.

'What? Really?' Claire asked, looking at the woman who had, only ten minutes ago, arrived. Claire had quickly taken to this woman, had explained about Robert and his search for Holly, which had set him on the path to try and find missing people. She told her about how she herself had been rescued, told her about a woman named Cynthia, about a man named Thomas and how she had recently begun a search for Holly, in memory of Robert, a search, she told Lea, that had begun when she found out about Holly's grandfather, Wayne, who had been lost, along with several other, when the Taciturn vanished into thin air. It was then, having intently been listening to Claire, that Lea spoke, saying that the bodies were recovered.

'Yes, let me tell you Claire, first of all thank you for sharing, getting our heads together we will surely find out what happened to Holly, you see, as I said, we shared an apartment, there was another girl too, but she went overseas, to France I think, anyway, not heard from her since, but, well, when I came home, that new year's day, there was a note, from Holly, it simply read, family emergency, have to go, will collect my stuff later, sorry, happy new year'

Lea stood up, they had been sitting at the dining table, just off the kitchen, looking down at Claire, she continued, 'We were quite close, we got on well, were at school together, but, well, led different lives really, anyway, my first reaction was that we needed to find another house mate, then, about two days, maybe three, I came home from work and noticed another note, Holly, or at least someone, had been there, taken all her stuff, left an envelope with two months' rent in it, and a note that said,' Sorry Lea, difficult family situation, hope to explain one day, love Holly'

'But you never saw her again?' Claire asked. Also standing up, then saying, 'Come on, we'll go upstairs to the engine room. Lea followed, answering the question, 'no, never saw her again'.

'So, why now? You must have done some research in order to find out about the ship that went missing, 'Claire said, punching the numbers on the keypad and opening the door.

'Wow, what an interesting room!'

'Please, have a seat, then tell me all you know, who recovered the bodies?'

'You say Robert searched for missing people? And worked from here?' Lea asked, sitting down in a comfortable arm chair across from where Claire had sat herself down after having collected a folder from the desk. 'Yes, he would be in here, practically all day every day. Listen, here I have a folder containing notes I had made and researched., regarding Holly, coming across the events on the Taciturn, captained by Wayne, Holly's grandfather, I also have discovered a report, put together by a Dutch journalist, Katja Wiersma, with the help of Holly's grandmother, Missy, who was Wayne's wife, I don't know how you have found out what you seemingly have, but, perhaps you could read this report, it is rather disconcerting, so much so, I spoke to Thomas and Tia about it, so….'

'Thank you' Lea said, taking the folder, then' I'll read this through, then I will share my findings, together we may have a clearer answer, I too am now a journalist, been working on this for a few years, off and on, but having not shared anything, though I understand your concern, I too have not openly shared this, so…'

Lea settled down to read the report. Claire got up, fired up the computer and set about to e-mail Thomas, informing him of the current development. Then turned and watched the woman read.

Looking up eventually and realising that Claire was watching her, she smiled and said' 'You have done well, this is some sleuthing Claire, and though I was aware of some of this, there are more details here that make this whole case, well, ….'

'Dangerous?' Claire suggested.

'We certainly need to tread very carefully, and we also need to find someone we can absolutely trust, here, let me share with you, what I have discovered' Lea answered, taking her own dossier from her bag. 'And might I possibly use the restroom?'

'Of course, it's down the hall, last one on the right' Claire answered, getting up to open the door and leave it open. Then sitting down to read, having also, a moment ago, received a reply from Thomas to say, keep us informed and take no immediate action, Tia is staying on another day, but I am nearly home'.

When Lea returned Claire looked up at her, said' I would like you to stay the night, we have a spare room, Thomas is flying over from Spain, and I agree, we need to be very careful'.

Lea nodded and sat down. Claire began to read, and as she previously was totally engrossed in the report by Katja, she was now equally so in this report written by Lea

The journalist, Lea Vaughn, wrote the account in the first person.

I have to admit that I was quite apprehensive. I had been let in to the building, a building that housed documents, naval documents, boxes and boxes of files that had not, as yet anyway, as far as I knew, been put onto computer files. I had a name, when I researched the disappearance of the ship, I came across several names, where to begin was a choice, I could go in the route of the shipyard that had built the ship, or actually, as I found out, had rebuilt, and adapted what once was a former icebreaker. But I was drawn to the fact that not fifty miles or so, from where the ship had vanished, there was an American Naval base, near Rochester. I opted to go down this route and hoped to find a file on the commander at the time, a Vernon webster. It had taken me several months of digging, but finally found someone who might be helpful, I shall not reveal who that person is, but it was this way that I gained access. It was a bit creepy, walking about the large warehouse with only a few lights. Torch to hand, my satchel over my shoulder I searched, and found a box with a title on it that intrigued me. 'Ontario Project'.

Claire looked up from the report and said, 'Ontario Project' It is what Missy and Wayne discovered when they were in their teens.

'Katja's report, that you discovered, also mentions it, yes it was Holly's grandmother, Missy, she knew, she had taken photos and Wayne had come across that label, please, read on' Lea answered,

I had to climb up a few shelves to reach it, but managed to get it down and placed it on a nearby fold up table, both the box and the table were very dusty. My heart leapt when almost immediately I found a file with the commander's name on it...

Claire was totally engrossed in what Lea had found out, regarding the Ontario Project. The submersible had, upon its return for a final test run, become ensnared in a cable of sort, which had twisted the craft and subsequently pulled it towards the bottom. Engines had failed and the sub had stopped dead in the water at close to five hundred feet. There was no way, no equipment to begin any sort of rescue, free diving was out of the question and even if that had been possible, there would have been no way to extract the two men, due to the pressure of the water at that depth. As the project was classified, the records were gathered and sealed. There was however a problem as to what to do with the armed missiles it had on board and moreover the four canisters with a new developed and highly dangerous gas. Air ran out for the crew and the submersible became their grave. Two nights later a small boat went out to the very spot, and guided by sonar reading, dropped a heavy cable like net to cover the site.

Claire looked up and asked, 'This was in 1943, this secret submarine?'

'Yes, the site was left, with the hope that the netting they dropped into the waters would cover and secure the craft' Lea answered.

Claire continued reading.

The information contained in the files that Lea read that night in the warehouse under poor lighting, made her forget the creepiness of the place as she was totally absorbed. The Naval Facility had a small file on Nicholas Robbins. *Canadian, aware of sunken sub, unlikely to discover but keep tabs.'*

They knew about the ship, Taciturn as well, but, as the report stated, what was about to happen was not foreseen. One of the canisters of gas attached to the sub, became dislodged, headed for the surface as it was designed to do, then released the gas which in turn created a white cloud, all at the exact moment that the Taciturn was entering the area. This was a disaster, moreover, it could be argued that perhaps the canister was released on purpose. Action needed to be done, and immediately.

Two boats were despatched in the early evening and radar showed, thankfully, no other ships on the lake in the area over the Rochester Basin at the time. The cloud of white had, by the time they reached the scene, evaporated, but the gas had done what it was designed to do. Three men boarded the vessel, discovered the bodies. The two-man crew on the second boat circled the area focused on the distant shore to ensure there we no witnesses. The three men on board the Taciturn got the ship moving and headed for the base. Though the ship was too long to totally fit into the dock area of the base, they managed to manoeuvre it just over halfway inside as it was wide and deep enough to accommodate the ship. Then all hands to the pump as it were to begin to camouflage the back half of the ship, so as to make it unrecognisable. Then the subterfuge began, the second boat had stayed in the very area where Taciturn had slowed to a halt, and from there, created some false signals that would create the illusion that the ship had disappeared from those co-ordinates.

'Wow, what a cover up!' Claire said, when she finished the report.

'Indeed, but how does it help, to find out what happened to Holly?' Lea said, 'surely it is connected, don't you think?'

'Yes, I do, but as you said, we must tread very carefully'.

In San Francisco after only a few hours' sleep, Alison rang Simon's number, then paced the lounge as she heard it ring.

'Hello?' a woman's voice.

Alison's heart pounded in her chest, her throat felt very dry, and she felt herself blush. Who was this woman? 'Oh, hello, is, is Simon there?'

There was a moment of silence, then, 'Are you Alison? '

'Yes'

'Hi, I know about you….' A pause, then, 'I'm Felicity Smith, I…'

'Yes, I know the name, Simon mentioned you…. Are you…' Alison said, feeling that what she indeed had thought, was now likely to be so, Simon had re-connected with this Felicity girl…

'Yes, I called in to see him, in the new year, and…well…'

'That's okay, anyway, just say hi from me, all the best….'

'Thank you, I will, you too… 'Fliss answered, feeling the awkwardness in the conversation. The connection was broken, and Felicity sighed deeply. She had seen a few photos of this Alison woman, a stunning woman indeed. But when she had called, that New Year's Day, he had welcomed her, they both felt the connection that had been there before, and it seemed only natural that they bonded again. She moved in with him three days later.

Alison stood still in the lounge. Phone in hand. Simon was no longer hers; she had a feeling, she was glad she had rung, she too had felt the awkwardness in the conversation with this Felicity woman, but she sounded nice, sounded friendly.

Taking in a deep breath, Alison turned, headed for the kitchen, and made up her mind, she then made the arrangements and checked when the next flight would leave San Francisco.

THE PAST; Period 6

The year 2011 – San Franciso

Josh De Garagoa was a mean-spirited man, approaching his thirty-eighth birthday. He was known to the police, had a criminal record for theft, disturbing the peace, running a brothel and illegal gambling. Pacing his plush apartment in an up-town part of the city, he was looking out the window and was determined to change his fate. He had a view over the harbour in the not too distant, watched the nighttime traffic for a moment and gave his predicament some serious thought. Another trip to the police station in the morning, another fee to pay his lawyer, another citation on his already lengthy record. Would they throw the book at him this time? Would he face prison time?

How could he possibly avoid this, was the question foremost in his mind as he kept staring out the window. Looking past his own reflection in the glass, he knew the answer. The witness would have to be eliminated!

Josh, having been giving the nickname, Posh Josh, considered a plan, a plan that sprung up in his mind and began to grow. A plan that not only would help him escape prison time, but, even better, would put serious pressure on one of his rivals in business. A night club owner named Phil Madison. This idea was starting to really appeal to him, as he walked away from the window heading for the kitchen, he pondered as to how to go about doing it. For the next hour he scribbled notes, checked data and called nearly a dozen people. Josh, although his given name was Jose, named after a forefather who had been an influential man in Bogota, Colombia, was slight in built, has a variety of tattoos on his arms and chest and relied on two even meaner than him, body guards as he went about town, for he was intently disliked, known for being abusive to women and demanding money from a number of vulnerable people for so-called protection.

A woman had been assaulted, had been left for dead, witnesses had come forward suggesting it was Josh De Garagoa, but the account had been too varied, and the police suspected that these had been made to incriminate him, some from whom they knew to be business rivals, other from whom it was suspected had come together in an act of revenge. The only true witness was the woman herself, but she was in hospital, and still in danger of succumbing to the wounds she had received.

After much thought and deliberations in his mind, after the string of phone calls and after having thought about the options open to him, he sat down, slumped almost, on the couch in his seventh-floor apartment. He was no closer to resolving his problem. The only upside was that, as yet, they had not arrested him, no doubt waiting for the woman to regain consciousness. Even though it was now close to midnight, he needed some air, headed for the hallway wardrobe opened it and immediately saw a solution. There, hanging on the far-left side of the wardrobe, was a sports jacket, an expensive jacket with the city's baseball team, the giants, emblazoned on the back and the logo on the front. Josh frowned, he pushed the garment next to it aside, studied the jacket and noticed it was stained. He suddenly felt his legs tremble and his heart pounding loudly in his thin chest. This was not his jacket. He nearly jumped out of his skin when there was a loud knock, in fact several loud knocks, on the door.

Less than a mile away, Phil Madison got up from the bed, splashed himself with cold water, put on a robe and went to the kitchen, leaving the woman he had recently married, Belle, fast asleep. He was disturbed because earlier in the day the police had arrived at his nightclub and had questioned him, in connection to a rape. Though he was, much like his rival Josh, known for being involved with illegal gambling, drugs and theft, and like Josh also had a criminal record sheet, he had, since marrying Belle, settled down and had promised her and himself, he would go straight from now on. The police questioning him, was a blow. Thankfully he had an alibi. Even so, according to the detectives that had called, they had witnesses saying that they had seen a man of his description at the scene.

He drank some juice from the fridge and a shiver ran down his back. He was suddenly worried, what if they could stick him with this crime. He had not been happy here in this city for some time, if it was time to move, then now surely, would be a good time. He would talk it over with Belle in the morning, and then ring a good friend who owed him a favour. Nico Rozzini.

Late afternoon the following day Isaac Javed called into the police station where Josh had been taken to and was being held, charged with assault and attempted murder. He was a defence lawyer. An expensive defence lawyer and had on previous occasion successfully defended Josh in court. This time it would not be so easy because the woman, an exotic dancer who had been raped and then assaulted, had briefly regained consciousness, had been able to make a statement to the detective present and had fallen back into a coma. Her testimony would be damming. Sadly, she never came out of the coma and died three days later.

The papers covered the crime, the death of the dancer and the arrest of Josh De Garagoa. Phil was relieved. There had been tension in the industry, his nightclub often been visited by rival businessmen, including Josh. Having contacted an old friend who owed him a favour, Phil and Bella felt it best to get away. He put the nightclub up for sale which was sold within three days. Then he and his wife took a holiday before heading to Halifax in Canada where he had been offered the job of warehouse manager by Nico Rozzini.

Pleased with the results of the sale, he and Bella flew to Miami for a week's holiday whilst a transport company packed all their belongings and shipped it to their new home.

Isaac Javed worked hard for his client, had an investigator searching for any clues and follow up on what, according to the police, the witness had said, before falling back into a coma. The statement given was that it had been Josh, who had taken her from the dancefloor that evening, had walked her to one of the changing rooms in the back of the establishment and had raped her. But, according to the very shaken dancer, he had left and someone else had come into the room, a young man. It had been him, who had hit her to the side of her head with a baseball bat. She didn't know who he was.

There was no doubt that Isaac would be able to keep Josh out of prison this time but was working on obtaining the lesser crime. His investigator was making a search for who this young man might have been that had assaulted the dancer, and why. The police, he was told, were also looking but couldn't comment on an on-going case. Isaac had several informants and investigators that he could call on, he chose this one because of her connection to the call girl and exotic dancer scene. Marilyn Montrose was a former dancer, now in her forties she enjoyed sleuthing but was the one who had approached Isaac, what had happened to the dancer was horrible and she wanted to get to the truth of that and find out who it had been that had struck her with the baseball bat. Glad that the slimy pervert, Josh De Garagoa was in prison, she was determined to find the second culprit.

Friday 5th March

Marilyn Montrose, now in her early fifties, had once more taken up the search for the gold. Ten years had passed. She had successfully tracked down the young man, Bartholomy Southall, nicknamed Barty, nineteen years of age. He had regularly visited the exotic club and watched his favourite dancer, Kiki, he was obsessed, had on several occasions asked if she would go out with him which she had, every time, courteously declined. But he wasn't to be denied, he was going to keep asking her. There had come a point when the manager had thrown him out, at Kiki's request. Then one night, when he knew she was going to be on, he bided his time, then when an opportunity arose, he entered through a back door that led to the kitchen area. He found a place to hide, close by where he knew the dressing rooms were. In his full statement to the police, he said that he saw her coming from the stage, head for the dressing room and then noticed a man had quickly followed. He didn't know this man, but the description he gave, matched that of Josh De Garagoa.

He waited, then eventually the man came out and left. He entered the dressing room, saw her and when she screamed at him to get out, he lost control, noticed a baseball bat right there, within reach.

In prison Josh was told of the chain of events. Though he would still be charged and imprisoned for rape, at least he was cleared of the murder. He still had no idea how the jacket, stained with blood that proved to be that of the dancer, Kiki, had made its way into his wardrobe, into his apartment. A damming piece of evidence. But in fairness the police detective on the case, felt it was too damming and too convenient and though having discovered that it had been planted there, and, by whom, when the actual culprit of the murder was brought to justice, he filed the information away and closed the case.

Marilyn was pleased with her catch, her boss Isaac, was pleased, but she had found something else. When searching for any clues in the apartment belonging to Josh, to which she had been given the keys by Isaac. She found some letters, old letters and with them some old deeds, documents relating to land in Colombia. This piqued her interest. Josh was going to prison, for at least five years, she figured. Marilyn took the papers she had found, which had been placed in a carton and shoved on top of a wardrobe in one of the rooms. Over the next few months, she studied what she had found, however, there was nothing of any value in the deeds she had come across regarding the land in Colombia, near the city of Bogota, which, she had learned, had once belonged to an ancestor of Josh, a landowner by the name of Jose De Garagoa. Nothing she could do about those deeds; they were no longer valid. She did however discover a report, written in Spanish, along with some letters, also in Spanish, which she translated. Threse proved more interesting, for they referred to a chest full of gold.

But however she tried and researched, she got no further other than the gold had at one point been in silver city, back in the year 1862. It wasn't until recently, in fact only a week ago, that she picked up on a special exhibit being held in the Albuquerque Museum of art and history, that she gasped and read the details. The gold, the very gold that had once belonged to the Garagoa family, had been stolen by Spanish soldiers and had eventually ended up in Silver City. Marilyn began to wonder if she could lay a claim on these, she would certainly try and after all these years she was once again on the search, deciding she would travel to Silver City to see if she could dig up any more information from that period. How had those coins, soon to be displayed in the museum, end up being buried for some one hundred and twenty-six years and be discovered by this Professor Emily Parker.

THE PAST; Period 7

the year 2014 – Monaco

Lea Vaughn decided she would change direction. Reaching for her satchel that she had placed on the seat next her, she opened it, reached in, and pulled out a green coloured folder. She threw a look outside as she heard the rain on the roof. A heavy downpour. She smiled as she saw people huddled down sort of running with their luggage trying to quickly board the train. She was glad she had arrived early and had settled down in a seat in the first-class compartment. An elderly man, whom, she noticed, showed signs of Parkinson disease with the right hand visibly shaking, boarded just ahead of her, also into the first-class section of the train.

He took the first available seats on the right, and smiled at her as she entered the carriage. She smiled back thinking that this man must have been quite the charmer in his day. She placed her small suitcase on a seat, opened and withdrew the satchel and then placed the case into a slot between the seats. Taking her coat off which she hung neatly on a hook provided, Lea sat down. Smiling to herself again as she thought about the man, with that contagious smile, she wondered if he still wasn't quite the charmer.

Another passenger entered, smiled at the man, walked on, and chose to sit in the seats two rows behind her. Lea gave her a brief smile as she walked past which she returned and busied herself in settling in. also taking her coat off and shaking her brunette hair loose, then sat down and too watched the rain as it suddenly came down. Lea took the folder and opened it, began flicking through the pages. The rain kept lashing at the windows, the wind had picked up and the sight of a blond woman running past, caught her attention. Moments later she entered the carriage, managing a large handbag and a mustard-coloured suitcase, which she almost threw onto the seat opposite, on the first set of seats on her left, then sat down and she too smiled at the old man who sat across the aisle from her. Lea watched as, two rows ahead of her, the blond woman was standing, seeing to her wet hair, and rummaging in her suitcase. A whistle blew.

And almost immediately the train set in motion. Lea opened the green folder and began to flick through the pages. She had come to France, had then travelled to Monaco in search of a story that would be of interest to the readers of the magazine for which she was a free-lance reporter. A magazine that was aimed at women, containing a vast array of fashion, and featured every month a woman who had made a history in her field in whatever occupation that was, especially from days gone by when often women were overlooked when it came to accolades of achievements. Lea had started her career when, after having finished college, she was taken on by a local Portland newspaper. It was her coverage of the woman's hockey team that had brought her into contact with Holly to whom she had an instant connection. When they again bumped into each other at the party of a mutual friend, a third girl, a retail assistant in a clothing store, bonded with them and only a week after that the three of them joined together and rented a very nice four bedroomed apartment.

So many changes, Lea thought, as she stopped reading and looked out of the window. The rain seemed to have eased now and she took in the French landscape as the train was smoothly speeding upon the rails towards Paris. So many changes, and when Holly had left a note that New Year's Day, thirteen years ago, though disappointed that she hadn't since contacted her, life went on. They soon found another girl to share the apartment with, in fact they found two, so all the bedrooms were now occupied, the rent was even easier and on top of that, she fell in love with the brother of one of her new flat mates. She worked as a journalist for several years, then had an offer from a newspaper in Seattle. By then she had married. He had an offer to work in New York, but she really wanted the job in Seattle. Neither backed down. They realised their bond and love for each other was not as strong as they might have hoped.

So many changes. Lea again looked up from what she was reading, threw a glance out of the window and wondered where the years had gone. She was now thirty-eight, worked as a free-lance reporter for a well-known magazine with its base in Seattle and had been well rewarded, both financially and with awards. Having been asked to do a piece of French wines Lea had flown to Paris, and when on her first evening, having settled on dining in a small bistro, tried a particular wine that was on their list, noticed it was from a vineyard in Monaco. Having always wanted to visit the principality, she decided then and there, she would investigate this business, established way back in 1590 by a woman named Viana Vanetti. The Italian woman had arrived in Monaco in 1578, had fallen in love and married a year later, her first born, a son, Pietro, was born in 1580 and eventually became a sea captain, his sister was born in 1586 and four years after that Viana set up the vineyard, naming it the Vanetti Vineyards. All this was interesting, and she had enough material to write a piece on this woman who had originally come from Rome. But it was when she was investigating the timeline of the vineyards, the history of it since it started, that she came upon the name Umbrego, who ran and operated the business in the early nineteen sixties. Following that name and that family, she then came across a Natalie Umbrego, and then she found something about this woman, who was, according to her findings, a reporter, which took her into a whole new direction. The woman had vanished, along with others on a ship called the Taciturn, in Lake Ontario. It was when following this strand, that she came across a name that she recognised. The captain of the ship was Wayne Koppell, and Lea knew, that this was Holly's grandfather.

So many changes. Though she had this article pretty well covered, had enough to put together a nice report and layout for the magazine, she knew that she had to follow up on what she had discovered. Was Holly's sudden departure connected to her grandfather? Lea closed the folder, placed it back into the satchel and sat back and reflected. Little could she even imagine that she was in close company to three people that she would learn about. The elderly man who had so charmingly smiled at her, was the forger, Robert Solari, the bedraggled blond woman who had arrived late, was a criminal, going at that time by the name Steffie Beartjens and the brunette woman sat a little behind her was Alcina Patronas who was at that time in search of the whereabouts of Sam Price.

A change of direction, she would focus on finding what really happened to her one-time friend Holly, and she knew that at the time she left, she had a boyfriend, Robert Pentegrass. That would be her first port of call.

Friday 5th March

'So that was the turning point, investigating one thing, then, out of the blue, something pops up and takes me in a new direction, finding that this girl, Natalie, was on a ship that vanished into thin air, that this ship was captained by Wayne Koppell, who I remembered, was Holly's grandfather, and I recall that she mentioned that story, so, it made me want to find out, what really happened, where did Holly go, and why did she never make any contact? '

'That's the way it goes with investigation,' Claire said, 'I sort of know how Robert worked, how his mind worked, the smallest of things could easily mean the greatest clue, but this was, what, six or seven years ago?'

'I know, time does get away with you sometimes, but I had bills to pay, I still needed to write stories for the magazine, and this investigation, well, it had to be done carefully and I was looking at it from an exclusive journalistic report, a scoop, though also wanting to make sure that Holly was safe somewhere. Eventually, having collected a larger number of clues and stories, one day I thought about her boyfriend at the time, Robert, I just had no idea that he had died, I did discover that he was known by the Portland police, as the searcher, surely some interesting stories there Claire, including your own, anyway, how about we team up, from what I gather we need to tread even more carefully now, in view of what you and I have found out.

'That would be great, let me get some fresh drinks, also, Thomas is on his way, and I'm not doing anything moving forward, until he gets here, okay?'

'Okay, I don't suppose I could eat something?'

'I do a mean omelette' Claire answered, 'come on down with me, now that you mention it, I am hungry too.'

'So, Lea said, as they were going down the stairs, 'tell me more about, this Thomas and Tia, did you say? Are they a couple?'

Meanwhile on board a flight to New York Chrissie was on the phone to Alison, 'You are no longer a couple?' she asked, looking at Sam next to her.

After listening for some moments, Chrissie said, 'Oh Alison, I am sorry, tell you what, Sam and I are going to New York, why don't you come up too? This Bella woman is now in jail, we can all come together and talk about it, also this doctor chap, who, I heard, Tammy is rather fond of, will have the answers, okay?'

'It's the decision I had also made Chrissie, thank you, I will see you there'.

THE PAST; Period 8

the year 2019 – Town of Harris – New Brunswick Tuesday 30ᵗʰ April.

At the police station the chief and his deputy were in deep discussion, slightly flustered and somewhat feeling uncomfortable. 'Nothing for it Slim' the chief, Faulkner Brown, said to his deputy, 'we need to get someone on that Yank woman, keep an eye on her, see what she does'

'I'll get someone there' Dusty Kerr replied, ' just observe?'

'For now, Mr. Rozzini will get back to me later today, with a plan of action'

Wednesday 1st May.

Alison Hudson stepped out of the train station, having looked at a plan of the city of Halifax, she turned left, past the bus station and walked over towards the waterfront. Eight minutes later she saw the building. A large warehouse. CP Holdings was clearly written on a sign above the large double doors. There were a couple of lorries and she noticed that there was a rail track leading away from the large building, this track, she knew, would lead to another large building owned by CP Holdings, a smelting factory where ore from the mine in Harris would be crushed, filtered, smelted and sorted. She stood there, contemplating on if to go inside or not. After some moments, she turned and went back to town. This is no good, she softly spoke to herself, it's too dangerous. Deciding she would check out the shops along the boardwalk before some lunch and then catch a train back to Moncton, she walked away from the warehouse. The sky was very cloudy, and rain was imminent. Checking her watch, she calculated how much time she had before the train was due to leave.

From an office window, upstairs in the warehouse, Bella Madison had spotted the blond woman, knew straight away that it had to be Alison

Hudson and picking up the phone she called Nico. Then went to find her husband who was on the warehouse floor getting another shipment ready.

'Hey hun' she called out as she approached him, ' just called Nico, that woman is here, she was outside, watching, she knows too much, you need to get Karina, we have a plan.' Then, walking away, she said, ' I'm going to follow her, she what she does, or where she goes, I'll call you later'

An hour and a half later Phil was driving Karina towards the Amherst filling station, a big rest area for truckers, coaches and cars, with a few shops and a restaurant. Bella had called back to say that the Hudson woman had come to Halifax by train and knew the schedule when the next train would depart for Moncton. She also informed him that at Amherst two men would arrive in a van and would take Karina back.

Phil spoke little as he drove, having given Karina detailed instructions and what payment she would receive upon completion. It began to rain. Karina West was prepared. She had the necessary equipment and was going through the plan in her mind.

Detective Inspector Murray Canney put the phone down. He sat still for a moment, this was a strange development. It had been Nico Rozzini, and he needed a favour. He was in debt. He was often in debt. Gambling. Closing his eyes for a moment, he then got up, left the police station on the south side of Moncton, saying he would be back in about an hour and headed for his car. He knew the address he had to go to, and all he had to do, is to make sure that it would be open, that the door was not locked and that there were no alarms in the house. A simple job. He just had to make sure that he was very careful and that he would leave no fingerprints.

Phil Madison dropped Karina off and drove back to Halifax. The rain was heavier now and as he concentrated on driving in these conditions, he was also thinking about the plan that had been made regarding the Hudson woman. A plan he didn't much care for, but he wasn't able to challenge it.

Bella in the meantime had kept on eye on the blond woman right up to the time that she boarded the train. Then made the call to confirm she was on her way back. Unlike her husband, Bella approved of the plan that she and Nico had come up with. A plan that was shared with Julien, Nico's brother and his wife Sandra, who, Bella noticed, was very quiet and said little. She wondered about her loyalty.

Deputy Dusty Kerr met up with the two men, gave them the keys for the van, told them all they need was in the back and that they must follow the instructions to the letter, that the woman they were to collect from Amherst would tell them.

Meanwhile, with the rain coming down quite heavily, Alison Hudson sat deep in thought as the train headed for Moncton. She had felt uneasy ever since she had decided to go into the police station in Harris. Maybe she should have stuck with her original plan, which was to confront Mrs. Debra Rozzini, Nico's wife, who's address she had found through her work at the Shapeshifters health club. But it was too late to go back in time. Her time in Halifax had not been fruitful. But she did have confirmation of the existing of the warehouse, of the fact that Julien was a manager or director there and the best thing she could do now, is to contact a detective in Portland, Oregon, who had been trying to assist her all those years ago, ten years in fact, when her ex-husband had taken their daughter away.

At the train station Karina and the two men were ready and waiting. The rain still coming down. They could see the car, the red sports car, that belonged to the woman who was their target. They had the home address of this woman, had been told the door would be open. She had explained the plan in detail to the two young men, both either late teens or early twenties she thought, and they knew of the exact place where the woman was to be taken that night.

The train arrived, the driver switched on the engine, Karina and the other lad were in the back, ready. They saw her, had a description, quite tall, slim, blond, wearing a long red coat. There she was. Walking quickly towards her car. Karina watched through the windscreen, the wipers doing their work in clearing it, then said, 'Now!'

Friday evening 5ᵗʰ March

The three of them arrived together by taxi. Sam, sitting in the front, paid the driver as from the back seat Chrissie and Alison exited the cab. Terri, who had been keeping an eye out and had, not long after she had been notified that they had left the airport, Sam and Chrissie deciding to stay at the airport and await Alison's flight from San Francisco, gone down from the twenty-eight floor to await them in the foyer.

As soon as she saw the taxi pull up, she headed outside and when her mother spotted her, she rushed towards her daughter, and they embraced. Taking her face mask off, she wiped away some tears, kissed her daughter on the cheek and turned, to then introduce Chrissie, who by now had also taking her face mask off as had Sam. Terri, also tearful, warmly embraced her, then, realising who the man was bringing up the rear, said, 'And you must be Sam' and through her tears and smiling, she then flung herself at him and hugged him tight. They embraced for some time. Terri had of course heard all about Sam, knew he was the man who had rescued her mother, he was the man who, with the help the Canadian policewoman, detective Saunders, had made it possible to be reunited. She would be forever grateful.

Pulling herself away, she followed Chrissie and her mother into the foyer, then the four of them together rode the smooth elevator to Tammy's luxurious apartment.

Less than ten minutes later they all sat in the lounge. Tammy having greeted the newcomers and between her and Chrissie had organised refreshments. 'Sam, would you like to begin? You have a way of relating the sequence of events' Chrissie said, sitting next to her husband to be on one of the three-seater couches that surrounded a two separate coffee tables, both identical, with curved wooden legs and glass tops inserted into the oak frame. There was a second three-seater, and then a further two armchairs that easily fitted in the space of the large lounge with a panoramic window that overlooked Central Park. Alison sat next to her daughter on the other couch and Tammy had made herself comfortable in one of the armchairs, tucking her legs right under her. Sam put his coffee mug down, then sat back and began to speak. 'Okay then, right, well, it all began when Debra Rozzini called on the health club, where you Alison worked and spoke to the receptionist, Rita, asking for your address, well, she was suspicious and spoke to detective Saunders, who also thought it was suspicious, she in turn, called me. That was the beginning.' Sam leaned forward, picked up his mug, took a sip, placed it down again, then sat back and continued, 'That same night, detective Saunders, Karen, who had taken a few folders from work to see if she could perhaps find some clues as to why Debra, Nico's widow, was interested in finding out where Alison lived, and particularly, why now? Anyway, when it came to around midnight, she noticed a strange car, with an occupant, in her street, had a bad feeling about it, and sent me a text message. When we didn't hear any more, Chrissie and I became worried, without hesitation we decided it best to get to Moncton, in the meantime Chrissie spoke to Alison and wondered what the interest was in finding her. Also, I believe at that time, we began to wonder, if it was really you, Terri, that was of interest.' Sam paused here, and Alison took over the conversation, 'Yes, Chrissie and I came to that conclusion, though still not sure as to why this would be, that Terri was of interest, but, following through, I told her to be on the lookout.'

'Yes,' Terri said, now taking up the story, 'and a good thing too, because, I had only just spoken with mum, when, as I was having my lunch, a woman called at reception and asked for me. I almost got up to see this woman, but, then decided to make an excuse, managed to see her heading to her car and took a few photos which I sent to mum'.

'Yes, and there was something familiar about the woman in the photo, I was sure I recognised her, so, I sent it to you Chrissie' Ally said.

'Yes, and you were right, I recognised her too, it was Bella Madison, the wife of Phil Madison, who was instrumental in your abduction Ally, anyway, by this time, we were of course already in Moncton, and just as well, because Sam, with the help of Daniel, a fireman, got into a dinghy and went up river, I went with the police by car to the ravine road and well, you know how all that unfolded'

'All the action in Moncton,' Terri said, then more action in your house mum, this would really make a good movie!'

Tammy, sipping her drink, listening to them all, now chipped in, ' Well, just to show that I have been following all the action, yes, brave Sam, recuing Karen, falling from that same ledge, goodness, then, someone who had once tried to stab you, came to your rescue when this Bella woman, who is obviously very skilled in breaking into people houses, was set to attack you.'

'I know, I was totally surprised and yes, a little in shock, but angrier that this woman, I mean this Bella woman, was in my house! And yes, Constance, bless her, who had been checking out where I lived to, which was her original plan, see me the following day to apologise to me, well, she spotted Bella sneaking around the house, didn't hesitate, and decided to see what was going on. Her sudden appearance was a shock to me, but even more so for Bella. Who, thankfully, is in jail right now.'

'Time to bring into the story, somebody else, someone who none of us have so far, ever met, a young woman named Claire' Sam said, once again taking up the story, ' she had a surprise visit from Sandra Rozzini, wife of Julien Rozzini and guilty of being part of the plan to kidnap you Terri, when you were just seven, and take you to San Francisco. But, so many years later, when you, Ally, were taken, she began to get worried, no longer wanted part of what her husband was up to, and so left Halifax, flew to San Francisco, where she couriered a full written confession, with all the details she could remember, and then flew to Hawaii, were, to date, she had not been found. When she came to the house and spoke to Claire and was then made aware of Bella looking for Terri, she had an answer, as to why. And you, Tammy, spoke with her'

Tammy untucked her legs from beneath her, leaned forward to place her cup on the table and took up the story,' Yes, she had come to give herself up to the police, after first having wanted to visit her brothers grave in Myrtle Creek, she told me that the reason Terri was taken as a child, was because she had a rare blood type, AB negative, moreover, there was a gene in the Rozzini family, one that affected only the male line, a gene, that when reaching a certain age, anywhere between twelve and twenty, would cause a debilitating disease, causing breakdown of the body's function to strengthen bones. Now, we know that Debra Rozzini, Nico widow, has two children, both boys, but we found out that they aren't Nico's kids, they are from an earlier marriage. So….' Tammy said, then looking at Terri to continue.

'So, 'Terri said, 'why the reason, for my kidnapping, why the reason for mum to be, well almost killed, and why was Bella so intent on finding me, well, it turns out, that, prior to marrying Phil Madison, she had an affair with, wait for it, not only Nico, but also Julien Rozzini. She got pregnant, doesn't know which brother, but definitely a Rozzini. She had a boy, now in his teens.'

'This is when I remembered we know someone, who might be of help' Tammy said, again taking up the story, 'having followed the story of the mosaic swallow Alison, sorry, may I call you Ally?'

'Of course, absolutely' Ally said

'So, I knew of the police report, that you, along with Simon, oh sorry Ally, I mean about Simon?'

'No, no, its fine, not to be, carry on' Ally said, blushing slightly. Terri noticed and took hold of her mother's hand.

'The police report detailed all that had occurred at the site where the tornado struck, and amongst the evidence, was a report from Raphael Morton, a medical examiner, who discovered, when he researched the relevant documents, that foul play had indeed occurred, well, I got hold of his contact number, explained who I was, how I knew about him and then about Terri. I asked him if he could help, he was very charming and helpful indeed.'

'What Tammy means is, she fancies him!' Terri said, smiling and it was Tammy's turn to colour slightly, and making a scowling face at Terri.

'Tammy and I went over to Yonkers, met with him and he took my blood and made several tests. The results of which came through only a little while ago, we must go back and thank him, don't you think Tammy?' Terri teased.

'And?' Ally wanted to know

'Yes, do tell' Chrissie added, secretly amused that Tammy was being teased, as often it would be Tammy doing the teasing.

'Turns out I do have a rare blood group, Rapheal is going to make a card for me to carry, in case I'm ever in an accident, but, and here he was able to obtain a blood sample from the police in Moncton, from Karen actually, from the blood when Nico Rozzini killed himself that day in Harris. I don't have the gene or the right bone marrow that could be possibly helpful if Bella's son ever developed that disease.'

'So, she attempted to kill detective Saunders, actually killed two people, the deputy and the nurse, through that car crash, and what, was her plan for mum? Anyway, all for nothing!'

'Glad it's all over Ally said.

'Still hope this boy doesn't get this disease though'. Terri said.

'Very true, Terri, still, time to celebrate, anyway know a good restaurant to go to?'

'As long as I don't do the cooking this time' Tammy said, 'Good idea Sam, let me make a call'

THE PAST; Period 9

The year 2020 Quantico Virginia

It was a very cold, rainy – and blustery-day late January. Deputy director of the Naval Criminal Investigative Service, better known by the initials NCIS, ignored the sound of the rain lashing against the window of his office as he was engrossed in reading a report. It was quiet in the offices of the headquarters that were situated on Telegraph Road in Quantico. The director and several of the civilian staff were absent due to having contracted the Covid 19 virus. Others, including a few special agents, were working either from home or had moved to a temporary base within the Naval Academy in Annapolis.

One floor below, in an office, she shared with two other agents, Special agent Charlotte Cartwright focused on the laptop screen, but found it hard to concentrate. It wasn't because of the rain that was making quite a sound against the glass window behind her. It wasn't because several of her colleagues were ill or that others were working from home or had moved to rooms vacated for this purpose at the Naval Academy. No. It was because of the report she herself had compiled and written, over many years, and one that she finally felt was ready to be shown and had delivered to him upon his arrival. What would her boss think? What would he do? How would he react?

Charlotte pressed a few keys on the keyboard and the screen returned to the home screen. She swivelled her chair and looked out the window, but due to the heaviness of the rain, it was almost impossible to make out anything outside. She did see, though very blurry, a couple of nearby trees swaying in the strong breeze. It hadn't been until, she had, in her own time, investigated for nearly two years, that she knew that what she was slowly uncovering, was sensitive. She then titled her report 'Underwater Undercover' With the virus pandemic raging around the world, she felt the time was right, to show her findings. Five years, since she began.

It had all started at her twenty first birthday party that several friends had organised for her, in co-operation with her parents. It was held in the Dale City Courtyard Tennis club, of which mum and dad were members. There was music, food, soft drinks and wine. A small group consisting of her parents, two aunties and one uncle, and six of her female friends, along with four young men, one of them being her boyfriend.

There were banners and posters and balloons. There was a cake. The evening went well, with party games and dancing. A table was set up for presents and Charlotte was well content. Her parents had also, of course, brought out the baby photo album, as well as a few other albums with a selection of photos. By eleven thirty the party was drawing to a close and Charlotte helped her parents in loading things back into their station wagon. It was a little before midnight that she sat herself down and picked up one the photo albums. Opening it she realised that she couldn't ever remember seeing these before and was soon absorbed. When her mother came and sat alongside, leaving her father to pack the remainder of the things, she pointed to an old black and white photograph, and asked, who are they?

'Ah, well, that's your grandfather, your dad's father, and standing behind him, is his father, your great grandfather, his name was Billy.

'He died in a type of submarine, a prototype of sorts, back in, let's see, yes, 1943, this was in Lake Ontario, a secret Naval operation, all hush hush, they never recovered his body' Her father said, as he had come up behind them. Then said,' come on, it's midnight, time to leave'

Charlotte swivelled in her chair, outside the rain seemed to be easing a little, she swivelled back pushed a few buttons on her keyboard and wondered how far into her report the director was, and what would his reaction be?

Checking to see if she had any fresh e-mail, she then once again thought back in time. It was that photo, and what her dad had told her, about his grandfather, her great grandfather, Billy Cartwright. Secret operation?

Hush hush? Body never recovered? Charlotte was intrigued, hooked on this mystery, a family mystery, and on the way home in the car that night, she whispered a promise to herself, I will find you, find out about you.

That was five years ago. A lot had happened since. The phone on her desk rang.

Frederick Thompson placed the handset back in its cradle. He then put his hands together, as if in a prayer mode, brought them to his face and then rested his chin upon his thumbs. He was puzzled, astonished and in somewhat of a quandary. How to proceed from here? The report was detailed, well formulated and there was no doubt in his mind, that Charlotte had thoroughly followed up to describe the events in accurate details.

The phone on her desk buzzed. She picked up the receiver, listened briefly, then said, 'Right away' replaced the phone and got up from behind her desk. Two minutes later she entered the office of the deputy director.

'Please sit,' Frederick Thompson said, then, holding the folder with the report in his hand, ' this is some report, I see that it has taken several years to complete, although complete might not be the right word, for I think there a more details to discover, however, this does present a problem, quite a problem, actually, what you have uncovered, most of it anyway, has to be, classified, I mean classified above even my security level, so, it needs to be very carefully handled. What you have here, or, I should say, having read it through twice, what we have, is, or potentially could be, a legal minefield, not to mention an international and diplomatic dilemma'.

Charlotte understood, once she had gathered momentum into her research, she had often thought about what it was that she was uncovering, hence it had taken her much time, to eventually decide to bring it to someone's attention, she had thought that it had to be the director, but as he was ill with this virus, the deputy was the next best thing, furthermore she felt at ease about approaching him, trusted him, and felt it the best route to take what she had found, to a next level.

'Yes, I realised, well quite early on, that this was, well, had to be, classified, I wanted to make sure that I had the information correct, checked and double checked, that's why it has taken me this long, but, well, personally I would like some answers as to what happened to my great – grandfather, furthermore, the incident in 63 when the canister broke free, there has to be more, a ship the size of the Taciturn, doesn't just vanish, and I'm sure evidence could be out there, of course, that evidence would also be classified, still, if I have found out this much, its likely someone else finds this too, and, if that information gets into the hands of, well, unfriendly people, then we will have an issue, better we are in control of this, I feel' Charlotte answered.

Frederick Thompson placed the folder back down on his desk, looked across at her, nodding, then said, 'I agree, we need to take ownership of this, then guide it through to the best outcome'. After a pause, he said, 'I feel it needs to be taken further, this has to be done, for now, however, I am going to leave your connection out of it, do you understand?'

Charlotte nodded in agreement.' Understood' she said. 'Thank you'

Frederick nodded and Charlotte stood up and left his office.

Walking back to her desk she pondered for herself as to what to do, though she totally trusted the deputy director, she was glad that she, kept very safe indeed, had another copy of her findings.

Entering her own office she wondered, was there anyone else, who knew what had occurred, back in 1943, and what had occurred, on 4th of June 1963? A few hours later she called the deputy on the phone to say she was heading home and was there anything he needed her to do. He said no and wished her a good day, and, he said, thank you for this report, it will take some time to decide what to do with it.

Leaving her office, she took the elevator down to the ground floor and fished out her car keys. couldn't help but think about the conversation they had earlier. He was going to investigate further, he had said, and was going to leave her name out of it he said, it was going to take some time he said. This was all good, for some time now she had felt a weight upon her shoulders with the information she had, over the past five years, gathered. Charlotte exited the building and headed for where her car was parked. She was glad that it had stopped raining.

'Hello, miss Cartwright' a female voice said, startling Charlotte as she quickly turned around, and about to reach for her sidearm.

'No need for the gun' the woman said, 'my name is Holly, Holly Koppell.'

'How did you…' Charlotte began.

'Get on the base?' Holly finished, 'I have clearance, just noticed you coming out, we have to go back inside, see your director, or, I believe, your deputy?'

Charlotte sensed no danger from this woman, who, just so suddenly, out of the blue, had just appeared. Holly Koppell, she knew the name, it had been Wayne Koppell, her grandfather, who had been the captain on the Taciturn. She had an oblique reference regarding Holly in a file she found amongst papers in the Portland police station, and the name Robert Pentegrass was connected, but she didn't know why.

'Deputy Frederick Thompson, earlier today I handed him a report on my findings for the past five years, regarding your grandfather's ship, among other things.' Charlotte said, closing the car door and started walking back to the main entrance, wondering why it was that this woman had clearance? Or so she said.

'Other things being the accident with the submersible? Speaking of grandfathers, yours was on the Ontario One… 'Holly answered, then after a short pause, ' sorry for your loss, although it has been nearly eighty years ago'.

'You seem to have a lot of knowledge, are you part of the…'

'Cover up?' Holly completed, figuring out what this woman was thinking. 'Yes and no, really, I will explain, when we get inside'.

They reached the main entrance and Charlotte swiped her card to gain access. Neither woman spoke until they reached the deputy's office.

'Sir?' Charlotte began as she knocked and entered, and when he looked up, 'this is Miss Holly Koppel.

Forty-five-year-old Holly swept passed Charlotte and having retrieved a folder from her bag, said' Here are papers, forms, the US Espionage act document, also the Canadian National Official secrets act document. Please, read these, in the meantime, perhaps Miss Cartwright and I could grab a coffee?'

Frederick Thompson looked at the documents before him, recognised the forms, looked up at Holly and simply nodded.

Charlotte saw the nod, then said to Holly, 'follow me, I could sure use a coffee myself now.'

Holly followed the agent and felt quite relieved, it was almost time for her to come out from under the shadows, almost time for her to be able to leave a life without the pressure of this secret pressing on her shoulders. These past twenty years had not been the best. Her grandmother had died. The Dutch journalist, Katja, had left to go back to her homeland and Holly had never heard from her again. Her father had not taken his mother's death very well. It was shortly after that, in fact not long after the funeral, that two women appeared, the same two who had escorted her from the new year's party that day, which, at the time, had been three years earlier. They came with documents and forms. They questioned her and her father for nearly an hour and then were told to sign to the form, also being reminded that anything they shared would be seen as treason and would result in life imprisonment. This totally shook Holly, for up until that moment she had thought the women were saving her from a potential danger.

Her father had, at first, been okay with this, even had a sense of importance to know things that others didn't, but it eventually weighted to heavy on him. Two years after signing those documents he drank too much one night, got into a fight and fell into the harbour. Death by drowning was the verdict. Holly, who had moved into her grandmother's apartment, settled herself in as best she could, tried hard to make new friends, joined a local field hockey club and even had several relationships. But none were anything like the connection she had with Robert.

She shook out of her reverie when she heard Charlotte ask her how she wanted her coffee.

In his office Frederick made a call to a number listed on a cover letter that accompanied the various forms Holly had given him, asking him to make contact.

Charlotte and Holly stood in the narrow galley and slowly drank their coffee. Neither speaking, each with her own thoughts.

Holly thought back to when she discovered that Robert had died. A year ago. She had cried. She had also been angry, and she was at a point of wanting this secret to let go off her life. She knew much of what had happened, to the submersible, to the crew within who had died. She knew about the ship the Taciturn, about the lethal gas about the accident and about how it was all, for national security's sake, covered up. She knew where they had buried the ones on board the vessel. She knew where her grandfather had been buried. She knew about the ship itself, its transformation and knew about how the rescue attempt had been severely falsified.

Time for the truth to come out. Time enough had passed.

Just as seaman Albert Green opened the bible to a passage from Ecclesiastes and Billy Cartwright whispered the words, *'A time to die'*, in 1943, and as Millie parker thought of words from that same passage when finding that note book her husband had written, *'A time for war and a time for peace'*, so Charlotte brought to mind from that same piece of Scripture, the words, *'A time to keep silence, and a time to speak'*.

Both women finished their coffee at the same time and looked at each other, then Charlotte said, 'Come on, let's see him.'

'Ah, there you are, Miss Holly, this here,' Frederick said, handing over a folder, 'Is a report, made by Miss Cartwright, it is very detailed, could you please read that and certify the truth of it?' Then looking at Charlotte, said, 'I believe Miss Holly here has report, which I have just been informed of, and have the approval for you to read it'

Holly delved into her bag, pulled out a folder and handed it to Charlotte, then took the folder the deputy gave her and both women sat themselves down and began to read. Frederick left them to it, went to fix a drink for himself and was quite relieved for the forms he had just read authorised him to use the full knowledge of both incidents as he saw fit. That he could liaise with the Canadians and with the Secretary of the Navy as to how to proceed.

Saturday 6th March

Cynthia Barnes stood on the balcony and looked down at the short runway that lay on this side of the hacienda, mug of tea in her hand. It was early in the morning, but already quite warm. She smiled at the memory of her driving a car onto and into the plane, the twin prop aircraft that stood outside the hangar. He had not long ago travelled to Bilbao to catch a flight back to the States. Thomas. Taking a sip of tea, she smiled again, a man, who, when he was a boy, a teenager, she had been mean to, now a man, a handsome man, a brave man. A gentle and courteous man. A man she now was very much in love with. Thomas, she briefly thought about all the information that Claire had found, quite a lengthy report that she had told them over the phone, quite disturbing, potentially dangerous and it was right that Thomas was flying over to assist her and to think through what, if anything, needed to be done next. Finishing her tea Cynthia, known by her nickname by most as Tia, re-entered the lounge from the balcony and again looked across at a far wall where the painting hung. It was a beautiful painting, so masterly created by the artist Tiziano Vecelli, better known as Titian. A painting of a man, in regal clothes, standing by a black horse. It was around eighteen inches wide and three feet in height. The frame was gilded and made of wood that was ornately carved. It was not its original frame for it had come to the auction house in Boston without one, but the art dealer there, a man named Moshe, had fitted it with a frame befitting its stature. The man, king Charles V, wore a red heavy coat finely detailed by the artist who painted it in the early 1500's. Continuing through the lounge toward the door and heading for the kitchen, she was still smiling and shook her head slightly, for it had been this painting that had set in motion a chain of events that had led Thomas and her here.

Entering the kitchen moments later, she smiled and said hello to the housekeeper, Maria, placed her cup near the sink and headed for the study where she and the owner of the big house and land and factory and plane had worked together, studying legal documents and reading up on the law of the land. Letitia was there already, sat behind the desk that had been her father's. He along with her older brother had died in a boating accident some years ago.

'Buenos Dias Tia' she said, looking up and smiling, then went on to say in her accented English,' we are getting somewhere, yes?'

Having brought in a small pine table from the factory, Tia had been sitting at it in a comfortable swivel chair and had perused through many documents and looked up references to land ownership and legal requirements. She had been, prior to joining forces with Robert Pentegrass, a successful lawyer.

'Morning Letitia, yes, we are getting somewhere, almost ready to submit our findings and file a court order.'

'Thank you so much for helping, sorry it has taken much of your time' Letitia said, standing up from behind the desk and continued' We have breakfast soon, okay?'

Tia nodded, sat behind the table and started to sort the papers together. They would be off to the courts in a few hours. She reflected on the past, when she would be submitting various legal documents in the cases she worked on when, after having passed the bar exams, she began working for a law firm in Portland. So long ago, she mused, and so much had happened since, so many changes in her life. She thought about Claire, the young woman she helped rescue from human traffickers, all with the valuable research that had been done by Robert. She knew that Claire would likely, at some point, investigate her own files, investigate how Robert had located her. She would likely find out some information that would upset her. Tia knew this information, but, as it concerned a person who was no longer alive, she felt it best left alone. Thankfully Claire had, at least so far, not looked into her own files. However, and this was such a nice gesture Tia thought, she was going to try and find Roberts missing girlfriend, Holly. For this was how Robert began his research, this was why he started to focus and learn about missing people. For the next twenty years he would do so, earning him the title of The Searcher, by the Portland police. It was from them, through one of their officers, that she heard about Robert Pentegrass, picking up on a conversation about him being the searcher. She knew the name, then, painfully delving into her own mind and looking back at her own past, she realised who he was. When at high school, she and her co gang members, at the time quite pleased with what they had been called, the ABC girls, with a reputation for being mean and for being bullies. He had been one of their victims. A time she hardly ever looked back on, mostly because she blamed herself, when her younger brother, after he had started the same high school, had been severely bullied, likely because of what she, along with Barbara, the leader, and Alison had done. It was because of this, that one day he took his life. A moment in time that still brought her to tears, and despite all the love from her parents, despite, in these last months, the love from Thomas, she could not forgive herself.

Even now, as she had gathered the files and walked alongside Letitia, making their way to the Spanish woman's car and setting of for the nearby town of Ampuero, she felt the onset of tears. Tia sighed, opened the passenger door and got into the car.

Though Letitia was speaking at one point, she could hardly take in what was being said. All this court business had taken her back, to when she worked for the law firm. 'Sorry Letitia, my mind was elsewhere, what did you say?'

'You are missing Thomas?' she asked, turning and smiling at Tia, recalling the time when she had come out of the house, armed with a shotgun and had confronted her and Thomas.

'Yes, I had a text that he arrived safely, is with Claire to sort out a problem that Claire had come across in the search for someone'

'Si, yes, I remember Thomas saying that his friend, Robert, I think, was very good at finding missing people?'

'Yes, Robert, I worked with him for many years, became his assistant in rescuing people that he had, somehow, located, he was very good at it, Claire is now doing that too'.

'Si, you tell me earlier, you found her, this Claire?'

Tia smiled, turned to look at her new friend, then answered, 'Yes, though it was Robert who knew where she had been taken, I just followed directions'

'You and Thomas, good people' Letitia said, driving into town and drawing up into the parking place by the police station, 'thank you'.

THE PAST; Period 10

The year 2021 – Myrtle Creek – Oregon

'He was a good man' Holly said, standing by his grave and reading the tombstone.

'The searcher?' Charlotte asked, standing beside the woman who until recently had been a mystery. A part of the intriguing story that she had begun to unravel so many years ago. A story about the death of her grandfather, a story about a likely cover up. A story that rolled into another story, one about a missing exploration ship, a ship which had been captained by Holly's grandfather. She threw a sideways glance at her, saw the sadness, saw the tears. She had told of this man, this Robert. A boyfriend she had to leave behind, a boyfriend she could never see again, a boyfriend she couldn't even contact.

'Yes', Holly answered, ' I found out, not even that long ago actually, that he was very helpful, instrumental in fact, in searching for and locating missing people. The young lady we are going to see, is one of those he rescued.'

Holly took out a small lace handkerchief from her pocket, blew her nose and smiled at Charlotte, 'Come on, your sources tell me that the journalist is there at present, we have to nip this in the bud.'

'Yes, indeed we do, so, about this Thomas chap, how does he fit in?' Charlotte asked as they moved away from the graveside.

'Thomas, yes, well, actually there is also a Cynthia, Cynthia Barnes, she was Roberts assistant on the outside, he hardly ventured out from what I have learned, bless him, anyway, so, yes, this Cynthia and Thomas, who inherited the house, it was left in Robert's will, they seem to have carried on with what Robert had started, more than twenty years ago…'

'You say he, Robert, began when he started looking for you?' Charlotte said as they reached the car. Holly gave her a brief smile and got in behind the wheel. The Ontario Project, she thought, was coming to an end. NCIS had closed the file, there were no loose ends left, other than the journalist, Lea, Holly's former flat mate, and this Claire, along with Cynthia and Thomas, who, they felt, would surely know about it. The Dutch journalist who had uncovered a great deal, leaving a report which Claire had discovered, was no longer alive. The chemist, the Holly who had deciphered the formula and had informed the Katja woman of this, was also no longer alive. Perhaps there were others who might know something? But as far as the agency was concerned, these were the last known reports to deal with.

They had only recently arrived in Myrtle Creek, having arrived in Portland on a flight from Washington DC and rented a car. It was early evening by now, and, as charlotte's sources had confirmed the presence of a reporter, they would call on the house tomorrow, Saturday.

THE PRESENT; New York

Saturday 6th March

Ally stood by the window in the kitchen, having made herself some breakfast and now sipping some juice she looked down at the scene below. It had been a wonderful evening, her daughter, Chrissie and Sam, and Tammy. She felt blessed to have such good friends. She felt blessed to have her daughter back. Closing her eyes she brought back that day, the rain coming down, when she had come out of the train station, when she had walked, half ran really to her car. Then, how quickly it had all happened. Opening her eyes she thought, what if? But her very good friend Chrissie, had told her off once, for even thinking like that, she remembered the stern look Chrissie had given her, saying, 'What if and if only, are dead end streets Ally, don't go down there, there is no upside to it.'

Smiling she drank her juice and knew how right she had been, how right it was, not to go there. Sam had been there. Sam had seen what happened and he had spotted her car that night. It is how it is. She was truly blessed.

Meanwhile in Panama City, where it was an hour earlier, Murray Canney felt totally different. A knock on his hotel door stirred him to wakefulness and seeing on the clock by the bed that it was a little after five o'clock in the morning, he mumbled something and got out of bed. It had not been a good night for him, he had rolled into bed shortly after midnight and it had not gone well for him at the tables in the downstairs casino. Making his way to the door he thought it might be a manager wanting to ensure he had enough credit left to pay his bill. Opening the door, he was taken aback, and his eyes opened wide. He took a step back, frowned, wanted to say something, but could not find his voice, not even think of anything to say.

Several hours later, the postman delivered mail in Myrtle Creek. Claire was in the kitchen, heard the mail drop and went to get it. Thomas was in the 'Engine room' upstairs, talking with Tia who was on her way back from Spain., and Lea was in the lounge going through her files and writing further reports. Claire saw there was post for her. Opening it she was surprised and happy. It was an invitation to the opening of the Emily Parker exhibit in Albuquerque as a special guest and came with airline and hotel tickets. Open-mouthed she took it all in and ran upstairs to share the news with Thomas. Then there was a knock on the door.

Going down the stairs again she got to the door and opened it.

'Hello Claire' one of the women said, 'I'm Holly'

For the second time that morning, Claire stood open-mouthed.

'And I am Charlotte Cartwright' the other woman said, then showing her credentials, NCIS, special agent.'

Claire found her voice, asked them to come in and called up the stairs, 'Thomas!' then entered the lounge and said, ' Meet Lea, I think you know her, Holly?'

It was Lea turn to gape. She then stood up and the two women rushed towards each other and embraced. 'I knew you were alive,' Lea said, ' but here you are!'

'Sorry Lea' Holly said, pulling away and looking at her former friend, ' I will explain, oh, and this is special agent, Charlotte Cartwright'

Just then Thomas walked in, suspicious at first, wondering if the situation was alright as he had just heard a woman being introduced as special agent.

'I trust we are not all under arrest' he said, his voice deep and resonating through the room and all four ladies turned to look at him.

'You must be Thomas' Holly said, ' and yes, 'I remember you, from our high school days, you were a good friend'

'Holly, my word yes, Robert's hockey girlfriend' Thomas answered, smiling and shaking the offered hand.

'Charlotte' the agent said, also offering her hand which he shook.

'I'm guessing that my story, our story, all our findings, end here?' Lea asked.

Holly smiled at her, ' let's sit down, and we will explain it all, in every detail' Holly answered.

'And yes, it ends here' Charlotte added.

Saturday 13th March

The Museum on Mountain Road in the city had been opened in 1967. Specialising in Art and history of New Mexico it contained a vast amount of works and exhibits and the doors were about to be opened and a new exhibit revealed to the public. Already a crowd was awaiting near the entrance, but inside a selected group of people had arrived earlier, having been personally invited to preview the exhibition. The mayor and the museum curator welcomed the group of nine who had flown in from various place.

The exhibition was in recognition of the work and life of Professor Emily Parker, with a particular emphasis on the discovery made on a Mayan excavation in 1988. The mosaic tiles, depicting the image of a swallow, were Roman, but what lay beneath would trigger a series a dramatic event. Gold coins, Spanish in origin, minted in Colombia in the early 1800's. These had been stolen from the Spanish by a wealthy landlord, then in turn, stolen from him by a group of Spanish soldiers and eventually buried, the remaining 740 out of an original 800, near silver city in 1862, by Juan and Lena Castagnet. One hundred and twenty-six years later it would be Professor Emily Parker who would discover these. The day was severely marred when a tornado struck the site. The exhibition not only showed the professors work and lifetime but paid carefully attention to the events surrounding the gold coins and mosaic tiles. The display was well laid out, there was the complete square metre of tiles, which had been cleaned up and recovered from the home of Constance Shelton. There was the letter written by Juan and Lena, explaining the reason why they buried the treasure and, out of the seven hundred and forty coins, four hundred were also present, some placed beneath a few loose mosaic tiles, other in a chest, the whole exhibit having ensured extra security as it was estimated that the coins would be worth an estimate of three hundred thousand dollars. Then, in a sequence of handwritten sheets, a story was told for the visiting public. A replica spade to the one marking the site where they had died, was displayed, with the names of the victims. Professor Emily Parker, her assistant Mr. Donald Alredo and two students, Josie Morton and Kathryn Smith.

Then there was a written sheet thanking several people for their contribution in solving the events of that day. The curator introduced the invited guests to the mayor. Detective Inspector Roger Mantell, from the city police, Miss Millie Parker, daughter of the professor, who had flown in from Milan, there was Nueva Santos, who had been a student on the dig that day, Miss Claire Symonds, from Myrtle Creek who had followed up on the original research that had been done by Robert Pentegrass. Alison Hudson, from San Francisco who along with Millie had also been investigating, then there was Rapheal Morton, brother of Josie Morton whose medical examination proved valuable. He had travelled from New York and had brough Tammy with him, who had been delighted when he had rung and asked her to come. Simon Lightfoot was introduced along with Felicity Smith, the sister of Kathryn Smith.

After the introductions the group took time to study the exhibit. Alison and Millie walked slowly along together, both with memories of their search. Tammy was in deep conversation with young Claire, whom, she had noticed, seemed a little forlorn. Raphael and Simon chatted and Felicity, after a few moments, excused herself and headed towards where Alison and Millie were standing. In another part of the sizeable exhibition Detective Mantell was in conversation with the curator and with Nueva Santos, whose conversation with Claire had set in motion the search for Eddie Philpott, sadly having died from the Covid virus, but who had brought fresh information to complete the truth of all that had happened.

'May I speak with you?' Felicity, though preferring to be called Fliss, asked.

Alison turned, then said to Millie who was standing next to her, 'excuse me a moment, then stepped a few paces to one side, looking at the petite blond woman who was at least five inches shorter than her, then stopped and said, 'Hi'

'I don't really know how to begin, but I'll come right and say it, are you going to fight me?'

Ally smiled as she looked at her, thought for a moment, then took in a deep breath and said, ' You know, I once fell in love with a guy, madly, but, there was another woman, who was also in love with him, and, well, when I saw one day, how much she loved him, I walked away, let him go, I didn't want for him to have the pressure to choose, nor, to be honest, did I really want to hear what his answer might be, though I had a fair idea, anyway, Felicity, I know about you and Simon, and, well, what are the chances of this kind of thing happening to me twice? I can see that you love him, you two have known each other for quite some time, you have been together, at one point, for quite some time, so, no, I'm not going to fight you.' Alison said, smiling and then followed it on, by saying, 'How about we hug as friends?'

Fliss felt enormous relief and practically flung herself at the tall woman before her. They hugged and she said, 'Thank you' when pulling back, then gave a brief smile and turned around. Simon, who had noticed Fliss heading over to see Ally, sighed with relief when she came back to him, smiling.

'What?' she said to him, 'did you think that there was going to be a catfight? Did you hope that there was going to be a catfight?' she asked, smiling. Simon felt himself colour slightly and said nothing, but leaned forward and kissed her cheek.

Tammy, still in conversation with Claire, had also noticed Ally and the blond, she knew now to be Felicity, talking, then beckoned her over.' Hi, say, have you ever met Claire here?'

'No, hi Claire, so nice to finally meet you, and thank you, for all that you have researched, I believe you are still deep in some mystery?'

'Before you get into that with Claire, I'm going to chat with Rapheal, but you and her, Simon's girl, all okay? I was thinking that a confrontation might be happening the way she strode over to see you.'

'She was determined, and looked a little worried, but I can see Tammy, that she loves him, so…'

'You're a very kind person Ally, come here, give me a hug, then talk to Claire' Tammy said, embracing her friend and then walking over to where Rapheal was now chatting to detective Mantell.

The exhibit was due to open to the public in less than ten minutes. Millie had now also joined with the detective and Rapheal and saw Tammy approaching, who said, 'Hi, sorry we had little time to chat before the reception, but, nice to meet you, the person who translated that book for us, you still live in Milan?'

The curator called attention to the invited guests and asked if they all would come to the foyer and entrance to the special exhibit where the mayor will officially open it to the public, there are also refreshments and drinks available, he said and moved towards the doors in readiness to open them to the waiting public.

Chantal Brewer was near the front of the queue of folk wanting to enter the museum. The doors were about to be opened. The forty-two-year-old brunette had been waiting this moment for some time, from when she first heard about the story of the mosaic tiles and the gold coins. She had heard the story before, it intrigued her, where had she heard it? The crowd began to move and enter the museum. In the large foyer, the city mayor spoke a few words and cut a ribbon to officially open the exhibit. Chantal, though excited to see it, took her time, followed the crowd and after a while when the early rush had subsided, she took some refreshment, checked her phone which she had used to take several photographs, then had a second look, taking in the artifact, the display and the notices.

It was a fascinating display; she was particularly drawn to the letter. The letter, writing in Spanish, by Juan and Lena Castagnet. She stood there for some time, reading it through several times.

'I remember the first time I read that letter'

Chantal turned to face the voice that had spoken. Studied the woman for a moment then frowned and asked, 'You mean before today?'

'Yes, hi, I'm Alison, I just noticed your special interest in it, you seemed, thoughtful, I take it you can read Spanish?'

'Chantal, is my name,' the brunette answered, then focused on the letter on display, said, it reads... *No amount of gold will equal the satisfaction of challenges overcome. No amount of gold will bring the growth in our nature and character...when difficulties are faced and conquered. No amount of gold can measure the value of true love...' then turning briefly to the woman next to her, she said, 'and then it says, '... We leave it here, as we have all that we need and what we want...is still an aim and a purpose that we may strive for to obtain a true sense of worth... Juan and Lena Castagnet'*

'You can read Spanish, it took me quite a while to translate it, I was on a plane from Portland to San Francisco, I feel that this is important to you? I mean, the exhibition, yes, but this letter in particular?'

Chantal faced the woman, looked at her, then said, ' Yes, and, for you?'

Ally smiled, looked at the letter, recalling when she had first seen it, then looked back at the woman calling herself Chantal and said, ' No amount of gold can measure the value of true love...it seems, well, it strikes me today more than it did when I first saw this letter, when I first really took in the words that are written there, anyway, sorry to intrude on your thoughts, I just saw an emotion in you as you stood here'

'Alison, yes, you are one of the invited guests that arrived earlier, I take it, in fact it must be that you are one of the people involved in solving the events surrounding the death of the professor, her assistant and those two students?'

Alison nodded.

'Juan and Lena Castagnet are my ancestors' Chantal said, then offering her hand, said, Chantal Brewer'.

The curator of the museum was happy indeed. There were far more people that had come than anticipated and he walked among them, greeting a person here or there as he walked throughout the museum. The mayor, having done his duties, had stayed only for a while. In a small café area, which was full to capacity Tammy had secured a table and sat with Claire. Raphael had joined them earlier but left them to it whilst he wanted to have a talk with his mum and dad who had arrived to visit the museum, saying that he would introduce them to her later.

'So' Tammy said, when Raphael had gone and she watched him as he left, ' tell me about Thomas and is it Cynthia?'

Claire was well pleased that she had come, though apprehensive to begin with, travelling all the way from Myrtle Creek and thinking that there would be no-one that she knew, was happy that Tammy had come to chat with her. She felt immediately at ease with the New Yorker whom she had heard a lot about. 'Yes Cynthia, though she prefers to be called Tia, well, 'Claire continued, feeling she wanted to relate so much to her new friend, ' Tia and Alison, or Ally, Terri's mother, used to be friends, long ago, at school, they were, maybe you know this, but, they were, along with another girl, called Barbara, called the ABC girls, and, well, anyway, Barbara is the sister of Eddie, who had vanished, disappeared, that time, back in 1988, it is what set this whole chain of events off, because it was Robert who had begun the search for Eddie'

'I recall, and, it was Thomas, I only briefly met him when he flew us to Paris last year, who started to follow up on what Robert had found, but then you, clever Claire, took it on when he and Tia had to go to Spain' Tammy interrupted.

'You are very clever, I know you know about this case from what you have read and heard, you have a good memory, and yes, that's right, I followed up, spoke to a lady, who is actually here today, a lady that was a student back then, who knew the professor and all about the tornado, it was she who gave a very good clue that helped to establish a fact that there was foul play afoot' Claire said, smiling at her own Sherlock Holmes reference and pleased that Tammy thought her clever.

'So, yes, 'Claire continued, this Barbara, was a third girl in this gang, I suppose, Tia told me, the three of them were bad, were bullies in school. It was Ally who found her, went to see her and got the papers that once belonged to the professor back, along with that letter you've seen in the display, that written by Juan and Lena Castagnet. I remember hearing that when Ally showed Millie, she had not recognised, that the stains on the folder that belonged to her mother, were actually blood stains. Bless, I spoke to her earlier, she lives in Milan now'

'I spoke to her as well, she was so helpful when Terri and a lady called Sophie? From Paris, have you heard of her?' Tammy asked.

'Aha, Thomas mentioned her, it was to her that that painting of the monk was sent, wasn't it?'

'You have a good memory too, no wonder you are good at your research, yes, she was helpful in translating a book from Italian, anyway, I really want to get back at what you said earlier, I know when you rang asked about Terri, that something else was going on? You were searching for, Roberts old girl friend? Holly?'

Claire drank some of her coffee and putting the cup down, she looked across at Tammy, knowing she was totally trustworthy, and said, 'Yes, something rather sensitive and…well, classified really.' Claire answered.

'Do tell Claire, could this be dangerous, if so, I am happy to help in anyway, as, I'm sure are Sam and Chrissie, and Ally.' Tammy said, speaking softly.

Claire smiled, then said,' Thank you, and yes, it might be a wise move to have a pow wow all together, work as a team, by the way, thinking of Ally, you were showing some concern when this blond lady, that was with Simon, was walking over to her?'

Tammy smiled, then answered, 'Yes, you see, you probably know, but Ally was involved with Simon, but before her, he was involved with Felicity, now, it seems, that she is once again with Simon, the way she strode over to Ally, well, …'

'Darn, you think there may have been a scene?'

Tammy smiled, 'To put it mildly, yes,'

Raphael at that moment came back with his parents in tow.

Meanwhile standing by the entrance to the exhibit, detective inspector was in conversation with the curator who was saying, 'The trouble is, now that this is all very much in the public eye, we are faced with legal challenges'

'How so? Roger Mantell asked, studying the man he had not met before today, Neil Miles, the fifty-eight-year-old former lecturer, now the curator of the museum.

'There is a family in Colombia who are challenging that the gold was stolen from them, and want it back, then, the Spanish, who say the gold was originally theirs, but was stolen by the Colombian family, and should be returned to Spain, they, by the way, have kept the remainder of the coins buried by the Castagnets, who laid the mosaic tiles covering seven hundred and fifty coins, Constance Shelton had four hundred, which, along with the tiles, as you know, we recovered, the other three hundred and fifty was taken by the then dean of the university who eventually fled to Spain, he has, again as you are aware, died from the virus, but, they found three hundred and forty eight hidden away inside the frame of a bicycle, they also discovered that he had sold two of the coins, well, the Spanish are keeping these, but still want the ones we have, so then, as out lawyer has claimed that these coins have been on American soil for over a hundred years, they should be able to legally challenge that they belong here, but' the curator continued, 'but, we have another avenue come to light, there is a woman here who is a direct descendant of the Castagnets, in talking with her, just a few moments ago, and explaining the situation, she said that she would look into challenging the claim, for the coins belonged to her family, she said that if successful, she would certainly make sure the coins stayed in the museum'

'Goodness' Roger said, 'and you say this woman, this descendant is here?'

'Yes, 'Neil looked around, spotted her and said, 'Over there, her name is Chantal Brewer'

Roger thanked the curator and walked over to meet this woman, seeing as he approached that she was talking with miss Alison Hudson.

EPILOGUE

March had rolled into April and April became May.

In Moncton

Detective inspector Karen Saunders pulled up in the parking lot by the Shapeshifters health club. She was dressed in light blue jeans, feet into pink and blue sneakers, wore a dark blue sweat top and with a casual bag slung over her left shoulder and wearing a pink facemask entered the reception area.

'Hello Rita' she said, greeting the receptionist who, though almost ten years younger, she had over these past weeks bonded with, since she had called about her suspicion when Debra Rozzini had called asking about Alison Hudson two months ago.

'Hi Karen' the receptionist, a tall redhead with a figure that would turn many a man's head and leave many women envious, answered, an ideal front person for the health club for she looked a picture of it.

'I came, firstly, to give you this' Karen said, taking an envelope from her bag and handing it over.

Rita took the envelope, looked at the detective with a quizzical frown and opened it. It was an invitation to an engagement party.

'Wow, you and Daniel, he's the hunky fireman, isn't he?' Rita said, smiling and amused to see Karen blush. 'Thank you, that is so kind, I'd love to come.'

'Good,' Karen answered, smiling back, then said, ' I'm in the gym for an hour, so please sign me in, and, oh, you can bring a friend, if you like'.

'Great, go ahead, perhaps afterwards you can fill me in on how Alison is?'

'Of course, yes, we will chat.'

In Myrtle Creek

'Okay, come on, it's time, let's all chat' Cynthia said, flicking her long brunette hair back and sitting down in the room that Thomas had now dubbed as the engine room. 'I've missed all of it'

Thomas smiled, sat opposite her and Claire was on the leather swivel chair behind the desk, the computer showing the screen saver that Robert had put there, and that Claire would never take off. ' But you have your own tale to tell as well' she said' in Spain'

'True, just legal stuff really, but that is all sorted and everything is fine for Letitia, now, come on, you, young lady, start talking.'

Claire smiled, briefly thinking back, all those years ago, when Cynthia had come to her rescue, and, looking at Thomas, how impressed she had been when he decided to get involved in hoping to rescue a woman who had been abducted in England. She was so pleased to have such good and loyal friends in these two. Smiling at each in turn, she said,' Goodness, well, where to start…'

Meanwhile across on the east coast in Boston

'Right,' Chrissie said, having settled herself on the couch in the front room, the very place where she had sat, with Sam sitting in the same chair by the window, that time he had first knocked on her door. 'Start, you are so good at recapping, so, just remind me, about, well, everything!' she said smiling.

Sam smiled back, also recalling the time he first met her, the time that he was amused when noticing how she curled and uncurled her toes on the carpet. Thinking how happy he was that she was to be his wife.

'Okay then, here goes' he answered, closing his eyes briefly, he then took his glasses off, placed them on the coffee table in front of him and started speaking.

'First of all, after I had that long chat with Karen, yesterday, let me start with all that she told me, Sandra gave herself in to the police in Portland, but, for her, no jail, a twelve month community service, mainly due to the fact that she wrote that confession which was couriered to Terri's school, and, her part in all of it was small, also, she was not involved at all in assisting the attempt on Karen's life, so, that's all good. Phil Madison has been released on bail, again, it had since come out that his involvement was very little indeed, it was mainly Bella who was behind it all, she, by the way, has been extradited to Canada, to Halifax where she will serve whatever sentence they give her, her court case is due any day and Karen thinks she'll get at least twenty years. Julien remain in prison, and he has another two years to serve. Finally, Karen told me that her and Daniel, the fireman, are engaged!

'Sam!' you couldn't tell me that yesterday?' Chrissie said, throwing an exasperated look at him.

'Sorry, I know, anyway, moving on….'

'I'll sort out a card for them, better leave that to me' Chrissie said, 'Men!'

Sam smiled,' shall I continue?'

Chrissie smiled back, 'Go on, recap away' then remembered something, 'wait, what about that other detective, Karen's old boss?'

'Ah, I was waiting for you to notice….'Sam began

'Liar!'

'Okay, just forgot about him, thank you dear, ' Sam replied, smiling broadly, then continued,' Yes, former detective, Murray Canney, turns out he was involved when they abducted Ally, also with other back handers and bribes, he was stripped of his rank, obviously, also he will lose his pension and face jail time, they caught up with him in Panama City and he will be transported to Moncton.'

'Good.' Chrissie said, then asked, ' by the way, did Karen say anything about the mayoress?'

'Yes, just that she is well and back on duty and we can expect a nice letter from her in the near future'

'You'd forgotten about that too, hadn't you?' Chrissie said, then got up, sat herself on his lap, something she had done a few times before. They kissed.

In New York

Tammy, dressed in pyjamas and a silky dressing gown, strode from the kitchen into the large lounge, carrying a bowl of cereal and a mug of tea. Placing the mug on one of the tables, she ate from the bowl and stood by the window. It was all quiet. It had been so good to have them all here. Chrissie and Sam, Terri and her mother Ally. Taking another spoonful she thought about Raphael. Yes, she had feelings for him, and he for her, she was sure of that. Smiling, she remembered when she had first seen him, that day in Yonkers, six years ago, when she had visited the law firm, when she had learned about her grandmother, when she had gone on that quest and how she now came to be a wealthy woman. She had seen him that day, so strange, all these years later, that they should connect. She had been so thrilled when he had called to ask her to come to Albuquerque with him, to the exhibition. Taking another spoonful of cereal, Tammy turned away from the window, sat down in her favourite chair and began to recollect events in her mind.

When the covid pandemic was at its worst, and she wasn't able to run her restaurant, she had, like her good friend Chrissie, decided to do some family tracing, delving back into time, and had been fascinated at what was out there to be found, even though it was, often, tedious and time-consuming work. She thought about young Terri, the adventure she had with her and with her friend Sophie in Paris, when they had together been involved in the case of the three monks. Young Terri, Tammy was glad she was safe, but couldn't quite figure out what Bella's plan was, it was all about a genetic disease, a rare disease, she knew that, and Tammy had a rare blood type and might have the right bone marrow to help fight this disease that her son might get. But, why the hunt, why the killing? A desperate woman for sure, but, why? Tammy put her bowl down, drank some tea and thought some more. Getting up she walked back to the kitchen with her bowl and mug, saw the time on the clock on the wall, then walked down the corridor, past the three seascapes that hung there and headed for her bedroom. She would get showered and changed, then head over to her restaurant and give Raphael a call, not necessarily in that order.

South of Washington DC, in Quantico

Charlotte Cartwright was putting all the files together, having confiscated the reports from Lea and Holly, and having signed forms from them, she could now put this to bed. All the information that she herself had gathered, along with the findings of Holly and Lea, she had the full story. Everything detail of what happened to her great grandfather Billy, still, along with able seaman Albert Green, in the submersible, in Ontario One, over five hundred feet below the surface. She had the full story of what happened when the gas cylinder broke free and the 'Taciturn' was caught in its deadly cloud. What happened to the recovered bodies, what happened to the ship itself. She knew it all, and now it had to be sealed and stored. She thought about Holly, whose grandfather had been the captain of the 'Taciturn' and thought about the misunderstanding that had so completely altered her life. Putting the bulky folders into a metal box, the closed and sealed it.

San Francisco.

Terri was back at work in the museum. In her office she was going through her schedule for the day and already on her second bottle of water she smiled as she thought of the recent events. Twice, she thought to herself. Twice she had been in an adventure, the first time was when she was held at gun point, when they had come to steal a painting, the one of a monk, which had begun a great adventure along with Tammy and Sophie. Then, the danger from Bella. Like Tammy in New York, Terri was also wondering why it had to be this way, why did this Bella woman had to go to such lengths, why kill, why threaten? Shaking her head she looked again at her schedule and taking a sip of water, set about her work.

On the other side of town, Alison was reading a letter. A letter that had just arrived, from Milan, from Millie, along with a package.

Dear Alison, it was no nice to meet up with you at the exhibition. What a wonderful display the museum has put together and of course an outcome of which you were so instrumental. Again, thank you for that. I have decided to stay in Milan and when some of my belongings arrived, I found these journals. They were sent to my great grandfather Carlos, actually arriving on the day my mother was born. I was told that my mother read these when she was about fourteen and that it inspired her to become a geologist. These journals tell of the life of a man who befriended my ancestor in Peru who then at some point moved to Mexico and then San Francisco. I am giving these to you as I saw how good you are at solving things, which your daughter has obviously inherited as with the search for the three monks. Also, I noticed you met up with an ancestor of the couple who buried the gold, I think her name was Chantel, and believe it or not, Henry Hopkins met one of her ancestors at some point, flicking through I spotted the name. Have fun with this and show her.

Alison picked up the three journals, noticed they were numbered and put the second and third ones on the table. Opening the journal which had a number 1 stencilled on the top right-hand corner of the black cover., she immediately saw the very neat writing. 'The Trading Post at Caracas' was the heading on the first page, and underneath the date was shown. 'It was early October in the year 1803'.

Closing the journal, Alison got up, headed for the kitchen and wondered about who this Henry Hopkins was, and how he would connect with an ancestor of Chantel's?

Preparing for herself a glass of juice she then returned to the lounge and said to herself, 'Well, one mystery solved and ended, another to figure out' smiling at her own foolishness. Then continued speaking aloud, 'Here's to you Henry, whoever you are'

THE END